W9-AQW-435

Praise for *Red Right Hand*

"*Red Right Hand* is a beautiful, terrifying nightmare of a book. Stylish and nerve-wracking, it held me constantly in an iron grip as I read it . . . and has yet to let me go. More, Levi Black!"

—Nancy Holder, *New York Times* bestselling author of *The Rules*

"Imagine that one of Lovecraft's Great Old Ones showed up at your door and said, 'You work for me now.' That's the premise of *Red Right Hand,* Levi Black's grim and gory tale that takes urban fantasy into the darkest places of both the universe and the human heart. Riveting in both senses of the word: it grips your attention, and it feels like bolts punching through your flesh."

—Alex Bledsoe, author of *Long Black Curl*

"Levi Black mixes deft characterization, vivid description, and H. P. Lovecraft's cosmic horrors to create a thoroughly engaging urban fantasy."

—Richard Lee Byers, author of *The Reaver* and *Blind God's Bluff*

"With *Red Right Hand,* Levi Black gives us an exciting, pulse-pounding mash-up of urban fantasy and Lovecraftian horror. Charlie Moore is a great entry into the pantheon of urban fantasy heroines, and the Man in Black is a Mythos character made even more terrifyingly real. I can't wait for the sequel."

—Gini Koch, author of the Alien/Katherine "Kitty" Katt series

"Levi Black's *Red Right Hand* is a perfect fusion of noir, action, and horror. Urban decay, Lovecraftian madness, and emotional desperation are only a few of the ingredients in the mix that powers this breakout novel. The engine on this beast is burning high-octane fuel and running hot. Highly recommended!"

—James A. Moore, author of the Seven Forges series
and *Alien: Sea of Sorrows*

"Sleek, savage, and brutally well-written, Black's story hurtles you into a world where the elder gods view humans as expendable playthings or tasty snacks. Even as you obsessively turn the pages, you'll be rooting for good to triumph over endless evil. A brilliant blend of horror and urban fantasy, *Red Right Hand* proves that truth is chaos and hell is only a tentacle away."

—Jana Oliver, award-winning author of the Demon Trappers series

"If Mickey Spillane had delved into the Cthulhu Mythos, he might have turned out something like this. Hard-hitting and truly scary, *Red Right Hand* is a postmodern Lovecraftian nightmare of a tale. Dark and bloody and bad to the bone."

—Charles R. Rutledge, coauthor of *Congregations of the Dead*

Levi Black

A Tom Doherty Associates Book

RED RIGHT HAND

This is a work of fiction. All of the characters, organizations, and events portrayed in this novel are either products of the author's imagination or are used fictitiously.

RED RIGHT HAND

Designed by Greg Collins

A Tor Book
Published by Tom Doherty Associates, LLC
175 Fifth Avenue
New York, NY 10010

www.tor-forge.com

The Library of Congress Cataloging-in-Publication Data
is available upon request.

ISBN 978-0-7653-8248-1 (hardcover)
ISBN 978-1-4668-8760-2 (e-book)

First Edition: July 2016

Printed in the United States of America

0 9 8 7 6 5 4 3 2 1

Dedicated to the Missus,
who chases away all the chaos gods

ACKNOWLEDGMENTS

Things happen behind the scenes with every book. There are movers, and there are shakers, and without both the moving and the shaking there would be no book for you to read.

Here is a woefully inadequate bit of thank-you to some of the ones who helped bring this one to you.

Lucienne Diver: The baddest of badass agents. You rock so hard, and I am much appreciated in your faith in me.

Greg Cox: Editor extraordinaire. Thank you for loving this story as much as you do.

Melanie Sanders: Copyediting ninja extraordinaire. You really did bring the extra polish this book needed.

The Tor Books team: Thank you for all your most excellent work. You kick all the ass.

The Writers of Metro Atlanta: You critiqued this one. Thank you for your kind words, and thank you even more for your harsh ones.

The Missus: I appreciate how you let me go and write when I need to. Your support gets me through.

H. P. Lovecraft: You started this whole Mythos thing and let other people play in your universe. I appreciate that. Literally, without your Mythos this book would not exist.

Robert E. Howard: You, sir, have taught me so much about writing. Thank you. Rest easy in your Valhalla.

Thank you to all the women throughout my life who have trusted me with their pain. I am humbled by you all.

RED RIGHT HAND

1

THE CHEAP ALCOHOL burned as it splashed down my throat.

Fumes roiled up the back of my esophagus, making me choke. It felt like getting punched in the tonsils with a fistful of kerosene.

I sucked in a breath, swallowing hard.

Dammit, Daniel . . .

I really like you.

Holding the dented, plastic bottle of vodka, I smeared my arm across my face, wiping away hot tears.

The first guy I . . . and he knew. He knew.

I fumbled keys out of my pocket and held them up, jangling them in front of my face. They woozed and blended in a fuzz of eyestrain, tears, and alcohol.

Now you know there's nobody in this crappy world you can trust.

My rage had cooled on the walk home, devolving into a ball of hurt and anger and drunken fog. The stairs to the townhouse I shared were treacherous, threatening to throw me back down them with each step, but I wasn't going to let them get the best of me.

I'm stubborn that way.

Besides, it was cold outside.

The key in my hand stabbed at the keyhole, brass clicking on brass. I had to lean my forehead against the door frame to get the key to slide into the lock. It turned in a smooth motion, barely a click to tell me it had unlocked. I stumbled across the threshold, slamming the door closed behind me, harder than I meant to.

Dammit.

At least the night is over. Just go to bed and try again in the morning. You've got jujitsu at ten. You can take it out on the mat.

My keys hit the table by the door with a metallic clatter, clashing against my roommates' keys.

Keep it down, or you'll have the whole house up. Shasta'll want to know what's wrong, and you do NOT want to get into that. Not tonight.

I looked up the stairs to my room.

Bed.

Just get to bed.

I'd taken only a few wobbly steps when the first skinless dog stepped from the shadows.

2

My mind stuttered, jut-jut-jittering around what I saw.

I didn't have a dog. None of my roommates had a dog, and no one I knew had ever had a dog that looked like this.

It stood on the hardwood floor in four slowly widening puddles of goo. Wet ran in rivulets down its legs, the musculature of it strung tight over a rack of bones. It stood by the stairs leading up to my room, watching me with a low-slung head. Skinless hackles bunched over its neck in knotted cables of raw meat.

Adrenaline slammed through my bloodstream, driven in a stampede by my heart suddenly trying to pound its way out of my chest. It burned away the fog of alcohol, shocking me sober. The jug of cheap vodka slipped from my fingers, tumbling to the floor. It bounced, spun, and lay on its side, spilling astringent alcohol over my shoes in a splash.

The dog stepped closer, a low growl rumbling from its vivisected chest.

The growl echoed in the stairwell, doubling, then tripling as two more hounds trotted out of the shadows. These two were leaner than the first, their rib cages hollow and caved in. They stalked toward me, the three moving in unison with the same squelching lift of paws, then the same *click-clack* of crescent razor claws as descended again. Their shoulders moved up and down; heads swinging side to side, panting rib bones expanding and contracting in time with harsh snuffles as long, blister-pink tongues lolled out of jaws over-filled with bone-cracking teeth. The rasping sound of their breath scraped my ears like a nail file on the membrane of my eardrum, dragging down and flicking up with just enough pressure to never *quite* tear through.

Clickety-clack squelch, clickety-clack squelch, pant-pant-pant . . .

My mind screamed at me.

Move! Get out! Don't just stand *here!*

I wanted to turn, wanted to run. Panic clawed at the front of my throat. Somehow I knew that if I took my eyes off the hounds they would take me. They would lunge and snap and latch and drag me to the ground where they would rip me open and bury their snouts inside my shredded body. My mind bounced around, unable to latch on to any one thing, unable to focus, desperate for a way to escape.

The door.

You didn't lock the door.

I stepped backward, slowly, carefully. The hounds matched me step for step, their baleful eyes pinned me, glowing the color of rotten squash. Lidless, they stared at me from deep sockets of raw gristle.

I stuck my hand out, fingers twisted in a ward against the evil eye my grandmother always used on a neighbor she accused of being a witch. I don't know why I did it. It was just instinct, a fetish from childhood—worthless and, worse, ineffectual. I used the same sign whenever I thought a car might not stop for its red light when I crossed an intersection. A tiny, stupid, reflexive habit.

My keys still sat on the little table in the center of the foyer. I snatched them up. The weight of them hung familiar in my fingers, a sliver of comfort, the merest ease to my jangled nerves.

The first hound growled again. It stepped quicker, trotting closer.

My throat closed, the pounding of my pulse throbbing through each side. Tension stabbed inside my lungs, stilettos sliding in.

Breathe. Remember, you have to breathe.

The air between me and the hounds became a plucked string singing with tension. They stopped, raw haunches crouching, front paws *click-clack*ing against the floor as they spread apart, preparing to lunge.

Oh, crap.

Grabbing the table, I yanked it around me, tipping it over, letting it crash to the floor between me and the hounds. I turned to the door as they pushed off, leaping over the table. My hand had closed on the door knob when I felt the hot, sharp slash of claws down the backs of my legs. I was driven to the floor, knees banging *hard,* pain shooting up my thighs. My fingers scrabbled as my hand slipped off the slick brass knob.

A weight slammed into my back, smashing my face against the door. Pain blasted across my forehead, flaring white behind my eyes. My ears closed, turning the snap and snarl of the hounds all tinny and hollow. A blow knocked me sideways, scraping my cheek raw on the wood of the door. I tumbled across the floor, banging knees, elbows, and hips until the wall stopped me.

My body went numb, skull stuffed with cotton. Nothing worked. Panic screamed.

Get up! Get the hell up or you are dead*!*

My eyes were the only things I could move. I rolled them

around, watching the dogs as they circled. The big one lunged, snapping at my face. Its teeth clacked together, its lips pulled back in a snarl. A string of brackish saliva slung off those raw lips, slapping across one of my eyes. It hit, itching and burning like jalapeño juice on steroids.

The hound pulled back.

It shook its head, jerking from side to side. Its jaw distended with a loud *POP*, dislocating to take a bigger bite. Cold, baleful eyes were pinned on my throat. My fingers flexed, scratching the floor. Striated muscle on the hound's shoulders quivered as it prepared to lunge and tear my throat out in a spray of hot arterial blood.

I couldn't close my eyes. Couldn't look away.

My eyelids were glued open, eyes stuck wide in their sockets as the door slammed open and a tall man in a long black coat strode in with amusement in his glittering eyes and death in his red right hand.

3

THE HOUND JERKED around, its skinless head still looming over and dripping on me. The rumble in its chest shook loose fat droplets of slick liquid that drizzled across my arm, my shoulder, my neck. They splattered, as warm and thick as fresh milk. Its brother hounds moved back as the Man in Black filled the doorway.

The wind swept in behind him, blowing and billowing his long coat around a slender frame. The black leather *fwap*ped around his legs, the sound reminding me of bat wings. The wind cleared the air of the moist, green-rot smell of the hounds, filling my nose with the scent of woodsmoke and blackberries.

He stood, outlined by the streetlights behind him, his face in shadow. Just a shape, just the form of a man, all shadowed moving edges and hard silhouette. His eyes glittered deep in his face. Other than that I couldn't see anything about his countenance.

Then he smiled.

It was a shark-toothed grin, a glistening grimace from a mouthful of murder. A chill slid slowly down my spine. The gleam across his teeth was the same gleam that slid down the edge of a sword like a drop of quicksilver. Gooseflesh that had nothing to do with the chill night air rushing through the open door rose from the base of my skull to the bottom of my shoulder blades.

The hound standing over me growled from within its exposed rib cage.

"Shut up, mongrel. Recognize your better."

The voice was deep and clear, a tolling bell that echoed in the tiny vestibule. The hound tilted its head, watching the man with an unblinking sulfurous eye. Fear pulled tight every tendon in my body, squeezing like a python, making me want to scream. The tension in the air suffocated me and clamped around my chest, thick with the potential for violence.

The hound above me turned, snapping at its brethren with a hoarse bark and a *clack* of wicked teeth.

The two smaller hounds sprang in an explosion of deadly, liquid grace. They were a blur, hanging in the air at the same time. Ropes of spittle and foam slung from raw-lipped snouts as their teeth gnashed.

The Man in Black turned, flicking the black-bladed sword in his terrible, red right hand. The slender length of steel licked out, not slowing as it bit deep into the belly of one airborne hound. Muscle parted like water in a gushing plop of strange organs on the floor. The hound fell as if struck down by the hand of God. Both halves of it twitched, sloshing out more of the chunky stew its entrails had become.

With a twist of the red right hand, the sword's curved blade sliced the air again, cleaving the second hound's side with a hollow, drumming *thunk*. It struck deep, a hack instead of a slash, driving through contracting, skinless muscle and grating along the vertebrae of the hound's spine. The hellhound fell at the man's feet, spasming its life out in a gout of black, runny ichor that spread like sewage underneath it.

The Man in Black spun the sword, slinging gore off the blade. It flicked in a wet arc across the wall. He pointed the weapon at the last hound.

"Your move, cur."

The last hound took a half step back. *Clackety squelch.* It stopped, stood, and quivered.

Then it turned its head and latched its teeth into my ear.

Pain exploded, hot and immediate from my eyebrow to my chin. The fangs scissored in, puncturing the skin, the cartilage, and the flesh, ripping furrows deep in my cheek and temple. Saliva sizzled and popped like bacon grease in a hot pan.

I tried to jerk away from the agony. The skinless dog shook its jaws, worrying the meat in its mouth. It felt like my face was being yanked off the bone, pulled away like a rind from a melon. The teeth that had punched through my earlobe ripped free in a spit of hot, thin blood, but the ones through the rim of cartilage around my ear held fast, the gristle strung tight in the hound's mouth.

My ear filled with blood, but I could still hear the hound's breath *whuff* and hiss as though we were in an echo chamber. Blood ran down my ear canal, filling my brain with sound, the moist snuff of canine breath bouncing off walls of throbbing, pulsing agony.

My feet slid and slipped on the gore-covered tile of the floor. I jerked as an electric current of pain jolted all the way down to my heels. My nerves burned as one hand slapped against the smooth, skinless muscle of the hound's chest, trying to push away, the other cramped around the keys I still held.

Hard metal dug into my palm.

My mind went animal blank, panic slaughtering all rational thought, leaving behind only hollow, raw instinct. Deep in the lizard part of my brainpan, that base-of-the-skull place, a spark flared and my training kicked in.

I drove my keys into the hound's face as hard as I could.

The metal sticking up between my knuckles bit deep. Punching through muscle, scraping on bone. The long, serrated key to my car punctured a lidless eye, spilling spoiled aqueous liquid across my fingers like runny egg yolk.

The hellhound gave a shrill yelp, and my pain cut away in a wash of cool sensation as its teeth slipped free. I popped my eyelids open in time to see the Man in Black slash with his sword. The hound turned skeletal tail, bounding across the room. A wide gash gaped open along its flank, the meat split wide and peeled back. The hound didn't slow or turn or hesitate, and when it hit the corner behind the stairwell it disappeared.

The world flickered in my mind, sputtering like the end of a movie reel. The Man in Black knelt beside me, his dripping sword held out and away. The fingers on his left hand touched the side of my face. They were cool and clean. He smiled a crooked, shark-tooth grin. His voice came to me clearly, more inside my mind than out.

"Do not die yet, Charlotte Tristan Moore. We have much to discuss."

4

"Do you have cream or sugar?"

The side of my head throbbed, pulsing in time with my heartbeat. I could *feel* the blood lurching underneath the skin, slouching its way toward the Bethlehem of my face. It *hurt.* Like claw hammer to the skull hurt. Even my teeth were sore.

I held a towel against my shredded ear to catch the blood that poured out, running hot and sticky down my neck. The world sounded half muffled through the blood-soaked cloth.

I stared at the tablecloth in front of me, elbow propped on the red-and-white checked vinyl my roommate Shasta had brought back from her last visit home. The little red squares wavered with every pulse from under the towel.

What the hell is going on?

A dark hand sat a steaming cup of black coffee on the table under my face.

"I asked you a question, Charlotte Tristan Moore. I would appreciate an answer before this turns cold."

I looked up. The Man in Black stood close beside me. My neck hurt as I twisted my face up to take all of him in. Tall, he loomed, his head seeming to brush the ceiling—though some small part of me knew that was a trick of perspective, the angle I looked up from. A black coat stretched from his neck all the way down to the floor. It moved even though he stood still, shifting subtly, delicately, as though it was breathing. Not that coats breathed.

It must be a trick of the light.

Or my head injury.

Oh, shit. Do I have a head injury? Something cracked inside my skull, making me think weirdly?

The Man in Black held a second steaming cup in his right hand. My eyes locked on that hand. It thrust from the edge of his coat sleeve, the one bright patch of color on the doom-black darkness of him. This close, it glistened in the incandescent kitchen light. Wet, or possibly greasy—as though it had been flayed, dusky skin peeled off, leaving behind the raw red of meat, the exposed underflesh. Subtly shiny like it had been dipped in crimson liquid latex.

Or fresh-spilled blood.

Now that hand held my favorite mug, a bright yellow cup with a picture of George Takei doing heart hands to the camera.

I caught myself leaning away, threatening to slip off my chair and onto the floor, trying to get as far from him as possible. Dammit. I was cowering.

I pulled myself upright.

My voice didn't tremble when I spoke. That surprised me.

"My name is Charlie. Only my family calls me Charlotte. Sugar is in the cabinet above the coffee maker, creamer is in the fridge. Help yourself."

He nodded, turning away in a swirl of coat.

As he rummaged through the cabinet, I pulled my hand away from the towel. The hand moved, but the towel stuck, held to the side of my face by a clot of dried blood.

Great.

I pulled on one corner, tugging sharply. It peeled free with a tearing sound. I winced—I couldn't help it—the pain flaring hot and bright like a struck match laid against my skin.

You've been hurt worse. Get it over with.

My fingers closed on the corner of the towel, and with a swift, sharp yank I pulled the whole cloth free from the clotted wound. It felt like being slapped with a belt sander. I sucked in air hard and fast between clenched teeth.

*Damnthat*hurt*likehell!*

The man was there, next to me.

I didn't see him move—my eyes hadn't been shut longer than a second—but he somehow crossed the room to me. He was just there. As though he'd teleported. His red right hand reached for my face.

His voice came, a dark murmur. "Do not move."

My nerves locked, freezing me in one spot. That hand moved closer, drifting lazily near. It hung, exposed and obscene, from the end of his sleeve, almost limp, its fingers slightly curled like those of a dead man.

It became all I could see, all I could look at, blocking the whole world. Made of striated muscle attached to tendon and bone, stringy nerves laced over the entire surface like electrical feeds. It came closer, everything else going blurry with strain as I tried to watch, but it slipped out of my line of sight. I couldn't move my neck, couldn't tilt my head, frozen by his command like a field mouse hypnotized by a cobra.

The hand touched my ear. I felt a slight pressure and then . . .

nothing. No pain, no stab, no tear, no rip. None of the searing agony I expected. He pulled away, hand falling to his side, disappearing in a fold of that long black coat.

My own hand flew, touching my ear. It felt . . . strange. Odd. Hot with fever. I felt the rough, crumbly crust of dried blood. My hair was matted with fluid into a hard knot. As I felt around, the blood crumbled and dusted down my cheek, down my neck. My fingers moved the flaps of soft, spongy tissue where teeth had ripped through the earlobe, leaving it a tangle of skin strings. The hard rim of cartilage felt like a frond of plastic under my touch.

A gnarled, half-melted frond of plastic.

A chunk of scab came off in my fingers, and they were suddenly slick with new blood. I felt all that in my fingertips.

None of it in my ear or the side of my face.

That skin was dead. Rubbery. No sensation at all.

The Man in Black now sat across from me at the little table, a long-handled spoon clinking around the rim of the yellow coffee mug as he stirred in hazelnut creamer.

I hadn't seen him move. One second he stood at my side; the next I examined my ear; the third he was in the chair across from me.

"Did you heal my ear?"

He smirked, making the corner of his full lips twitch upward. Dark eyes glittered, smudged with deep hollows underneath. "Does it feel healed to you?"

"No, it still feels like shredded meat, but it doesn't hurt anymore. Why?"

He lifted the coffee mug. George Takei smiled at me. "I shut off the nerves in that part of your face."

"You did *what*?"

"Your eardrum is not damaged. You heard me."

"Is it going to come back? Will I have feeling again?"

The Man in Black sipped his coffee, not answering.

"Are you going to tell me what the hell is going on?"

"Tonight is your night of destiny, Charlotte Tristan Moore. You have been chosen to receive a great blessing."

"A chewed-up ear is a great blessing?" My hand banged against the table. Coffee splashed over the rim of the mug in front of me, spilling across the plastic tablecloth. "Quit talking in riddles and tell me what's going on."

Slowly, the man set his coffee on the table. His hands folded around the mug casually, lying loose and relaxed around the yellow cup, fingertips barely touching the smooth ceramic surface. His left hand had long, slender fingers, each one carefully sculpted and covered with smooth skin the color of the coffee in his cup. The nails were even and manicured. It made me think of the piano. His fingers looked like they would be able to seduce a tune from an instrument.

Stroke the keys.

Tickle the ivories.

Then my eyes fell on his other hand.

The right hand.

The terrible, red right hand.

The memory of it touching my face slithered through my brain. A chill ran up one side of my spine and tumbled down the other to splash against something low and deep inside me.

I tore my eyes away, forcing them up to his face.

He looked at me, gazing intensely from under a dark brow. His nose was sharp, hawkish at the bridge and widening at the bottom over full lips. He had an exotic face, feral and Semitic, the face of an ancient Babylonian or a time-flung Assyrian.

That sensation happened again, the sick thrill that churned deep inside me.

Fear wrapped itself around me. I felt like an injured swimmer in shark-infested water.

This time my voice did tremble, just slightly, just below the surface. "Who are you?"

"I am Nyarlathotep."

"Why does that sound familiar?" I'd heard that name before.

"Your uncle Howard Phillip Lovecraft wrote of me."

"My uncle Howard?" Who the hell was he talking about? Knowledge slammed into my brain. "You mean my *mom's* great-uncle? The dead writer?"

"You are of the Lovecraft bloodline."

This makes no sense.

"My last name is Moore."

A sip of coffee, a twinkle in dark eyes. "Your father's last name is Moore. You are a Lovecraft through your mother's blood."

"Wait, wait, wait a damn minute." My hands were flat on the tablecloth, holding onto something solid because the world had tilted on its axis. My brain fumbled around, trying to figure things out. "I read that stuff as a kid 'cause my mom made me. It was weird and boring and totally made up."

My mom took great pride in being related to a famous writer and wanted me to be proud too. She used to assign his stories to me like homework. I would sit on a Saturday and try to plow my way through words that filled pages like marching insects. Words that had been out of date when he wrote them, containing enough syllables to make my jaw hurt, and he used them as though it were his job. Four adjectives to describe one noun, and three or four nouns in a sentence. *Everything* became *eldritch, elephantine, horrifying, terrifying,* or some other ten-dollar descriptor.

Too wordy and dry for a twelve-year-old.

Too wordy for me now.

"Howard Phillip Lovecraft walked your planet as a prophet, able to see through the veil between worlds. He didn't understand his gift, passed to him from his own mother, a daughter of the original wardens. It very nearly drove him mad. He wrote stories to clear his mind and warn your kind of dangers they knew nothing about." He leaned toward me. "You have the same gift, Charlotte Tristan Moore."

"Stop using my full name. It's annoying. Just call me Charlie."

He shrugged and sipped his coffee.

"Let me get this straight. You're telling me that all this craziness is real, and I'm a prophet, and you're a demon named Nar . . . how do you pronounce your name?"

"Nyarlathotep."

"I don't know if I can say that."

"You may call me *savior.*" His lips twitched. Not a smile, just a flicker of amusement. "Or *master,* if the name is too hard to pronounce."

"Are you serious?" I stared at him. "Did you seriously just tell me to call you *master*?" Anger spilled into my voice, making it crack. "What the . . ."

"Stop talking."

Something in the tone drew me up short, some power catching my breath in my throat like an animal in a trap. His eyes flashed, crackling with the heat lightning of anger. Dusky skin flushed even darker, a shadow of a thunderstorm rolling over the horizon. His voice dropped into a hiss.

"I am Nyarlathotep. I *am* the Crawling Chaos. It matters not if you call me the Thing in the Dark or the Nightmare Man. I am that which you fear. I have been named Shaitan, Loki, and the Spider God. Know this." He leaned forward. "I have chosen *you,* Charlotte Tristan Moore, to be my Acolyte. That gives you leeway." A raw, red finger stabbed the table. The plastic tablecloth sizzled underneath it. *"But I will not be mocked."*

He sat back in the chair, his dark eyes boring into me. The words vibrated the air between us. They hung like a suicide, dangling loose and swinging slightly. The silence swelled, filling the air like a humidity, making it hard to draw a breath.

I clenched my teeth, keeping words trapped in my mouth. Sweat ran under my hair with a gut-locking sweep of fear. My mind raced, thoughts pinging off the insides of my skull, tearing along the twisted pathways of my brain and stumbling over each other.

Oh shit this is crazy why haven't Bobbi Annette or Shasta come down this is crazy what is he a man is he a man did he kill them in their sleep what the hell were those things when I got home why did Nyar . . . nuh-yar-la-THO-tep save me what the hell *is going on?*

Nyarlathotep waved his normal hand in front of me. "The other people who live here are asleep. They will not wake until I allow it."

My tumbling thoughts screeched to a halt.

"Did you just read my mind?"

"I did. Your housemates are locked in their dreams until I allow them to wake. I chose to not kill them. I am not a man. Those things were skinhounds, bidding-doers of the Ones Locked Away, sent to kill you before I could find you. I saved your life because you can be my Acolyte." He smiled. "Did that answer your questions?"

I pushed the chair away from the table. The legs grunted across the floor, loud and sharp. I needed to get up, to move around. This was weird, *too* weird, too strange, too *much*. I felt trapped on a train headed off a cliff somewhere down the line. I couldn't see it from my car, but I could feel the tracks were loose under the wheels. My skin twitched all over from the adrenaline pumping through my bloodstream. I paced beside the counter on the other side of the kitchen, as far away as I could get from the Man in Black while staying in the kitchen. He sat between me and the door. Somehow I didn't think he would let me leave the room.

I took a deep breath, making my mind calm down.

Think, Charlie, think. *Work the problem.*

"Why would those skinhounds want to kill me?"

"To stop you from becoming my Acolyte."

I put my hand up. "Stop that. Stop talking like I know what the hell you're saying. I don't know what"—my fingers jerked quotation marks into the air—"*become your Acolyte* means. Tell me what you want in plain, dumb, *human* English."

Nyarlathotep took a sip of coffee. He studied me over the rim of the mug with half-lidded eyes. Slender brown fingers held the cup to his lips. That awful red right hand lay somewhere out of sight, under the table or put away in the folds of his coat.

I didn't care, as long as I couldn't see it. That thing creeped me out. It filled me with a cold dread in the bottom of my stomach. Nyarlathotep drained his cup and placed it gently on the table.

He stared at the empty cup, his hand tented on the table just in front of it. After a long moment his hand twitched, fingers flicking out. The cup upturned and flipped to its side. It rolled until the handle *thunk*ed on the table, bringing it to a stop. Dregs of heavily creamed coffee slowly ran to the edge of the mug and spilled over to drip out onto the tablecloth.

His voice was clear. "There are things, gods if you will, beings of immeasurable cosmic power who covet the Earth. They desire to overrun it. Some want to destroy your species. Some want to enslave you as playthings. Some want to devour you as succulent prey. They are the Elder Gods, the Outer Gods, the Great Old Ones of time long forgotten. They ruled when this world was without form, and void. They were the darkness upon the face of the deep, slaughtering the ancestors of Adam, laying waste to Creation until they were bound, imprisoned on the edge of the universe. For eons they have tried to crash their cell gates, return to this world, and seek vengeance on the sons and daughters of the ones who slammed shut the door against them."

I blinked, my eyelids shuttering down for only a split second. When they opened, the Man in Black stood in front of me.

Everything inside my body locked down, every muscle tightening in alarm.

Nyarlathotep loomed over me. Sharply arched eyebrows creased together, obsidian eyes boring into the meat of me. The weight of his gaze lay heavily, a physical thing, pressing against my skin.

His voice came low, nearly breathy, pushed between too sharp and too many teeth. "After millennia of howling and gibbering against the gates, they have a new design. Now they slip quietly into this realm, squeezing through the cracks and the fractures and the fissures little by little, seeding themselves here in this reality. They come like a thief in the night, growing in might and power until enough of their substance has crossed over to make a full and complete transition."

He leaned in, his sharp-angled face inches from mine. I didn't flinch, didn't draw back.

I didn't.

"I have grown fond of your world, of your little humanity. I do not wish to share my playthings with Old Ones who would destroy you all. If the human race is to die in glorious slaughter, it will be by my hand or none at all."

I took a slow, careful step back. Like you back away from a dog that may or may not bite you, but definitely will if you move too fast. "What do you need me for?"

"Only the Lovecraft bloodline carries the gift of Sight. I need you to be my hound, to help me hunt the avatars of the Old Ones that have already crossed the threshold before their power grows too great to stop."

"I've never seen anything like what you're talking about. Not until tonight. Not until you."

"The magick lies dormant inside you. After I place my Mark upon you as my Acolyte, your gift will spark. You shall be of me, and I of you. *Then* your magick will be accessible to you."

Dread sat like lead in my stomach. I didn't want anything to do with this. I just wanted to get away from this . . . this Man in Black and his craziness. I felt stuck.

Trapped.

Trapped like . . .

I shoved that behind its door, locking it away.

No! Not like that. Never like that again. Keep it together, Charlie. Play along until you get your chance.

"What do I have to do?"

"Simply give me your hand." His right arm moved out of the folds of his coat. His hand hung, red, raw, and sticky-slick. I pulled back. I didn't want to touch that hand. I clenched my fist and shoved it in my hoodie.

The Man in Black looked amused.

"Do not fight me on this, Charlotte Tristan Moore. I will have your hand one way or another. It would be best to give it willingly."

Slowly, I unfurled my arm, stretching out my palm like a sacrificial offering. His dreadful crimson hand fell quick and terrible, clamping around the bones under my skin, rubbing them against one another. My mind loosened. The shiny cinnamon skin touched mine, firm and slick like scar tissue. I thought it would be sticky and tacky, like semicongealed blood. For a second it almost felt pleasant. Comforting.

Then the pain struck. Small and quick, like a biting cuttlefish under the water. Just a sharp nip that faded before I realized it had happened.

That wasn't so . . .

And then the cutting began.

A jolt of agony slashed across my palm. My mind filled with the image of my dad using a woodcarving tool: the spiral blade spinning furiously, carving grooves into a piece of wood clamped to the worktable. The pain burrowed deep in my palm, and it *moved,* zigging and zagging across my grip, building and building and building, crashing and clanging inside my brain like a crescendo, a cacophony of agony. I tried to jerk away, but the red right hand clamped harder, grinding my phalanges together until they felt shrill and spiral-fractured.

My muscles yanked and stretched, threatening to tear tendon from bone as I fought to break the grip. My mind babbled at me, overloaded from my nerves being set afire, the edges gone brittle and crackling like spun glass, threatening to shatter.

He let go.

I fell backward, ass banging on the kitchen floor, jarring my spine in a *click-clack* of vertebrae. My jaw slammed shut, teeth tearing through the sides of my tongue. Blood dripped and splattered on the linoleum around me, sizzling as it landed. My hand was smeared with it, looking like a kindergarten finger-painted version of his. I looked at my palm.

The flesh had been excised in lines and whorls and squiggly trails. The raw wound was in the shape of a symbol I'd never seen before. It looked like a pentagram, but there were too many lines, too many swirls. The edges of the skin were crisp, the cuts deep, grooved all the way to the pink flesh underneath. Blood, my blood, pulsed out in time with my heartbeat. Each pulse matched a sick, queasy throb deep in my belly.

His voice rolled like thunder. Pronouncing, "Charlotte Tritsan Moore, you have been Marked as my Acolyte. Now you will be able to See."

I looked up.

The Man in Black was gone.

In his place stood a monstrosity.

I AM GOING insane.

I couldn't see it all, couldn't take it all in, my vision breaking on the edges like cheap windowpanes, crackle-fracturing from the outside in. The thing in front of me filled the room, a mass of limbs and tentacles writhing in knots. The tentacles roiled against each other, worm-white membranes tearing as they rubbed. Clear ectoplasm gushed, lubricating the smearing caress of alien flesh against alien flesh. From this mass jutted spindly limbs ending in grasping, many-fingered hands with too many joints, each finger capped by a talon black and curved to pull meat from bone.

I don't, I don't, I don't . . .

The massed tentacles were split-seamed with gaping mouths, gnashing rims of razor-sharp chitin crowding and pushing each other in jutting, jagged rows, piranha mouths designed by a mad, sadistic creator. The teeth chomped together, the noise a cacophony, driving into my mind like a drill.

. . . *understand, no sense, what, what, WHAT* . . .

Hundreds of orbs of all sizes dotted the oily membrane skin. A few were as large as my face; some were the size of a pea. Unblinking they stared, drinking in my human frailty, my weakness, my lowly pathetic life. They looked on me without pity, seething animosity in their cold, unmoving stare.

. . . *toomuchdontknowwhatiamlook* . . .

Over this sloppy, slithering form lay a shaggy hide, still raw and bloody from being cut off its original host. It moved on its own, rippling around the chaos it clothed, trying to pull away each time its sore subcutaneous inside brushed against the skin of the chaos god who wore it. Each kiss of contact raised a sizzle and a thin wailing scream that cut through the teeth-gnashing noise of a hundred hungry mouths.

My mind broke, sanity washing away like sand on a crumbling beach. I already knew fear; since that night it had been my constant companion, living in my bones, stalking my shadow, always waiting for a trigger to come screaming back into my mind.

A certain look from a man, the smell of Sax body spray, carpet against my skin, four men in a group, my face touching the bare mattress if the sheet slipped in the night, that song . . . that damned song that *still* haunts me. These things and a hundred others had stalked my life since that night, looking for any opportunity to take me and drag me back to the edge of madness.

That was *nothing* compared to the terror that ripped my soul at seeing the Crawling Chaos in his true form.

A tentacle slithered toward me. My eyes locked on it, unable to blink or look away. It slapped around my arm like an obscene bracelet, the membrane cold and greasy as it curled around my right wrist. Its touch turned the thick line of scar tissue running up my arm into a throbbing current of ice. It ached deep in my tendons, racing along my carpal tunnel. My fingers opened, uncurling to reveal the symbol carved into the flesh of my hand. A scream tore out of my throat.

The chaos moved, surging toward me.

Something hot and wet hit my palm, setting it afire.

The world exploded.

6

I SNAPPED BACK to the real world in a harsh, pulling jerk.

I found myself on my knees, still on the kitchen floor. Nyarlathotep stood over me, hand clamped around my wrist. His normal hand. The red right one held my now empty coffee mug from earlier. Something sticky ran down my arm in a twisty, winding trickle. I looked. Coffee. Coffee mixed with blood streamed down my arm, dripping off my hand onto the floor. My mind tumbled into working order and my first coherent thought became:

Who's going to clean up this mess?

The bones of my wrist *ached* under the Man in Black's fingers, and the scar that ran up my forearm thrummed with cold.

Let me go!

I jerked down and to the inside, like I'd been trained to, and slipped my hand out of his grasp. I scrambled, my shoes squeaking on wet linoleum, putting as much distance between me and the Man in Black as I could. He watched me, his lips pulled into a bemused smirk. My back hit the wall. The wall was solid. It was real. Carefully I stood, sliding up, getting my feet under me.

A hornet's nest buzzed inside my body. I could feel my blood running under my skin, rushing and blasting through the veins. I felt high, charged, jolted full of some weird energy that made the world spin faster.

"What the *hell* just happened?"

Nyarlathotep smiled. "Blood touched your Mark, and your Sight activated."

"Stop." My left hand, the smooth uninjured one, flew up between us. "Stop using those words like they mean something to me."

I thought for a second, pulling it all together. I looked down, studying the symbol etched into my palm. My hands were shaking, vibrating and tingling like they were hooked into a live wire. The lines and swirls made grooves in my flesh, open and raw, but they weren't bleeding anymore. My hand felt sticky, but the stickiness had the sugary tack of coffee instead of the iron-tanged texture of blood. "You're saying my blood, on this thing *you* did to me, made me see . . . what the hell did I see?"

His normal hand swept up and down, indicating his body. "This is merely a glamour, a skinsuit I use to walk unhindered in your world. Your Sight revealed to you my true form on this plane of reality."

"It's ugly as hell, just so you know," I spat. The insult felt good. A tiny stab. It didn't change the fact that this situation had become completely batshit crazy, but it made me feel stronger, a little more in control.

The Man in Black shrugged.

I wiped my shaky hand on my hoodie. The material was tissue-soft from hundreds of washings, but it still felt like sandpaper across the symbol cut in my flesh. "No more blood on this, not ever. 'Cause I *never* want to see that again."

"You will need your magick, Charlotte Tristan Moore, if you are to be of service to me. I will require much of you before I am done."

"You can *require* whatever you want. I'm not doing it."

Nyarlathotep appeared suddenly there, in front of me, looming tall, much taller than me. Dark eyes glittered as he leaned in, voice low and sinister. "When the time comes, Acolyte, you will do *exactly* what I need you to do."

That close he was overwhelming, looming like a tidal wave pausing before it devastates the shoreline. He smelled like musk and grave dirt, something primal that pulled deep inside me. In a blink he was back across the room. "When you need your magick, it can be activated by touching your Mark with any bodily fluid. Blood is the strongest, followed by sexual issue, but any secretion will spark it to life."

Bodily fluid? Secretion? Sexual issue? What?

I pushed those thoughts out of the way.

Stay focused. Work the problem.

"Why should I help you?"

Dark eyes sparkled. "I could kill you."

The threat hit me like a slap. "Then do it and get it over with." Anger bubbled at his words, boiling away the fear I'd felt since seeing the skinhounds. I was *sick* of being terrified. I'd worked too hard to not be terrified every day of my life. *Nothing* was worth being stuck in fear. Fear grinds you down to bone dust and nothing, breaking your will, making you less than human.

Been there, done that, fuck you.

The Man in Black sighed and chuckled.

"Charlotte Tristan Moore, I am not the only one who will seek you out now that your gift has been activated. There are other things, things that crawl and slither at the edge of night, things that would find you. They will come, and they will not have the mercy I have shown."

"Mercy? I haven't seen any mercy from you."

"I spared your life from the skinhounds. I have not slaughtered your friends in their sleep, even though I could. I have not sought out everyone you love and care for and reduced them to mewling pieces of meat that cry for death as a relief from the tortures inflicted upon them." His red right hand tapped the tabletop. "You will not receive such kindness from those that will seek you without my protection."

"Wait a minute, *you're* the one who Marked me! If these things come, it will be because of what *you* did to me."

"That does not matter." He stuttered in my sight again, suddenly standing without having stood. "What matters now is your choice. Serve as my Acolyte and be protected, or refuse and die." He reached out his hand, his red right hand, to me.

My eyes narrowed. Anger twisted in my belly like a snake.

"You're a bastard."

The Man in Black chuckled in amusement.

7

My shredded ear throbbed as the cool night air brushed over it. It pulsed on the side of my head, still not hurting, but I could feel it.

"You should lock your door. You never know what might walk in if you do not."

I glanced at Nyarlathotep. He looked amused standing on the porch beside me, a statue carved from the night. His coat rustled around him, uneasy.

"You know your coat hates you, right?"

The Dark Man chuckled. "It has never forgiven me for filleting it off its original host."

"What is it?"

"It was an archangel who strayed too far from his appointed territory. Now it is my coat."

"You skinned an archangel? And you're trying to convince me you're the lesser of two evils?"

The Man in Black's smile gleamed in the shadow of his face. "I never claimed to be lesser."

I turned from the door, starting down the steps. He moved beside me, matching me step for step. My hip scraped along the handrail. I leaned as far from him as I could, desperate for his coat, the still-living skin, to *not* brush against me. If the dark god next to me noticed, he gave no indication.

My eyes scanned the short yard that buffered the parking lot from the row of townhouses. Once I made it past the handrails, it would be wide and open.

Hold it together. Remember what Sensei taught you. You're almost there. Distract him, then make your move and run like hell.

"That's my car over there." I pointed across the narrow yard to the parking lot.

Oh, shit.

A slender male figure leaned on the hood of my car. His shoulders looked narrower than normal, with his head down and hands stuffed in pockets. A thick lock of hair curled over his forehead, shadowing his eyes. He looked up as we stepped off the stairs and onto the sidewalk, the streetlight above revealing a clean jawline and a nose slightly crooked from being broken in a wrestling match in high school.

Daniel.

I stopped short.

This was the last thing I needed. Black magick and chaos gods and skinhounds had pushed me to the edge of my ability to cope, but this? This would be too much. I *couldn't* deal with Daniel and what had happened earlier, not on top of the rest.

No way.

Nyarlathotep moved on the edge of my vision, reaching for me. I twisted away, needing to not be touched, especially by him.

Daniel walked toward us.

No, dammit, no.

I stepped forward, holding my hands up, moving between Daniel and the Man in Black. "Go home."

"Charlie," His voice sounded husky, a raw rasp. Even in the dark I could see the fresh bruise that ran from the collar of his T-shirt and up to his jawline, wide and purple, so solid it looked like paint on his skin.

I guessed I'd gotten him good with that elbow.

He cleared his throat. "I'm sorry about earlier. I didn't mean . . ."

"Get out of here. Go." I shoved my words through clenched teeth. "If you know what's good for you, you'll leave."

I could *feel* the Man in Black looming behind me. I had to get Daniel away from him, away from this situation. Anger still bubbled in me about earlier, since he'd betrayed my trust, since he had tried to do what he had, but still . . . he didn't need to get mixed up in whatever the hell I'd stepped into with Nyarlathotep.

Pain filled his face, concern in his green eyes. He swallowed so he could speak again. "Whatever I did that made you react like that . . . I didn't mean it. You gotta believe me."

I lunged at him. "Get. The. Hell. Away. From. Me." My hands hit his chest, punctuating each word, shoving him backward. My mind screamed at him.

Go! Leave now, before it's too late!

I turned away, hoping he would take the hint.

He drew in a sharp breath. "My God! Charlie! What happened to your ear?"

I'd forgotten about my shredded ear.

"It's fine. It's nothing." My hand flew to the side of my face, fingers scrabbling, trying to pull too-short hair over the ruin of my ear. The hair didn't move, shellacked in place with dried blood that broke and crumbled under my fingertips like cheap dollar-store hair gel.

The Man in Black moved closer, coat *fwap*ping and *shush*ing.

Daniel looked up at Nyarlathotep. His hands clenched into

fists and he stepped back, bracing himself. "Who are you?" His eyes flashed in the low light. "Are you the one who hurt her?"

He's trying to defend me. He's going to fight for me.

Something surged inside me, the same something that had grown during the last few months with Daniel.

Something that eased the hurt from earlier.

It wrestled against the sure belief that the Man in Black could kill Daniel where he stood.

I had to get him to leave, for his own safety. There was a split second when my head turned selfish and ugly, a throwback to years of looking out for myself.

Leave him. He can be your distraction. Let him deal with the Man in Black, and you can get away, get safe.

I pushed that thought down *hard*, smothering it before it could take root, before I could seriously consider it. Daniel hadn't seen what I saw in the kitchen. He thought Nyarlathotep was just human and he would try to fight him.

For me.

I couldn't cut and run and leave him to be hurt. I just couldn't.

Before I could do anything, the Man in Black stepped around me, his coat brushing my legs as he passed and raising gooseflesh under my jeans. He lifted his right hand toward Daniel.

The air around us came alive with energy, crackling like it does seconds before a lightning strike. Fear clenched my stomach, and the hornets inside my body began to swarm and buzz, beating inside my skin like pellets in a hailstorm. My hands shook with the magick running wild in my blood.

That awful red hand hung, skinless and raw, in the air between the two men, pointing at Daniel's face. "Who do you think I am, Daniel Alexander Langford?"

The air split with his voice. I couldn't see it, but I felt it like a whipcrack.

Daniel's face *changed*, growing loose and slack. One second he scowled with anger, the next his features smoothed, the muscles relaxing, leaving his jaw slung open and his eyes staring at the red right hand before him.

His voice came, sluggish and drawn. "You are Lord and Master, fit to be worshiped in the night and the nightmares of men."

"Do you wish to worship me, Daniel Alexander Langford?"

"With all my heart and soul and mind, Master."

Daniel sounded like a drone. Horror climbed my throat. I'd listened to him talk a lot the last few months. He was quick-witted and funny, his green eyes lighting up whenever we would wordplay off each other. It was part of his charm, part of him.

Part of the reason I'd let him get close.

This . . . this was not him, not him at all, and it filled me with as much terror as anything else this night.

I shoved Daniel, pushing him back a step. He stumbled, loose-limbed inside his clothes, as if he'd been strung together with rubber bands. I whirled to face the Man in Black.

"What did you just do to him?"

He shrugged, making his black coat ripple from ground to shoulders. "I did nothing. Your species longs to worship my kind. Your entire existence on this plane has held nameless cults dedicated to dark and strange gods." He indicated Daniel with his normal hand. "This one is descended from a long line of such cultists. It is writ in his bones to turn to one like me in devotion."

"Stop it, change it, leave him alone."

"It is too late for that, Acolyte." He gave a flourish with his terrible right hand. "Besides, he is amusing to me. It has been too long since I've had a cult." He nodded sharply, his mind made up. "He comes with us."

"No."

Hell no.

Nyarlathotep turned toward me slowly, dark eyes heavy-lidded like a cobra. "Make no mistake, Acolyte. He has been marked by me as surely as you have. If you abandon him here he will be meat to the very things that will seek to harm you. The only safety for him is with us until our appointed task is finished. There is still one skinhound on the loose." He stepped closer, the edge of his coat brushing the front of my legs again. "Besides, he will be of use to us."

Daniel stared at Nyarlathotep, his eyes wide and unblinking as though he had never seen anything so amazing.

No.

This wasn't my fault. It wasn't. I didn't bring this weirdness into my life. Everything in me screamed to run, to bolt, to get as far away as possible from the Man in Black and whatever he wanted me to do.

I still could. He stood far enough away in his flappy black coat that I could be gone before he grabbed me. I'd had years of obsessive sprint training since that night, training so I could get away from people and situations. Those skills would pay off, and I would be gone.

But Daniel would still be here. Left behind. Left to the mercy of the Man in Black.

My ear throbbed at the thought.

I can't. I just can't.

"If I help you tonight, will you go away and leave us alone?"

The Man in Black nodded.

"Swear."

"Do your duty tonight, Charlotte Tristan Moore, and I swear on the sanity of Azathoth that I will leave you and he unmolested for the rest of time itself."

What does that even mean?

Did I trust him?

No.

Did I have a choice?

I couldn't see one.
Dammit.
My father's advice rang through my mind.
If you can't get out, then get through.
Simple words that are hard to walk but still true.
"Get in the car. Let's get this over with."

8

THE BLACK COAT rustled uneasily next to me, nearly quivering as it lay folded against the Man in Black. An edge of it curled to brush my knuckles as I shifted gears. A burst of noise, like a snatch of music when you're pushing the button on the radio too fast, garbled in my head, making me jerk away, grinding the gears of my Honda. The car, nearly as old as me and still on its original transmission, lurched violently.

Pull it together.

The coat fell away, slipping into a puddle of darkness.

The Man in Black filled the seat next to me with a solid presence, looking out the windshield as I drove. His saturnine face was all sharp angles and strange geometry cut from random lights as we passed. Sitting in my worn-down Honda Civic, he didn't even look real. Up close he was an optical illusion, a special effect in a low-budget horror movie.

That's fitting.

I glanced in the rearview mirror. Daniel sat folded behind us, feet up with no room for his legs. He wasn't overly tall, five-ten or so, but the Honda's backseat was pretty small and my floorboards were full of trash. I don't keep a clean car 'cause I just don't care that much. There's no food trash—my car doesn't smell—but anything paper or plastic I just toss in the back.

Daniel's eyes met mine in the reflection of the rearview mirror. They weren't back to normal, but at least they'd lost their mile-long stare. He had nice eyes, quick and kind. They nearly twinkled when he wasn't thinking with the hyper-focus of a student who could keep up, but not without work. He still had to be half drunk, as I'd been when I left his apartment, before the night turned vicious on me and any buzz had been doused from my system by fear, horror, and adrenaline. He did look stoned though, the micro-muscles in his face relaxed to almost strokelike looseness.

It was the same look my ex-boyfriend Thom had gotten when he went on a narcotic nod.

I never joined him, never that far, but I'd watched him slip off into the arms of Morpheus while dulling my mind on weed and pills. I did it just to be able to get through a whole day after . . . after what happened. My therapist at the time had prescribed a laundry list of pills to get me through, but those just deadened everything and put me to sleep.

Those drugs made sure I didn't think about what happened, but they did it by making sure I couldn't think about anything. Left dead awake, I wandered through my life not feeling, not caring, just sleepwalking and nearly nonfunctional. I *needed* to be able to live, to deal with the thing—but only a little at a time, holding it at a long arm's length. Working my way up to working my way through it.

So I self-prescribed, dropping into behavior I'd only been *around* before, never involved in. I burned out my brain cells and short circuited the memory so I could get to the end of *that* day and damn tomorrow for not being real.

Thom had been the way I accomplished that.

I'm a terrible person.

He was a nice guy, a sensitive art type who never met a drug he didn't like, so he had the connections I needed. He'd liked me for years during middle school and was enough of a nonjudgmental hippie to still like me after I got out of the hospital.

Guilt stabbed deep as I remembered pushing Thom to tie off, to shoot up, to nod away. He'd been headed there before me, but I *needed* him to give me painkillers and company without the threat of sex. Threat is the wrong word. He was too nice to push, never would if I'd given him the chance, but he'd want it, all boys do, and I just couldn't. Just before he would drop all the way gone, he would loll his head over, give me his crooked smile, pat my arm, and say, *Don't worry, babe, you're always gonna be my heroin.*

I wasn't proud of what I had done. Not at all. I hurt, and I saw a way out of it and, at the time, couldn't see anything besides that. It only lasted a few months. I got Thom to NA before I parted ways with him, but it was still shitty of me.

Shittiest thing I've ever done in a long list of shitty things.

Terrible person.

Don't judge me.

In the mirror, Daniel smiled softly. I cut my eyes back to the road.

Pay attention, or you'll kill us all.

Flexing my fingers on the steering wheel made the Mark on my hand sore. I adjusted in my seat, moving my kidney off the piece of broken seat plastic that jabbed me when I slouched. Outside the car my neighborhood fell away, streets opening to the rest of the city. Soon I'd have to turn off or run out of road.

"Where are we going?"

"We will be seeing someone who can give us direction."

"Direction? I could use some, unless you want me to turn the Kwikie Mart at the end of this road into a drive-through."

The Man in Black reached into his coat with his red right hand, the crimson of it slipping obscenely into the inky folds. His arm slid deep, deeper than it should have been able to, disappearing into the leathery darkness. I watched from the corner of my eye as I drove.

Where is his sword?

It wasn't in the car. I hadn't seen it since the foyer of the townhouse. Had he left it there? Would my roommates find it in the mess of gore and blood of the dead skinhounds? Shasta would freak *out* in the morning. They all would. If they woke up at all. The Man in Black had said he'd placed a spell to keep them asleep. What if he wasn't telling the truth?

What was I thinking? What if he *was* telling the truth?

What kind of insanity had taken me tonight?

Panic rose in my chest. I clamped down on it.

I could only do what I could do in this moment. I would deal with this right now and deal with that when it came.

The Man in Black felt around the depths of the coat, too-sharp teeth biting his lower lip. He smiled as he found whatever he'd been looking for and began to pull his arm out. The smile scraped the points of his teeth over the thin skin of his lip. Black blood trickled from a dozen pinpricks. It pooled along the bottom edge of his lip, quivering as it thickened, hanging, threatening to drip. His tongue darted out, sweeping across and scooping up the droplet. The tongue was too long, scabrous, and red like a boiled lobster.

The sight of it ran a chill up my spine.

His hand slid out of the coat. Held delicately between his fingers was a tiny white object. The fluted ends gently curved to a narrow center. He studied it for a moment, turning it carefully in front of him. My scalp began to prickle, hot and itchy under my hair.

The light ahead switched from yellow to red.

I coasted the Honda to a stop. "What's that?"

He didn't answer.

Raw red fingers flicked the tiny object into the air with a gentle spin. His other hand plucked it before it began to fall. I watched in dread and fascination. I didn't see his red right hand snake toward me until it snatched a hair from my head with a sharp, sudden shock.

"Ow! What the hell!?"

The Man in Black didn't answer. He held the single hair between his fingertips. It was short and dark, curling on itself in twists. My hair is a complete pain in the ass. Tight, dark curls that I can never straighten or even really brush. Even more so since I had cut it short—short enough that it couldn't be grabbed, couldn't be used against me.

As I watched, he placed my hair inside his mouth, holding fast to the end of it. Closing his lips around it, his jaw worked for a brief second. He pulled, drawing it slowly between his lips.

It came out straight as a needle.

He jerked his chin, pointing forward with the fingers not being used to hold my hair.

"Drive, Acolyte."

I looked up. The light had turned green. Shifting and punching my foot down, I accelerated, still watching him from the corner of my eye, my scalp still itching with some weird feeling from the thing in his hands. He took my chaos god spit–stiffened hair and laid it against the small white object. Holding it in place with his thumb, he wound the hair like piece of wire.

A low noise filled the car, harsh and guttural, banging against my eardrums. The Man in Black began to chant under his breath.

The air in the car grew thick, cloying, and oppressive, heavy with the scent of rotten honey.

It made the energy, the magick, inside me boil and the hair on my arms rise.

A glance in the mirror showed Daniel leaning back, his eyes closed, a smile on his face as if he were listening to Mozart instead of the whine of my car and the bickering between me and the chaos god in the seat beside me.

"Turn left."

The Man in Black held the hair in his fingertips, suspending the fluted piece of ivory in the air. It leaned left as if the whole world had tilted on its axis.

I turned where he indicated, holding the steering wheel tightly to keep my hands from jittering. The Mark on my palm hurt. "What's that thing?"

"It is a compass. It will lead us to the one who can reveal the hiding places of the gods."

The wheel spun in my hands. "Okay, it's a compass, but what's it made from besides my hair?"

He stared at the piece of ivory. Now it dangled forward, against gravity.

"It is the finger bone of a murdered child."

I hit the brakes.

The Honda jerked, black smoke ribboning from under the car as retreaded tires screamed in protest. Daniel slammed into my seatback with a grunt.

Nyarlathotep scowled. "Why are you stopping?"

Disgust rolled inside me. My mouth twisted with it. "*What* did you say that is?"

"It is the finger bone of a murdered child."

"If you want me to drive, you need to explain to me why you have that thing!" My voice turned shrill, tilting into a higher pitch, brittle with anger at each word. This was too much. The face of every child I knew flashed through my mind. My younger brother; my niece, Sara; my nephew, Rolf; the kids I used to teach when I worked at a daycare. This was over the edge of what I could handle.

"Calm yourself, Acolyte. It was not a child you knew."

Daniel pulled himself up by the back of my seat. He touched my shoulder. "Hey, Charlie. It's okay, it's all right."

"It's not *all right*." I jerked his hand off my shoulder. "You have no idea how not *all right* it is right now."

"Drive." The Man in Black pointed across the front of the car. His voice burned with heat. "That way."

"No. That's it." I pounded the steering wheel. "That. Is. It. No more! That thing is too much. You show up, you kill some stuff, you drag me into this freak show of a night. My ear is messed up. He's"—I indicated Daniel in the backseat with a wave of my hand—"acting like a zombie. You do all this *weird,* black magick shit, and so far I've been here going along with it. But that"—I jabbed my finger toward the dangling fingerbone—"*that* is *too much*!"

My fist smashed into the steering wheel. Pain sliced through my hand, running along the symbol incised there. I welcomed it, pulled it into myself.

Bring the pain.

It was sharp, and bright, and clean inside my mind, cutting through all the confusion. A lifeline in the whirling, swirling storm-tossed sea. Everything started to crash around me, pushed over the tipping point by the finger bone, the tiny, delicate finger bone of a murdered child. Logically, I knew I didn't know the child, didn't know how old the bone might be. It might have been a hundred years old, and it didn't truly matter anymore.

The thought that it might not matter sent a spike of guilt through me.

Lights flashed into the interior of the car as a van topped the hill behind us. I didn't move, didn't reach for the button in the center of the dash to spark the yellow hazard lights.

Let them hit us. At least it would stop this crazy night.

The car shook as the van whipped around us, its horn blaring. I flipped a middle finger at them even though they couldn't see it, anger boiling over inside. They rode their horn until they disappeared over the hill ahead of us on the road.

Nyarlathotep shifted in his seat.

"Tonight is about saving your kind from extinction. The longer you delay us, the less likely that becomes possible."

I shook my head, not looking at him. "You are *not* the good guy. Don't play that card with me."

"You have seen me in my true form. I am not the worst of my kind. There are things on the edge of the darkness, things we are trying to stop, that would use this world as a feasting board. They would spill every drop of humanity's blood until it runs a river for them to bathe in. Your race would be gristle in their teeth and meal for their bread."

An image of Nyarlathotep's true form charged to the front of my mind, making me close my eyes and shake my head. It rattled behind my eyelids, horrible and terrifying and lodged deep in my cerebellum. That image, the thing I saw, would fuel nightmares for years to come. I could just feel it. The thought that there might be more of his kind out there, and even worse than him, turned my guts into ice water.

But that finger bone, that child . . . "You aren't any better, not if you can use a thing like that."

Daniel's hand touched me again. "Maybe we should . . ."

"Shut up, Daniel." Pulling the parking brake, I turned the car off. I didn't look over, didn't look around, just kept my hands on the wheel and stared straight ahead. "I'm done here. Find someone else."

I meant it.

Silence filled the car, broken only by my strained breathing, the cooling tick of the engine, and the rustle of the angelic pelt the Man in Black wore as a coat. It fluttered around his legs, quietly *fwap*ping in the dark.

Headlights shone over the hill ahead, cutting through the dark like a pair of spotlights. They grew brighter as the vehicle they were attached to drove relentlessly our way.

The Man in Black turned in the bucket seat. Dark eyes looked past me.

"Daniel Alexander Langford."

I watched in the rearview mirror as Daniel turned toward him, his eyes wide and unblinking.

An eighteen-wheel semi truck burst over the hill.

"Step out of the car. Stand in the road."

Stiff-shouldered, Daniel reached for the door handle.

The semi cleared the crest of the hill, barreling over, picking up speed on the other side.

My throat closed in terror as I realized what was about to happen. I couldn't speak, couldn't scream *NO.* My fingers scrabbled desperately at the safety lock button. It engaged with a *click* from all four doors.

But Daniel had already pulled his handle.

He stepped out of the car, shutting the door behind him. He took three long steps and turned, his eyes closed as he stretched out his arms in supplication.

The semi roared down the hill.

He'll see him, he'll see him, the driver will see him and stop.

Daniel stood in the road, dressed in a black hoodie and dark jeans, in a puddle of darkness between wide-spread streetlights. We were only a few feet away, and I could barely make out the shape of his face.

I grabbed my door handle. I had to get out, to get him. There was time. I could get him out of the road.

Pain clamped around my arm, jerking me against the seat. Black spots fuzzed my eyesight as all the air rushed out of my lungs. Nyarlathotep leaned toward me, his face drawing close. Under his red right hand the pain turned cold, an ache stabbing deep, straight into my bones. His face thinned, drawn into a feral mask. Sharp, jagged rows of teeth meshed as he hissed between them. "You chose this, Acolyte, so you will watch. *This* is the price you pay for disobedience."

He shoved me, making my head jerk toward the window. My eyes fell on Daniel, standing still in the street, docile as a Hindu cow. The headlights of the truck threw his silhouette into harsh relief.

The driver saw him, the semi's air horn blaring out into the night and brakes locking in a scream as thin asbestos pads tried to stop twenty tons of vehicle rushing headlong at eighty miles per hour.

The truck didn't even slow.

My mind jolted with images of roadkill, burst organs and shredded fur.

Thirty feet.

Acid geysered up the back of my throat.

Twenty feet.

My heart clenched like a fist.

Ten.

I screamed.

"ALL RIGHT, I'LL DO IT! I'LL DO WHAT YOU WANT!"

Nyarlathotep let go of my arm. The fingers of his red right hand flashed together like matches being struck. The skinless hand made the same *crack!* my father's snapping fingers used to make. A burst of light slapped me in the face, searing my eyes, flash-frying my optic nerve. The world went white, then red, then black. I blinked away tears, and my vision returned like a slowly developing photograph.

Daniel sat in the backseat, the same look of serenity on his face.

The Man in Black pointed across the dash and out the window with his red right hand. The fingerbone swung gently at the end of my strand of hair, which was curled around two skinless red fingers.

I started the car. The keys jangled in my shaking hand.

"Thou shalt not tempt the lord thy god, Acolyte." The Man in Black's red right hand fell away, disappearing in the folds of his coat. "Now drive."

I looked in the rearview mirror. Daniel looked back at me. He smiled. I didn't smile back. My throat still tasted like stomach acid.

I put the damn car in gear and drove, hatred burning in my heart for the Man in Black.

9

THE LOW-SLUNG BUILDING sprawling in front of us was on the brink of collapsing in on itself.

It lay end to end in square architecture made for order and expedience instead of artistry. Windows lined the graffiti-covered brick wall illuminated by my headlights. Most of the glass had been broken, replaced with plywood gone gray from exposure. The brown, knee-high grass and weeds weren't enough to hide all the trash scattered on the ground.

I asked, "What is this place?"

It looked creepy as hell.

The Man in Black tucked the finger bone compass into his coat. The coal of hatred in my heart flared again. "It is the lair of an old . . . acquaintance." He opened the door, stepping out of the car.

Daniel scooted across the seat, his fingers on the door handle. "You coming, Charlie?" He looked expectant, his face unlined by concern. He looked like my kid brother climbing out of the car in the parking lot of the county fair, all wide-eyed and excited.

Jesus, he has no idea how jacked any of this is.

For a moment, a split second, the urge to crank the car, jam it in reverse, and *run,* run as fast and as far as my broken-down Honda Civic would take me, sat *hard* in my chest. It lay so heavy my heart felt as though it beat inside a plastic bag filled with syrup.

The Man in Black watched me through the windshield.

He shook his head.

"Yeah, yeah, I'm coming." I unbuckled the seat belt.

My door creaked, the sound rolling along the front of the building. I'd parked between a jacked-up, piss-off, stereotypical redneck truck that towered over the Honda, its wheels almost as tall as me, and a sleek, high-performance convertible so new it sparkled even in the dim, yellow light of the streetlamp. My eyes scanned the tiny parking lot. Cars of all makes and models, in all states of repair, filled almost every space, crowding next to each other like family at a reunion before the bickering started, before grudges fueled by alcohol sparked fistfights.

Daniel touched my arm.

He needed to stop doing that.

His voice was soft, low. "The Master's waiting, Charlie. We should go."

"Don't touch me." My face felt hot. I lashed out. "What's with this 'the Master' crap? Don't you know what's going on here?"

Daniel glanced at the Man in Black. His hand moved, hovering next to my arm but not touching it. He blinked, long and slow, his eyes closing then opening, locking with mine.

They were clear and bright.

And oh so green.

The anger inside me melted, just a little.

He looked away, running fingers through his bangs in a nervous gesture. "I *don't* know what's going on. All I know is that I feel . . . weird around him. Something I've never felt before. I want to . . . I don't know the word to describe it, but if he needs something, anything, I *want* to be the one who gives it to him." A look passed over his face. "Things are pretty screwed up in my head."

Damn.

My mind tried to sort it all out. I'd seen Nyarlathotep do things, things I couldn't explain, and he said Daniel had to worship him. I thought about the eighteen-wheeler and the look on Daniel's face as he waited for it to run him down.

Realization thundered in my mind.

He doesn't have any choice. Not one drop.

Daniel's hand touched my arm again. I didn't pull away this time. I couldn't. "The only thing that's not screwed up in my head is how sorry I am for whatever happened earlier. With us. I'll make it up to you, I promise. Whatever I have to do."

He really means it.

Fingers slid down my arm, warm when they brushed the skin of my hand. "I like you, Charlie. A *lot.* I hope I didn't mess that up."

Oh shit, oh shit, oh shit.

Daniel wouldn't look at me, his eyes turned just slightly away.

The Man in Black was suddenly there, next to us without moving. "We have things to do." He turned, his coat flaring out to brush against our legs. Gooseflesh rose where it touched. "Come, Acolyte; come, minion; follow me."

Daniel dropped my hand and stepped in behind the Man in Black.

That coal of hatred flared hot and sharp behind my breastbone as I followed the two of them into the building. I swore in my heart that somehow, some way, I would fix this. I would find a way to get Daniel away from the Man in Black, no matter what I had to do.

Walking into the run-down, burned-out hotel, I hoped I'd have the courage to keep that promise.

10

DARKNESS FILLED THE inside of the building.

Not pitch-black, but gloomy. Spooky.

Shadows cast by a multitude of burning candles danced along every nook and cranny. Tallowed light filled the room with a runny yellow glow.

In its glory days the place had been a "no-tell motel," a haven for third-rate romance and low-rent rendezvous. A feeling washed over me: impressions of desperate passion and sweaty flesh pressed to service empty souls and broken hearts. It swept around me like a graveyard breeze and left me feeling cold and a little shaky. The magick inside me had cooled to a low simmer but was still there, bubbling away.

We walked through the lobby, check-in counter on the left, dust-covered square furniture on the right. Candle wax had dripped from the edge of the counter in a glacial waterfall of various colors and lengths. Wax stalactites hung, some only an inch or two from the lip, some forming lumpy columns that stretched all the way to the floor. They piled across and spilled over the sign under the counter with raised lettering that read Pinecrest Inn.

Looking around, I took in the acoustic tiles falling from the drop ceiling, sagging and broken. Yellow insulation spilled out of the black openings like sulfuric cotton candy. Trash lay in piles on each side of a candlelit path that led deeper into the hotel and, all I could think was:

Fire hazard much?

A sour, clotted smell hung in the air. Part candle soot, part ripening meat. Nyarlathotep didn't stop. He strode along the path of candles, his coat flaring like bat wings, snuffing candle flames as he went. In the gathering darkness he became a silhouette, the shape of a man carved from starless midnight. As the gloom deepened, he seemed to stretch and grow. It was a trick of the light.

I hoped it was a trick of the light.

Candle glow glimmered along his red right hand, edging it starkly like a drop of blood on a sheet of black velvet.

Daniel followed him, close behind.

I hurried to keep up, not wanting to be caught in the dark. The thought made the skin under my shirt crawl with tiny electric jolts.

I'd caught up to only two steps behind them when we rounded the corner and ran into the line of people.

They stood, front to back, men and women of all shapes, sizes, and social standings, stretching down the hall leading to a room whose doorway had no door. Some of them turned as we rounded the corner, naked hatred pulling their faces into snarls.

A man in a black cowboy hat, a plaid shirt, and dark skintight jeans growled, an ugly animal sound rolling from deep in his chest. Red and purple spots mottled the caramel Aztec skin of his throat, spilling up onto a jaw clenched like a pit bull's, baring square, unnaturally white teeth. I watched foam fill his lips, spilling out of his mouth as though he were a rabid dog. He took a step toward us, hands curled into ripping claws.

Nyarlathotep's fist flashed, cuffing the man across the cheek in a casual backhand.

He fell as though he had been shot.

The line shuffled forward, the person behind him stepping on his back with her six-inch, thousand-dollar, spiked heels.

"What are all these people doing here?" I asked.

The Midnight Man kept walking. "They are here to worship."

I looked behind us at the line of people, taking note of their details, cataloging them in my mind. A man in an Armani suit texted on his cell phone; a mechanic with grease on his coveralls and skin hooked his grimy thumbs in drooping denim pockets as his fingers tapped his thighs in some rhythm I couldn't catch; the woman in the high heels had her legs spread to shoulder-width, keeping a ramrod-straight spine centered over the six-inch spikes; a tuxedoed groom grinned ear to ear while arm in arm with his white-gowned bride; a man older than my grandfather stooped in a set of striped pajamas; three cheerleaders in their uniforms looked unblinkingly at the brightly glowing screens they held; two soldiers in their uniforms held hands; a human so covered in filthy rags they had to be homeless hung on a pair of dented crutches . . . The line had over twenty people in it, and none of them fit with one another. The diversity disturbed me for some reason I couldn't identify.

"What are they worshiping?"

The Man in Black reached the open doorway. He stepped back, bowed, and gestured inside with a flourish. "They are worshiping her."

I moved past Daniel, between the chaos god on one side of the door and a saffron-robed Hare Krishna on the other. Crossing the threshold of the room made my head swim. The blood in my veins lit up as the magick simmer became a roiling boil. Ache settled in the Mark on my palm, the lines hot through to the back of my hand. The air inside clotted around us, thick and moist with a fog of humanity. The smell went to spoiled meat and crawled into my nose, coating the insides of my sinuses. The line of people followed the wall, leading to a bed in the center of the small room.

On the bed a man held himself up by his arms, the muscles of his back outlined in the flickering light of the guttering candles. Naked, he hovered over someone hidden by his body and the shadowed light.

The sight of it was a punch in my stomach.

I grabbed the wall, wounded palm flaring in sharp pain. My knees went weak, threatening to kick out from under me. A band of iron clamped around my chest, squeezing the air from my lungs, compressing my heart, and making it beat like an animal trapped in a heated cage.

That's not you. It's not you. It's not them. It's not then. *Feel the wall, feel the floor under your feet.*

You.

Are.

Okay.

I took a step, moving to feel myself move, to remind myself that I was still myself, that I *wasn't* pinned to a filthy mattress. Pushing deep breaths in and out of my lungs, I studied the situation, fighting past the trigger.

I've got this. I can handle this.

I could see most of the man's face as his head jerked up and down with the thrust of his hips, and I latched onto that. All of that was happening outside me, proof that I was in the room, not on the bed. Reality formed a dam against a flood of bad memories, and I held to that desperately. The man's contorted face wasn't over me; it was across the room over someone else. That reality gave me the stability to really look, to see the man and his actions.

I recognized him from a big-network hit dramedy that aired every Thursday.

He thrust violently, jerking spastically as if he'd been plugged into a live wire. The moist sound of skin slapping skin became a staccato rhythm section to the high-pitched gurgling grunts he made with each jerk and gyration. He thrust deep, the muscles in his back trembling like plucked cables as he roared out in climax.

He rolled away as the Man in Black stepped behind me, Daniel in tow.

The actor grabbed his clothes, clutching them to cover himself as he stood and moved away. The woman left on the bed reclined in a valley of soiled cotton; the mattress cupped her sprawled form, beaten into a cradle after countless interchanges. She lay, legs spread without shame, thighs and groin glistening, slick and swollen to deformity, the mattress under her damp and soaked through. Dark eyed and dark haired, her skin golden in the candlelight, she turned and looked at me. A claw of a hand rubbed across pendulous breasts that hung like overfilled wineskins to each side of a pronounced rib cage. A curving nail picked at a scabbed sore, one of hundreds dotting her body in a constellation of infection. She smiled and her lips cracked, chapped into snowflakes of dead skin. Her voice purred from deep in the back of her throat, smoky and seductive as she looked past me.

"Ahhhhhh, Son of Azathoth. To what do I owe the honor of this visit, my long lost friend?" She smiled a black-gummed smile. "And you brought me presents! How thoughtful of you."

"They are not for you, Ashtoreth." The Man in Black stepped past me. "Send your worshipers away so that we may talk."

The woman on the bed smiled a crooked smile. It pulled her round face to the side as though she were a stroke victim. "But if I send them away, who will worship me?" Her crooked smile turned into a crooked pout. "Will you worship me, O Lord of Nightmares?"

"You will gather more. Like flies to spoiled milk they will come."

The actor had pulled on most of his clothes. He staggered past the Man in Black, leaning away from him. The coat swirled, wrapping the actor's legs and waist, slowing him as it undulated against his body. It stretched as far as it could, holding the contact as long as possible before being pulled away. The next person in line stepped forward, a young Asian man with thick, square glasses. He pulled a distressed-cotton T-shirt over his head to reveal a narrow, hairless chest.

The Man in Black pointed at him. "Stop."

The Asian man dropped his shirt on the ground. At Nyarlathotep's command his hands bunched into fists. He stepped forward, his voice wavering from deep in his bird chest. "It's my turn."

The Crawling Chaos slipped his red right hand under the coat, reaching deep inside the dark folds of the skin he wore. With his hand still inside, he looked at the woman on the bed. His eyebrow arched in an unspoken question. She twittered a laugh in response. The Man in Black shrugged.

When his hand came out it held the black-bladed katana.

The curved sword flashed in a circle of silver light, striking as it was drawn. The razor edge caught the Asian man just over his hipbone, shearing through skin, spine, and viscera. Blood splashed with the blade's exit, tumbling through the air, splattering across Ashtoreth's sex.

She writhed and moaned in a way she hadn't under the actor's gyrations.

The Asian man looked down, shock raw on his face. His face rose, looking at me, mouth working silently up and down as he tried to speak. Blood leaked from the red line across his midsection. His hand came up, reaching toward me as if to steady himself. The movement upset his balance, making him top-heavy.

His upper body toppled free in a spill of blood.

That wasn't what made my stomach revolt and empty itself on the floor. No, that part had been too much, too shocking to do anything but strike me numb. What pushed me over the edge into vomiting was the way the next man in line casually stepped through the puddle of gore soaking into the threadbare carpet and began to unbutton his shirt, glassy eyes only focused on the blood-splattered goddess sprawled on the bed.

Face flushed hot and sticky, I turned away.

My ears rang hollow, everything muffled and dulled as I threw up. Nyarlathotep's voice sounded far away even though he stood close enough for me to reach out and touch him.

"Send them away, little goddess, or I will carve them all into decorations."

My mind babbled, already brittle from what had happened so far. I wanted to go, to get away, to run. My mind felt like crumpled cellophane.

Oh God, oh shit, not more, not now, not blood, what? Nowhere to go. No way to run. Fight. FIGHT.

Breath dragging deep in my lungs, I fought the panic, shoving it away, compartmentalizing my mind the way therapy had taught me to handle panic attacks.

Picture a door with a lock.

A hand touched my back.

My now empty stomach clenched at the thought of the Man in Black touching me with that skinless hand of his. The panic boiled back up. I jerked my head around.

Daniel hovered next to me, forehead creased in concern. His hand lay softly on my back; he was trying to comfort, trying to help. I grabbed the panic and shoved it into the room in my mind, slamming the door, turning the lock.

Daniel whispered, "You okay?"

I nodded.

I will be. To keep my promise, I will be.

Straightening, I turned away from my sick.

Enough of that. Just a physical reaction. Be strong. Be a survivor. Get through this. You can, you have before.

I wiped my mouth without thinking. The rough-edged symbol carved into my palm smeared across my lips, becoming moist with my saliva and my sick.

A spark flared deep in my mind, tearing my vision apart.

11

The room swirled, tilting and then locking into place. In my eyes it looked like two films playing at the same time, overlapping each other.

I could still see the room. All the furniture looked the same, but distorted, my new vision twisting the perspective and opening the space around me, bringing some things closer, pushing some things further away, and melding them all in a funhouse-mirror version of reality. The people in line were all glowing pockets of light, threaded through with tendrils of poison-green energy that twisted around them like mistletoe choking the life from an oak tree.

Nyarlathotep stood next to me, still tall and dark and imposing, but his true form was wrapped around him like a ghost image. I could see it dimly, superimposed over his human guise like a swirling, tentacle-laden illusion.

Movement from the bed made me turn.

The woman still lay there, still sprawled obscenely on the soiled mattress—but now, *now* I could see her true form.

She was grotesquely female, still long limbed, but her flesh was now tinged blue with decomposition, as if she'd been drowned and dead for days. A vertical slash of mouth ran from brow to chin, two wide yellow eyes set deep on each side. They glowed sulfurically, casting shadows down her corpulent form. Her hair writhed across the mattress under her head like a nest of trapped snakes.

My eyes traveled down Ashtoreth's body, taking in the puckered sacks of breasts that ran down her rib cage like infected udders. Horrible fascination made me look, made me see the thatch of wriggling, twisting fibrils above a gnashing, tooth-filled cavity that nested between swaying, blubbery thighs.

I shut my eyes, scrubbing my raw, wounded palm on the front of my hoodie, trying desperately to shut off the Sight.

When I opened them, the world had slid back to normal.

Thank God.

The line of people had turned around and was silently shuffling out of the room. The body of the Asian man was gone, nothing left behind but a dark stain on the carpet. I pushed his death out of my mind.

Get through this. This right here and right now.

The Man in Black stood at the end of the bed, hands in the pockets of his rustling, restless coat. The sword was gone again. Daniel hovered near me, not touching but close enough to. Ashtoreth still lay on the bed. Flame burned blue-bright from her fingertips, touching the end of a broken glass tube held to chapped lips. She sucked hard on the crack pipe, dirty gray smoke billowing out of her mouth and swirling around her face. A sticky-sweet smell crawled through the air, rippling the back of my throat.

I had to ask. I couldn't help myself. "What are you?"

She laughed, more smoke streaming out of her mouth. "Child,

I am everything you desire. I am Ashtoreth." She sucked on the end of the crack pipe, the rock inside flaring the dark orange of a dying sun. Her mouth on the pipe made a wet hissing noise as lip skin sizzled on butane-heated glass, and her right eye shuttered up and down and up and down in a mad twitch as the noxious smoke did its work. She exhaled her next words in a cloud of poison.

"I am the reason men kill each other and women debase themselves. I am the flicker in the night, the moment of comfort. I am the reason to live or the excuse to die. Your kind have named me the Whore of Babylon, the Scarlet Harlot, Aphrodite, Ishtar, and Lilith." She smiled a haughty, black-gummed smile. "I am everything woman. I *am* the Goddess of Love."

The arrogance of it struck me like a blow. Everything *I* desire? Everything *woman*? I lashed out. "You look like a two-bit crack whore to me."

Ashtoreth turned to the Man in Black. "Oh, she has fire in her belly, this one does! There's an anger inside her that will bite like a serpent if poked and prodded too much." She wriggled, sitting up on the mattress. It squelched underneath her, and my stomach twisted. "You should give her to me. With her Sight, there are so *many* things I could show her."

"She is *mine*. I will not share."

Anger flared inside me at the possessive tone used by the Man in Black. Before I could protest, Ashtoreth turned her eyes toward Daniel. The look on her face hit me like a splash of ice water: a look of raw desire, of naked lust.

A look of hunger.

"Give me the boy, then, he's ready to partake of my gifts. Ripe for the plucking, that one is. Never known a woman, and he's long overdue." Her hand dipped low, slithering over jutting hipbones to move between her thighs. I kept my eyes pinned to the glowing crack pipe still hovering around Ashtoreth's angular, pock-marked face. After what I had Seen, I did not want to watch what she did with her hand.

The Man in Black shook his head. "He is also mine."

"He's a worshiper." Ashtoreth's voice was haughty, dismissive. "He can be easily replaced. You took one of mine and sent the others away. The use of yours would place us on even ground."

Nyarlathotep shook his head. "But we are not equals. I am the Crawling Chaos, and you are a filthy, worn-out receptacle."

Fury flashed across Ashtoreth's face, spilling out in a snarl. "This is still my lair, still my place of power!"

"Fear drives people further than lust does."

The Whore Goddess rose to her knees. The mattress suctioned off her back, wet linen peeling slowly from her skin. Bedsores the size of my palm were slapped across her back and buttocks. Heavy breasts swung left and right, *fwap*ping every time they impacted against her waist, punctuating her shrill and venomous voice.

"Love drives humans to overcome fear!"

The Man in Black was beside the bed in a blink, red right hand clamped around Ashtoreth's throat. He pulled her close, lifting her, making her dangle in front of him. Her dark eyes bulged from the pressure of that skinless right hand.

The Man in Black curled his lips into a sneer. "You have not inspired love for a very long time. You have fallen far, O mighty Ashtoreth." He flung her on the bed. She bounced into her hollow with a wet slap. "And you would do well to remember your place."

Ashtoreth crumpled on the soiled mattress. Locks of greasy hair hung over her face. She didn't brush them aside as she brought the broken stem of glass she still held up to her cracked, chapped lips. She stopped, one eye squinting through her lank hair at the crack pipe. It was empty.

A tear shimmered, spilling out and tracking down the dirty cheek of the goddess.

I felt sorry for her. Even after Seeing her true form and knowing what she was . . . I couldn't help it.

Pity drove through me in a quick stab, making me move forward. "You said she could point us on our way. Can we get that over with?"

The Man in Black turned. He smiled his shark-toothed smile. "Ah, Acolyte, so eager to run into the fray. Yes, let's get this over with." He pointed at Ashtoreth. "Do you know why I have come here?"

Ashtoreth shook her head, crack pipe clenched in her hand. "You are hunting your kind. What you have done fills the Void with screams. But as you have said, I am not of your ilk. You can't be hunting me. I have nothing to do with you or your kind, elder god."

The Dark Man sat on the edge of the bed. His coat rustled. Ashtoreth tensed, shying away like a dog that's been beaten. "But, little goddess, you do have something I need."

Her voice was a hoarse choke. "What could that be?"

"You have the ability to seek out those who desire, and my brethren desire this world more than anything. They lust after it with everything they are."

Ashtoreth looked away. "I can feel their appetite."

"I want that ability."

"You know I cannot grant you my gifts, Son of Azathoth."

"No, little goddess," the Midnight Man said with a smile, "but you can give them to my Acolyte."

12

"Whoa, whoa, what?" My hands were up as I took a step back, making distance between us. "I don't want another gift." The lines cut into my palm throbbed. "And I damn sure don't want another Mark."

No. No way did I want anything else added to me, cut into me, or done to me. I'd had enough of that.

Nyarlathotep stood in front of me without moving, inches away from my outstretched palms. His coat rustled, whispering out to caress my hands. It was soft, like the first fur of a newborn pup, the silk of an infant's hair.

He looked down at me. "You can only be Marked once. This gift will be a relic of Ashtoreth that will marry your Sight. It will allow us to hunt our enemies."

I pulled my hands away from the coat. They stuck, just slightly, as though I were pulling them from a bucket of paraffin.

I didn't want the gift.

"She has the gift; just bring her with us," I said.

The Man in Black laughed. "She is a whore in her heart, unfaithful and untrustworthy. She will not do for my purpose."

Ashtoreth said nothing at the insult.

Daniel bowed. "I would gladly bear the gift, Master."

Nyarlathotep ignored him, still staring at me expectantly. "The gift must be used with your Sight or it is worthless. It is the job of an Acolyte, not a minion." The Man in Black's face softened. His voice dropped to a low, seductive purr. "This will not hurt, Charlotte Tristan Moore. You will feel no pain, but it is necessary that you do this."

"Stop using my full name."

The weight of his stare fell on me, pushing against my will. So much had been done to me and around me that I wanted to just quit. To lie down. Hopelessness, that old familiar feeling, tickled the base of my mind. I just wanted this over with. Only a few hours ago, my life had been okay. I'd settled into living on my own. I had a boring job that didn't kill my soul. I was out of pissant, middle-of-nowhere Beaumont, Kansas, away from the knowing glances and pitying looks that never let me forget what had happened. I'd found a new therapist and a new martial arts school. Whole months had gone by without a panic attack.

And there was Daniel.

Until earlier tonight and the thing he had done, he'd been my first male friendship since . . . well, since. I'd taken strength from the new relationship. It was something I had wanted to explore further. I wanted that part of myself back, the part that had been stolen from me so long ago, and I wanted it to be with Daniel. Earlier tonight had just been too soon, too sudden, too . . . much.

At the time I'd been angry and hurt, but standing in that room I thought it might all have been a misunderstanding. If what he'd said earlier was true, and I believed it was, our conflict could be fixed after some time, some sleep, and some talking. We could be okay.

I wanted that life back.

Life before this train of weirdness had crashed into my night.

Life before chaos gods and Marks and black magick.

Do what you have to do. You can handle this. Get to the other side. You're a survivor, you've proven that.

And apparently if I didn't do this, the world would end. Literally.

"Screw it." I sighed, giving in. "Okay."

The Man in Black nodded and stepped aside.

Ashtoreth held out her arms. "Come to me, my child."

"I'm not getting on that bed."

That I will not do. No way in hell.

Ashtoreth giggled. A disconcerting sound, something that should come from a schoolgirl instead of an ancient Goddess of Whores, it scraped a raw nerve in my ears. "You are smarter than you appear, dear. Now stand close while I fetch your present."

The words sank an ominous feeling deep in the pit of my stomach. I glanced over my shoulder. The Man in Black stood impassive, obsidian eyes glittering beneath a drawn brow. Daniel gave me a reassuring smile. He mouthed the words *I'm right here*.

It actually made me feel better.

Then I turned to the bed.

Ashtoreth dug the jagged end of the broken crack pipe into her own arm, the blackened, brittle edges leaving a gash. The skin peeled open, gaping wide as it split, revealing a black and empty void inside. Cold spilled from it, drifting through the air like a breeze from the grave. I couldn't tear my eyes away, staring in horror at the eldritch depths inside the wound. A black so deep it wasn't even a color filled it, the utter darkness of the space between stars.

Alien.

Terrifying.

Ashtoreth reached inside the wound, scabbed knuckles slipping deep, twisting obscenely, and disappearing to the wrist. I watched her face as she fished around inside the wound. Her dark eyes rolled back in their sockets, eyelashes fluttering. A hollow moan broke free inside the goddess's chest, slipping out of a mouth gone slack and loose. Ashtoreth shuddered in pleasure.

I was caught between revulsion and fascination.

Ashtoreth's arm twisted, muscles flexing in her forearm. Slowly she drew her hand out; it slipped free with a moist sucking noise. She fell back on the mattress loose and sprawling, a lover spent from a night of passion. She held a circle of metal, gold highlights around its circumference gleaming with moisture in the candlelight.

She lolled her head over toward me, voice slurring as she spoke. "Lean forward child. Accept your gift."

I tilted my head nearer to the Goddess of Whores. Tension sang along my spine with the movement. I didn't want to get closer. The ring in Ashtoreth's hand looked harmless, a simple circle of metal that might have been iron save for the strange tinge and hue of the metal, like bronze accumulating patina for a millennium. Its surface was smooth and clean. In the center, a dirty green round orb on a disc the size of a pigeon egg sat like a fat spider in a web. Ashtoreth moved it toward me.

I leaned away, wary. "What is that?"

"Stop fighting every damn step, Acolyte. It is infuriating." The Man in Black's voice was a jaw-clenched growl.

I looked over my shoulder. "So far, accepting things from you people has sucked big-time." I held my hand up, palm out. "See? No pun intended."

You don't like it, pick another Acolyte. Oh, that's right, you said you can't.

Nyarlathotep's face twisted into a deeper snarl.

Ashtoreth spoke, her voice gone all smoky and seductive. "Look at me, child." I turned from the Dark God to the Whore Goddess. She dangled the circlet from her fingertips. "This torc is not a Mark. This is a talisman, an object of my power. It's a tool you can use or not. Remove it when you are done with the need of it. It will not harm you." She said it with a low, throaty purr, mouthing the words she spoke as though they were obscene. It tugged something deep inside me. That something I'd felt for the first time only recently.

I looked over at Daniel. He watched me closely.

I remembered my promise.

I reached for the torc. My fingers closed on it, curling around the metal, pressing it against the incised skin of my palm. It hummed in my grip, vibrating with a charge of power that made the magick in my blood sing.

It wanted me to put the torc on.

"What do I do with it?"

"Slip it over your head, child. It is meant to be worn about your neck."

It was smaller than my skull. I lifted it to my head.

This is going to look like a tiara.

The second the metal touched my scalp, it expanded, pushing against my fingers, sliding over my head like the collar of an old T-shirt until it lay against my collarbones. It was heavy, pressing down in a hard line. The metal went chilly, singing cold across its surface. Gooseflesh raised on my skin.

Here it comes.

I braced for the pain.

Nothing else happened.

I let loose the breath I had been holding, let my fingers drop away.

The torc shrank against my throat.

Choking me.

My fingers scrabbled, trying to dig underneath. Tight. Too tight. I couldn't find purchase. Black fireworks burst at the edge of my vision. Flashing in fast and staying, peppering their way inward, turning the world dark a little at a time. I spun, my narrowing gaze falling on the Man in Black. He stood tall and impassive, staring down at me.

Sonofabitch, he tricked me.

The torc *squeezed,* a circle of pain around my throat. As my lungs burned, my trembling knees broke. I slid down. Hands were on me, an arm strong around my shoulders, keeping me off the floor. I slipped sideways and saw Daniel, his face nearly covered with black specks, right next to me. His mouth moved, not making any sound.

The world blinked away to blackness.

The torc opened with a sigh, loosening its grip, settling to rest easy at the base of my throat.

Air, the sweetest air I had ever tasted, rushed into my lungs. The pitch across my eyes cracked, splitting open as I sucked in oxygen, dragging it into my lungs, clawing for it. The first sound I heard other than my own tortured gasps for air was Daniel calling my name, voice pitchy with panic.

The second was Ashtoreth's twittering giggle.

"Are you okay?" Daniel held me, keeping me upright.

The Whore Goddess cackled. "She is fine, cultist. The torc was merely becoming familiar with its wearer."

I pushed away, out of Daniel's arms, standing on wobbly legs. Fire pulsed in my throat but, dammit, I could stand. I pointed a finger at Ashtoreth. "You lied to me."

The Whore Goddess pouted. "I did not, child. You are not harmed."

"It feels like my larynx has been cut in two."

"Hurt is not harmed. You should learn the difference if you are going to play in the arena of gods."

My throat hurt as I said, "Fuck you."

Bitch.

I turned to the Man in Black. "Are we done here? I'm sick of this place."

Nyarlathotep turned dark eyes to Ashtoreth. "The talisman will let her find my kind on this plane of existence?"

"More than that, Lord of Nightmares. I have given your Acolyte the ability to not only find what you seek, but to take you there as well. All she has to do is use the Sight you gave her, and the talisman will carry you to the nearest of your kind."

"That is very generous of you, little goddess." His eyes narrowed, red right hand slipping from the folds of his coat. "*Too* generous, I think."

Terror crawled across Ashtoreth's face at the sight of Nyarlathotep's hand. She cowered, pushing herself farther into the hollow of the soiled mattress, her wide eyes pinned on that red right hand. "It is not a trick, Dark Lord! It is how my power works! Find and fetch are part and parcel of desire!"

The Man in Black took a step toward the bed, his red right hand rising slowly. A black energy crackled along the nerves laced over the raw, skinless flesh.

I grabbed his arm without thinking. My hand touched his coat and it rippled under my fingers, curling around them. An alien melody sang softly in my mind. Nyarlathotep turned, scowling, as I jerked my hand away, cutting off the song.

"We have what we came here for. She seems harmless, so let's go find the bad guys."

"Do not attempt to bar my action again, Acolyte. It will not end well next time."

I bristled. "Thanks to you, my night can't really get any worse."

A smile cut across the Dark Man's face. "We shall see about that, Charlotte Tristan Moore." His red right hand disappeared in the folds of his coat. "Let us be about our bloody-handed business tonight." With that he turned, striding toward the door.

Daniel looked at me for a long moment before turning and following. I squared my shoulders, took a deep breath, and started after them.

Out of the frying pan and into the fire.

"Child, wait," Ashtoreth called, making me turn at the doorway. Her mouth opened in a black-gummed smile. "Thank you for your mercy."

My words were as harsh as my voice. "It wasn't mercy for you, bitch. I just didn't want to see whatever he planned to do."

"Still, I owe you my gratitude." The Whore Goddess rose, kneeling on the unclean mattress. She stretched out her arms. The wound gaped open, starless void yawning wide. "Would you like to fuck my wound?"

Ashtoreth's terrible giggle chased me down the hallway.

13

The parking lot was empty except for my car, Daniel, and the Crawling Chaos.

Where the hell do these names come from? The Crawling Chaos? The Whore Goddess?

Actually, that one is kind of obvious.

Scratch that. I'd seen the Man in Black's true form. Crawling Chaos actually was a pretty apt description.

They stood on the sidewalk, Daniel looking at the Man in Black like a lost puppy and the Man in Black looking up at the stars. The door creaked as I pushed it open, chill night air hitting me like a slap. It smelled clean and clear making me realize my mouth tasted foul, the back of my throat burning from being sick.

I would kill for a mint or a stick of gum.

Nyarlathotep's red right hand came out of his coat pocket as I stepped up to them. The slick, bloodless fingers held a silver foil-wrapped object.

A stick of gum.

He held it toward me.

I stopped short. “I hate that. Don’t read my mind.”

He didn’t say anything, just stood there in his creepy coat holding out the stick of gum. It winked at me, the yellow sodium lights above us reflecting dully off the foil. I didn’t want the gum anymore, not from him.

The taste in my mouth intensified, curdling. I tried to swallow, to force it down, but it stuck to the back of my throat like a cold. Even with the taste choking me, I didn’t want that gum. I didn’t trust it not to be a trick.

“It is not a trick, Acolyte. It is simply what you wished for. What advantage could I receive from giving you a stick of gum? You can trust that no harm will come to you,” he purred, his voice tickling along the inside of me.

He’d read my mind again. It made me want the gum even less, although my mouth tasted so bad I felt sick to my stomach.

Trust him? I didn’t think so.

Daniel reached out and took the stick of gum. Unwrapping it, he let the foil flutter to the ground at his feet. Pulling the end off, he popped it in his mouth, chewed, and swallowed. He stood for a moment as we both watched him. After a long second he held the rest of the gum out to me. “It’s safe, Charlie.”

I took the gum. I still didn’t trust the Man in Black, but Daniel had taken a chance on my behalf, and that obligated me.

And my mouth still tasted like death.

The spearmint cut through like a winter breeze the second it hit my tongue. The queasiness broke, fading with each chew. I looked at the Man in Black. “I still don’t want you reading my mind. It creeps me the hell out.”

He shrugged, his coat’s flaps waving on their own. “It matters not what you want, Acolyte. The Mark you bear connects us; it is what will allow us to use Ashtoreth’s gift and complete the mission set before us.”

The second he mentioned it, I became aware again of the circle around my throat. It lay on my collarbones, bruising and heavy, making them sore underneath it. I wanted it off me. I wanted Nyarlathotep out of my life. I wanted this night to be over.

Something moved on the edge of the parking lot, drawing my attention.

A low, long shape moved next to the bushes that edged the asphalt lot. Its four-legged gait herked and jerked, all hackles and low-slung spine. The creature glistened in the sodium lights above us, one baleful yellow eye staring at me as it slipped into a shadow, the other a black hole in its skull. I stared at it, and it stared right back from the darkness.

"What the hell is that?" Daniel's voice sounded too loud, shocking me.

The Man in Black answered. "It is a skinhound. It will hunt her until the one who sent it is defeated."

Daniel stepped in front of me, hands curled into fists. "Then let's kill it before it can hurt her."

"He will send more if that one is destroyed." Nyarlathotep put his normal hand on Daniel's shoulder. "That one will remain at bay while I am here, but the only way for my Acolyte to be safe is if we complete our mission."

I hate it when people talk *about* me and not *to* me.

"What do we do, then? How does this . . ." I searched for the right word. ". . . *collar* work?"

"Your magick is intuitive. It is a part of you, the same as the mechanism that allows you to breathe or your heart to beat is a part of you."

I held up my hand. The Mark across my palm was red and raw and scabbed over. "I thought this was where the magick came from."

"That merely activated what already lay inside you waiting to be born."

I could feel the magick inside me. "What do I do?"

"Close your eyes."

"Why do I have to close my eyes?"

Thin lips pulled back to show gritted shark teeth. "Do you have to question everything, Acolyte?"

"I'm not the trusting kind. I used to be, but I learned my lesson the hard way."

He sighed. "You have to use your Sight to find the one we seek. It is easier if you shut off your vision of this plane."

"That's all you had to say." I closed my eyes.

The Man in Black's voice vibrated through me. I could feel it in my bones: a low, deep thrum. "Open your mind. The elder gods are out there. You now have the ability to feel the desires of others. The ones we seek desire to enter this plane of reality. Their lust for this world will call to you like a siren song."

As he spoke, my mind loosened. It slipped like a dislocated joint, popping out of its socket and stretching. It hurt in a long, slow ache. From the edges of my mindspace came little pinpricks, swirly white spots that sparked and flared in my cerebral cortex. Emotions connected to impressions swept through me, quick as mosquito bites.

A woman lusting after a bottle.

A man lusting after a woman.

A child lusting after a meal.

A woman lusting after a girl's youth.

A psychopath lusting after human flesh.

The pinpricks jabbed at my brain, stabbing quicker and quicker, each one crowding into a fuzz of white noise. They blanketed my mind like maggots on a corpse, my own thoughts covered like a child who'd fallen through the ice.

Two bursts of desire came in peals of thunder, rolling over all the ones before them, echoing each other.

They were vast.

Alien.

Other.

Crying out:

MUST

BE

FREE

My mind unfolded in a topographical map. I could See all the wants like a landscape. Towering over them were the two thunderous alien desires, standing like mountains, one much closer than the other.

My voice sounded hollow, tinny when I spoke. "I have them. There are two."

Nyarlathotep's voice was clear, vibrating through me, shaking the map in my mindsight. "Good, Acolyte. Now take our hands and complete the circle."

I cracked one eye. The world swam for a split second as it invaded my vision, but I held onto the map in my skull. The Man in Black and Daniel were in front of me, hands clasped; they both reached out to me with their free ones. My right hand took Daniel's left, a sharp, raw rub across the incisions on my palm as his skin touched mine. If he noticed, he didn't say anything.

The Man in Black held out his hand. His red right hand.

I hesitated.

The map in my head slid a little, breaking along the edges.

Dammit.

I took that skinless hand and closed my eye.

Power thrummed through me. It felt as though I'd been plugged into a circuit. My body hummed through my bones and my joints.

Daniel's voice came from my right. "Whoa."

I guess he could feel it too.

The map sharpened, becoming brighter in my mind's eye. "What now?"

The Man in Black purred, "Pick one and simply wish to be there."

"It can't be that easy."

"Acolyte . . ."

I took a deep breath, focused on the mountain of desire closest to us, and wished.

Dear God, please don't let this hurt.

He didn't listen.

14

At first it felt like a warm shower. Soft, fat droplets peppering my skin in a massage, caressing, nearly tickling. The sensation was nice. Relaxing. A relief after the horror I'd been through.

Then the sensation turned.

The droplets came harder.

Sharper.

Striking every inch of me like diamond-cut thorns even through the safety of my clothes. It felt like being scrubbed down with a cheese grater.

I fell to my knees, banging them on a hard surface. My eyes were open, but I couldn't see anything, the world washed all in red. My skin pulsed with my heartbeat, each thud of it against my breastbone washing me with a wave of raw, abraded pain. I fought to catch my breath, jerking air into my lungs. Even they were sore, as though they had been flash-burned from the inside out.

This must be what a hot dog feels like in the microwave.

The world swam to focus in waves, the pain receding with each pulse until I could sit up again, a concrete walkway hard under my knees. In front of me a building made of faux marble and brick soared into the night. The overly large but tastefully subdued sign over the swoosh-swoosh automatic entrance read SAINT YOGASHURA MEDICAL CENTER.

What the hell?

Noise made me look over. Daniel was on his knees about fifteen feet away, in the grass between the walkway and the building. He retched, throwing up all over the lawn in front of him. The smell of it rode the night breeze over to me, and I could see it, orange-brown on the perfectly manicured Fescue. Whatever had just happened had been rough, but it seemed to be fading fast.

Is he okay? Why is he sick?

Immediately I felt guilty at the thought. I'd been sick not even thirty minutes ago.

The air swished behind me, and I turned. The Man in Black stood there, looking exactly as he had before whatever happened had happened. Still tall, dark, and sinister.

I climbed to my feet. My skin prickled, but less and less each second, fading away with every heartbeat.

"What was that?" I started walking to where Daniel knelt on the grass. He leaned back over his feet, still kneeling. His head hung low to his chest. He looked absolutely exhausted.

The Man in Black walked with me. "Your term for it would be transdimensional teleportation. Ashtoreth's gift allowed you to step through the void between Time and Space, the narrow gap between the skin and the muscle of the universe, and to take us with you."

Why does he have to use the most disturbing imagery when answering a question?

By the time I reached Daniel's side, the pain from teleporting had faded almost completely.

For me at least.

Daniel looked terrible. Sweat ran in rivulets down his face, his skin waxy and pale. I'd seen him nearly every day since he'd started working with me, early in the morning for an eight AM shift and after all night shifts when he worked for someone else. I'd never seen him look so washed out. The hollows under his eyes were smudged black and sunken in. He sucked air in long, deep breaths as though he had just run ten miles. Squatting beside him, I put my hand on his face.

He was ice cold.

His eyes cracked open, the lids puffy and only half raised, and he turned into my hand. A tiny smile made his cheek twitch under my palm. His voice came out low, hoarse from being sick. "Hey, hey, Charlie. That was pretty rough." His hand reached for mine. "Are you okay?"

He's asking about me? He's the one who looks like hell.

His concern touched me. I spoke gently and quietly. "I'm okay."

"Good." He nodded, his eyes closing again. "Good. I was worried about you."

"I'm all right. I can take care of myself. Are you going to be okay?" A thought struck me. "We're at a hospital. Do you need me to get a doctor?"

"We are not here for that, Acolyte." The Man in Black loomed over us. His coat rustled, stretching as it brushed softly against my hip and caressed Daniel's thighs.

Anger sparked, hot and bright. "Look, he's not okay. Something about what just happened hurt him, and if he needs a doctor then, by God, we are going to get him one."

The coat pulled away, reacting to my anger. Its wearer simply looked down at me with glittering black eyes. He didn't speak, just stared at me. I stared back in defiance, locking my gaze with his. The symbol cut into my hand began to tingle and burn. I shoved it out of my mind, forcing myself to keep staring, to keep looking, to hold that gaze as long as possible. My eyes burned in their sockets. I rode my anger until it started to crumble underneath me. I held on, staring at those sinister midnight eyes as long as I could.

Blinking back tears, I broke and turned away.

Nyarlathotep's voice fell on me like the striking of a midnight bell. "There is only one god you need be concerned with, Acolyte. Now stand up. Both of you."

I hated him as I got to my feet. Hated him deep inside my heart. I helped Daniel up hating this nightmare of a night.

And I *hated* the Man in Black.

Daniel swayed on his feet. The Dark God stepped in front of him. "Daniel Alexander Langford, you will stand strong. You will follow me."

I watched Daniel steady himself, setting those wide shoulders in a line and straightening his spine. His skin was still pale, but he wasn't shivering or sweating anymore. He took a deep breath, held it, and blew it out between his lips. He nodded at the Man in Black. "I will follow you to the ends of the earth, Master."

The Man in Black turned in a swirl of coat and began walking toward the hospital. Daniel and I followed.

I still didn't like the *Master* crap, but Daniel was able to move and seemed to be better, so I let it lie.

For now.

We caught up to the Man in Black at the entrance of the hospital. He stood, staring at the doorway, both hands deep in the pockets of his coat. We stopped just behind him.

I hate hospitals. I hate them with the hatred. They suck. I haven't been to one since I got out of one. Just being on the sidewalk I could feel it, on the edge of my mind. A therapist once urged me to go to a hospital, just to try and deal with my phobia. "Face your fears; you'll be stronger for it," she used to say.

I found a new therapist.

Now I wished I had at least given her advice a chance. Already my chest felt tight, lungs stuffed with cotton like a cheap cigarette filter, hard to drag air through.

My hand clenched and unclenched. Pain twinged along the edges of the symbol cut into my palm, giving me something to focus on, something to help me stay outside my own head. I pushed away from my physical reaction and studied the waiting room on the other side of the doors. Empty.

Totally and completely empty, not one soul in sight.

Hospitals are never empty. Even at that time of night they had people. Patients, family members, nurses, orderlies, doctors all hustling and bustling, doing things and going places. The waiting rooms might not be full in the middle of the night, but they would never be empty.

The creeps climbed my spine.

"Where is everybody?" My voice shook. Just a little.

The Man in Black didn't look at me, still studying the door like a raven studying a carcass. "They have probably been taken."

"Taken? By what?"

"By the thing we have come here hunting."

Cryptic much?

"You don't know what we're here to stop?"

"This place is warded. That is why Ashtoreth's gift could only take us this far." He leaned forward, tilting slightly at the waist. Dark eyes closed as he drew a long sniff through his bladed nose. He held it for a moment then snorted it out. His jaw opened, jagged shark teeth pulling apart in strings of saliva. That long, scabrous tongue rolled out between them, flopping against his chin, forked and too long. A jerk of his head lapped it up against the air.

It crackled black sparks as it brushed a barrier I couldn't see.

That tongue zipped back into his mouth like a kid's party favor. His throat worked, savoring the taste for a long moment. Dark eyes glittered when he looked down at me. "You are in for a treat tonight, Acolyte."

I don't like the sound of that.

"What does that mean?"

He smiled but didn't answer.

Damn him.

His left hand came out of the pocket of his coat holding something. He held it out to me. "Here, Acolyte."

It was a stick.

"What is that?"

"It is your weapon."

I took it from him carefully, keeping my fingers away from his. The stick was twice as long as my hand and made of gnarled, rough-barked wood burned black to hard charcoal on one end. It was heavy, heavier than it looked. Heavier than it should have been.

"Ummm, am I going to be fighting leprechauns or pixies? This is a pretty dainty club."

The Man in Black pulled his red right hand from his pocket. Reaching over, he touched the end of the stick with a skinless fingertip.

A gout of fire burst from the weapon.

Heat blasted my face, singing my eyebrows and scorching my cheeks.

I dropped the stick with a curse.

The flame guttered out as it clattered to the concrete at my feet. My face felt tight. The scent of burnt hair filled my nostrils, all I could smell. *My* burnt hair.

"What the hell!"

Amusement twitched the Man in Black's eyebrow up. "That is the fire that Prometheus stole. You should be more careful with it."

Daniel bent and picked up the stick, holding it carefully between his fingertips. He didn't say anything, just held it out to me with a look on his face.

I waved it away. "I don't want that. You keep it." Heat throbbed under my fingertips where they'd been singed.

"I don't think I can use it, Charlie."

"He is right, Acolyte."

I looked between the two of them. "Why not?"

Daniel shrugged. "I'm not magick."

"Well, I'm not either." I realized the thing I'd felt inside me earlier had quieted. Did it go away? Had I used it up?

"You just teleported us here from Motel Hell by wishing. If that doesn't qualify you as magick, I don't know what does."

He had a point.

I took the stick. It wasn't warm or tingly or anything; it just felt dead and heavy in my hand. A thin curl of smoke came off the charcoal end.

Nyarlathotep looked surprised.

"What?" I asked.

"You did not argue with him."

"He made sense." I shrugged. "And he's not evil."

"And you think I am?"

"Aren't you?"

"I am the Crawling Chaos. Evil is a matter of perspective."

"Is that supposed to comfort me?"

The Crawling Chaos simply smiled, saying nothing.

I didn't think so.

He went back to staring at the air in front of him. It was discolored where his tongue had licked, like breathing fog on a window in winter. I shuddered, the image of his tongue bouncing around my brain.

Daniel spoke up. "How are we going to get inside, Master?"

"It will take a sacrifice of pain to open a way through the wards."

"I'll make that sacrifice for you." He stepped up, moving closer to the Man in Black.

Grabbing his arm, I jerked him back. "What are you doing?"

He faced me, but his eyes kept jittering toward the chaos god, who now studied us as if we had done something interesting. "I can't help it. I want to do what he needs so bad. It's worse than I have ever wanted anything before. Food, sex . . . anything." His eyes slid completely away from mine. His voice became strangled, like the next words hurt him to say. "Even more than I want you."

"Do not fear, Acolyte. I will not take the sacrifice from him. He could not withstand it. There is another way."

I turned. The Man in Black stood in the same place, his arms were wide, red right hand gleaming in the incandescent light of the entranceway. The fingers twisted, wrapping around each other as if they had too many knuckles or no knuckles at all. Watching them move made my head buzz. The tail of his coat shifted, stretching and rolling, becoming longer, long enough to curl and rise in inky tendrils of utter darkness. Its shape changed, transmuting into something with jagged curves and spiky points. A tendril rose in a corkscrew, turning as it lengthened to a needle-thin point in front of Nyarlathotep's face. He nodded once, a sharp up and down, and the needle tendril turned. It hung for a moment, a long moment, before driving itself against the discolored air.

It struck with a sharp *CRACK!* and the air splintered.

Three things happened. One, the air discolored, crackling where the coat stabbed with energy the sickly greenish color of a still-healing bruise. Two, my nose clogged with the stench of spoiled bacon cooking.

And three, my head filled with singing, a weird alien song not made by a human voice. It boomed into my mind, a choir of ill children, frantic, urgent, and desperate.

The coat screamed, and I could hear it.

My hands clamped the side of my head, but it did no good. I could still hear it, still *feel* it ringing in my ears, splinters of sound pricking the membrane of my eardrum. I watched the needle tendril spread, displacing the fogged air, pushing it wide, roiling into a bigger space. The screaming grew louder.

"Stop, you're hurting it!"

The Man in Black's voice was cold. "This is the sacrifice that must be made, Acolyte. Something must take the agony of the wards. It will not be me."

"I'll do it then. I'll take it if you will just stop hurting the coat." The screaming broke, crumbling into a desperate, whining mewl. A sound full of anguish and sorrow. A sound of hopelessness. I knew that sound. I'd *made* that sound. Memory rose, a physical thing moving through my body, coating my bones with lead. I knew the kind of pain it took to force those sounds from something. Fighting past it I said, "I'll be the one."

"You cannot. You are a mere mortal. The wards would burn you to ash."

His words were callous, uncaring.

The coat changed where it stabbed the air, morphing itself into an opening that kept widening. Curls of smoke lifted off it, and the darkness that made it quivered and shook. Inside my head I could feel the coat weeping in despair. It rang across my mind, sorrow rising up like floodwater. I knew what it felt like to be in pain so unrelenting that all you want is the grace of death, the peace that must come from giving up, lying down, ceasing to be. Pain that convinced you that whatever came on the other side of that door had to be better than what you were going through in that very moment.

Nyarlathotep's indifference cut through that, striking the chord of anger that ran through me, the chord that had been struck after that long-ago night. Rage, the deep and abiding rage that lived inside, boiled up in a conflagration. My hand lashed out, reaching for the coat to pull it free.

Daniel grabbed my arm.

"Charlie, don't. Don't make him angry."

Angry? Make him angry?

I was so furious that Daniel's words were a buzz. Temples

throbbing, blood hot in my veins, I looked at his hand on my wrist. "Let. Go."

"Calm down. You have to be cool."

I swung the stick at his head.

He ducked, his high-school wrestler reflexes still intact, and leaned back. His hand came off my arm. Fury boiled behind my eyes, making me headblind, only able to attack without thinking. I lunged, stick heavy in my hand, raised to swing. Daniel stepped in and wrapped his arms around me, crushing me to his chest, trapping me against him.

The anger doused cold with instant panic.

TrappedstuckcantmovecantgetfreeohgodohgodOHGOD . . .

I froze, my mind melting down. I couldn't move my arms. I couldn't escape the feel of his face pressed against mine, the smell of man.

I drowned.

He lifted me, my feet off the ground, and my stomach sickened with the feeling of motion; panic made me blind for a moment, my sight washed black. Forever seemed to pass before he set me on my feet, his arms disappearing from around me. My knees gave out. The ground hit hard on my hip and shoulder, driving out the breath I had been holding, jarring me out of panic with sharp pain. My vision swam clear in time for me to see the Man in Black step toward us through the hole in the air his coat had made. Once he was through, the coat collapsed behind him, falling to the ground as if soaking wet. The end of it lay in tatters, long and limp around his feet.

The coat fell silent inside my head.

15

"What the hell was that?" Daniel asked this time, yelling at the Man in Black. I sat up on the grass, still shaky from my panic attack. We were inside the wards.

"Apparently my coat and my Acolyte are forming some type of bond."

"What does that mean?"

The Man in Black looked down. His voice was sharp, a scalpel cutting through a clenched jaw. "You forget yourself, minion."

Daniel thrust out his chest, his hands knotted tightly into fists. "You have to stop hurting her."

"I have to *what*?" The Man in Black's voice burned hot. "Kneel before me."

Daniel's spine straightened with a jerk. I couldn't see his face—he stood between me and the Man in Black—but every muscle in his back quivered against his shirt. Narrowing his black eyes, the Dark God continued to stare at Daniel. Coldness seeped around

Daniel's body, brushing over me. My breath curled in white wisps of condensation as the temperature plummeted. My mouth went sour with the taste of dark magick. Daniel took the brunt of it, the focus of Nyarlathotep's attention.

I wanted to grab Daniel and scream at him to stop, just stop, before the Man in Black hurt him. I wanted to cheer him on. I wanted to give him my strength.

I wanted to kiss him for trying to protect me.

The magick rolled off the Man in Black, heavy and oppressive. Bricks stacked on a sheet of glass.

The Man in Black's hand, his red right hand, slipped out of his coat raw and glistening against the inky fabric.

The glass shattered into a million pieces.

Daniel's knees bent, slamming into the ground at the feet of the Midnight Man. His head dropped to his chest. "I am here to serve you, Master. My place is at your feet." The words came out in a strangled whisper.

"Forget again, and I will have you flayed, salted, and hung in my bedchambers for my entertainment."

"Yes . . . Master."

The Man in Black stepped around Daniel. I scrambled to my feet so he wouldn't loom over me. My knees were still weak, but I dragged myself up. I didn't want him standing over me while I sat on the ground. Horror lay heavy in my stomach.

What are we dealing with?

"Your mind is your own again. Good. We need to seek the elder god who is here."

I shook my head. "I'm not up for another teleporting act."

Daniel stood. He caught my eye and shook his head. I took it as a sign to let go of what had happened to him. I didn't know what else to do about it, so I did.

For now.

"Ashtoreth's gift will not be necessary to take us there." The

Man in Black's head tilted slightly. "Now pick up the firebrand and follow me."

I picked up the burnt stick as he turned and began walking through the empty lobby. Daniel moved beside me. As one we followed the chaos god and his trailing, tattered coat.

I had a very bad feeling in my stomach.

16

THE EAGLES' "HOTEL California" played softly through the elevator's sound system. The cheap speakers made Don Henley's voice sound hollow and karaokesque, turning the soft-rock masterpiece into something haunting and melancholy, a splintered bow drug across the violin strings of my nerves.

I hear you, Glenn. I can check out anytime I like, but I can never leave.

"Hey."

I looked over at Daniel. We were standing against the opposite walls of the elevator. The Man in Black watched the numbers count up, ignoring us. My back pressed *hard* against the little handrail that ran along the walls. I was still jumpy, still jittery. I wasn't flexing my hand; I wasn't panicking again; but I could feel it skritching at the edges of my brain. Normally I had distance between me and full-on meltdown mode. It took years of therapy to get it, but I had it. Now, after the small episode in the lobby, I wasn't even inches away. No, once I had one I was left raw and exposed, all my defenses torn away.

And the music wasn't helping.

Daniel's whisper filled the small, square space. "Did you know this is a Satan song?"

I blinked at him. "What are you talking about?"

"Yeah, it's true. This song is all about Satanism."

"'Hotel California' is about Satan?"

He nodded vigorously. "An evangelist came to my mom's church and told us all about it."

"I find that hard to believe."

"He did come to my mom's church. Brother Hank something-or-other. I was fourteen at the time."

This was a good distraction. I went with it. "I believe a guy came to the church. I don't believe Hotel California is about the Devil."

"You just have to listen to the evidence. I didn't believe it either when I was told, but now . . ." His eyes slid to the Man in Black, then back to me.

Ah.

"Explain it for me then."

Anything to keep my mind occupied.

Daniel moved over beside me. I watched him. His hands still shook slightly, but he had the easy grace of an athlete, every movement made with confidence. He leaned next to me and talked out the side of his mouth so we could both watch the Man in Black. His fingers ran through thick hair, pulling it forward in a cute, boyish, unconscious habit.

"Okay, it's like this. The song starts out with this guy on a highway, and he sees this hotel. When he gets there, he finds a girl who tells him it could be heaven or hell. Well . . . it's hell." Daniel's eyes were big, really wanting me to believe what he said.

"Then he calls for some wine, and the guy tells him they haven't had that spirit there since nineteen sixty-nine. Guess what was founded in nineteen sixty-nine."

"I have no idea."

"The Church of Satan! In a hotel that Anton LaVey bought in California." His hand grabbed my arm, emphasizing the fervor in his voice. "Wine is a symbol of the Holy Spirit. That hotel really *wouldn't* have had it since sixty-nine. And if you look on the album cover, guess who's on it, hidden in an archway?"

"Satan?"

"No." He shook his head. "Anton LaVey." He nodded as he made this point. "I saw it myself."

"Who's Anton LaVey again?"

"The guy who started the Church of Satan."

I looked sideways at him. "That's pretty thin."

His eyebrows creased together. It was kinda cute. "Then how about this. There's a line about stabbing the Beast with knives, but it won't die. The Beast is another name for the Antichrist, and in Revelation he gets stabbed in the head but doesn't die." His hand still lay on my arm.

I smiled. I hadn't expected it, but his enthusiasm for this explanation was contagious and . . . charming. *This* was the Daniel I knew. I pushed that out of my head, holding onto the balance the conversation brought to me, running with it. "I don't know. That's pitchy."

His hand moved away, his arms crossing over his chest, a playful pout on his face. "You don't believe it?"

"You do?"

His eyes cut meaningfully at the Man in Black's back. "Even more than I did before."

"I get that."

"I can hear you." The Man in Black didn't turn around. His voice echoed inside the elevator.

"So, is it true?" I couldn't help asking.

"John's Revelation has not happened yet."

"Was that a yes?"

The elevator chimed. The doors split open, and the Man in Black stepped through them without answering.

Neither of us said anything as we followed him, leaving our glimmer of a good mood eviscerated on the floor of the elevator.

17

We stepped into a recovery ward, closed off behind a nurses' station. Behind it sat a pleasantly plump woman in a gleaming white uniform. Hair the color of a new penny frothed under a nurse's cap straight out of the fifties. Her skin had the shape and shade of uncooked biscuit dough, making the hair look brassy and fake. Not like a cheap dye job, but the color and consistency of fine copper wire.

"Can I help you?" Her voice was chipper and high pitched. Pushed through a wide, saccharine smile, it squeaked like a dog toy.

Immediately my nerves were on edge.

Nyarlathotep stepped to the counter in a swirl of midnight coat. He stood in stark contrast to the nurse, sinister and saturnine against her gleam. Looming, his head tilted slightly, he spoke. "Stand aside."

A hand fluttered over pillowy cleavage. "Now, you

can't just barge in here! There are rules, and our patients need order."

My fingers tightened on the charred stick I held as tension clamped across the back of my neck, making the vertebrae grind. I looked around, stretching while I did. My neck popped and cracked and felt better. Studying the reception area put the tension right back where it had been.

I'd been in ICU, a recovery ward, and a psych ward. This place looked nothing like any of them. Those all had things in common. The same bland, abstract paintings on the wall, nonspecific track lighting to diffuse the atmosphere, pastel colors to set visitors and patients at ease. None of that could be found here. Everything gleamed as white as the nurse, unadorned and blank. Harsh light cut from bulbs set into the ceiling, striking the floor in bright pools. Only one painting broke the stark whiteness. It hung down the wall, angled *just* out of my direct line of sight. I could see it was abstract, but it wasn't bland. The colors slashed across the canvas like claw marks on bare flesh. I leaned back, trying to look at the painting, to study it, but my eyes kept sliding to the left, going out of focus until a headache started to black-hornet buzz behind them. I turned. "What kind of wing is this?"

Before the nurse could answer, the Man in Black's voice whipcracked at me. "Do *not* speak to her."

The nurse looked up at him, a wide clown grin plastered on her face. Daniel nudged my arm. He pointed at a sign over the automatic doors leading to the rest of the ward.

ONCOLOGY RECOVERY.

That explained a lot.

I don't just hate hospitals because of what happened to me. No, my hatred of them goes way back. Long before that night, at a time where my memories are lost in the fog of childhood, my dislike of hospitals had been cemented into who I am.

My grandmother died when I was seven.

She'd been old my whole life. In my child's memory she'd been ancient, not even human, just a collection of sticks wrapped in sagging, wrinkled skin. I have no memory of her other than the hospital. I don't remember when she got sick with cancer, or what she was like before.

I've seen pictures, a pretty woman who looked a lot like my mom, but that's not the image in my head. No, I remember her as a sad, inhuman *thing* lying in a bed, curled in pain. She moaned, low and constant, the undulating rhythm of low-yield agony broken only by the sucking in of more breath. I remember the *smell* of her, moist and decaying, the scent of her body betraying her bit by bit, strong enough to cut through the astringent bleach and medication smell that all hospitals share.

I love my mom. I really do. Caught in the sorrow of losing her mother, she had no idea what she did by making me go with her to keep vigil. As an only child, she didn't have a choice; there was no one else to be with my grandmother and no one else to watch me. So I went with her, every day, all day that summer, until my father came to rescue me, taking me home and leaving my mom behind to stand watch and witness the slow dying, the ebb of life with each thin, tortured inhale and exhale.

I was there the moment my grandmother died.

I can still feel it clearly. The very moment the moaning stopped and didn't start again. The machines hummed and beeped and whirred, but there was a hollowness in the air, a desolation scooped from the atmosphere as my grandmother ceased to live. My mother sat up and looked at me. Both of us were frozen, locked in time by what had just happened between one breath and the next. Neither of us moved for a long moment. Then my mother's face twitched and cracked and broke, tears spilling down her cheeks, running off her jaw, and splashing her shirt. She slipped off the chair, crumpling to the floor with a sob that turned into a scream.

I was a child. I didn't know what to do. I stood there, locked in fear, until strangers rushed in the room and shoved me away.

"Move aside. I will not tell you again."

Nyarlathotep's voice broke through the memory, snatching me back to what was happening here and now in front of me. His red right hand had slipped out of its pocket. It hung beside him, skinless fingers slightly curled. He looked almost casual, indifferent and unconcerned, but the air crackled with tension.

"Sir, I will not allow you to disturb our patients."

The nurse stood now. Her uniform puckered at the buttons as the fabric strained across a generous middle and spongy breasts the size of my head. Self-conscious, I hunched my shoulders around my own modest B-cup. The nurse's smile was still in place, cheeks pulled high, stretching lips tight against teeth that were so very white.

The tension between them vibrated. I had to speak, had to say something in the face of it. "She's only a nurse. Why don't we just go around her?"

"She is the guardian of this place." The Man in Black didn't turn when he answered me. "Stop asking questions, Acolyte."

The nurse turned her face toward me. Her smile got even wider. It looked painful, pulling her eyes into diagonal lines, thinning the skin over her brow and drawing tight her double chin. "Acolyte? Dr. Mason would love to . . . examine you." Her head swiveled toward the Dark Man with a snap. As her cheeks quivered and strained under the pull of that clown smile, her voice dropped a full octave. That smile hadn't faltered since we stepped off the elevator. "But you will not gain entrance."

The Man in Black didn't move. He didn't. His coat rustled, pulling its hem tiredly off the floor. It had been nothing, a simple shift, the tiniest movement of all.

But it was enough.

The nurse's face split in two.

It started in the corners of her mouth, twin ruptures like paper cuts, trickling translucent blood that zigged and zagged down the plane of her jaw. I could *hear* the skin ripping, like packing tape being pulled off the spool. The splits widened, yawning in strings as they tore all the way to her ears. Teeth ran to the very back of her skull.

In the blink of an eye her face swelled, expanding like a puffer fish and turning a dark shade of jaundiced, a rotten-lemon yellow. The top of her head flipped back to reveal an open maw crammed full of jagged teeth, all of their crowns wicked sharp and white. They circled an empty, gaping gullet like an enameled chainsaw whirlpool. Saliva sluiced out in a gush to spill over the counter and drip on the floor. From the neck down she was still human, with the same pudgy arms, still wearing the white uniform now obscenely see-through after being soaked with spittle. Putting its chubby, pale hands on the counter, the thing that once was a nurse pushed off, lunging at the Man in Black with her mashing monster mouth.

That terrible red right hand flashed, slapping her to the floor.

The thing that once had been a nurse tumbled off the counter in a sprawl of chubby arms and legs. It scrambled to its feet, the top of its head askew. Its face had deformed: eyes slit closed, copper-wire hair wadded around skin gone swollen and bright, dehydrated-urine yellow.

Its upper jaw clacked against the lower as it tried to speak, but words dribbled out in a chewed-up, mangled mess.

The Man in Black's red right hand curled into a fist. With one step, he drove it into the skull of the thing that used to be a nurse.

Its head exploded in a shower of pulp.

Tiny pieces of monster head splattered across Daniel and me. We hadn't moved. There hadn't been time. It was over in a moment, a breath . . . no, a thought. One second the nurse was talking, the next her head had been obliterated.

The Crawling Chaos turned to us. Blood and gore slid slow and chunky down his face. His eyes glittered with dark amusement, backlit with glee as he licked clean the fingers of his red right hand.

Finished, he looked at us and smiled under sharply arched eyebrows.

"What? Did you want me to share?"

18

The automatic doors shushed closed behind us, and the second they did I wanted to turn around and leave. The ward stretched out before us, twin rows of hospital beds captured in dull pools of low fluorescent light, the back wall lost in the hovering darkness. The fact that it was the middle of the night struck me like an openhanded slap.

The middle of the same *damn night.*

The room *breathed.* Slow and labored, the air dragged kicking and screaming into lungs too tired or frail or weak to do it themselves by machines that gave no consideration to the comfort of the people tethered to them.

Along each wall were beds, hospital beds, with people in them. They lay twisted, curled in on themselves, each person strung with wires, tubes, and hoses like human-sized science fair projects.

Or bombs.

I stopped walking. The room closed down around me like a hand on a throat. My mind teetered at the edge of a cliff; the sight, the sound, the *smell* of the ward pushed against it, trying to tip it over the edge and down the chasm of insanity.

I had woken up in a ward just like this one after that night.

It's not you.

This is not then.

Keep it together.

Keep it together.

I didn't feel my hand clenching and unclenching until Daniel grabbed it.

His brow creased with concern. "Hey, are you okay?"

His hand felt warm against mine, the skin soft. "I don't like hospitals. Hate them, in fact," I said.

"I know. I don't like them either. They remind me of the time I separated my shoulder in a match. Damn, that hurt." He shook his head, shaggy bangs falling across his eyes. "Pain sticks with you, ya know?"

I did. I had woken with the pain of three cracked ribs, a broken hand from fighting back, a dislocated jaw to stop me from fighting, and a dislocated hip from what they did after I passed out. Contusions, abrasions, tears, and lacerations had covered my body inside and out. I knew beyond a shadow of a doubt that pain sticks with you.

Breathe.

I pushed past it.

"Hopefully we won't be here long." Daniel pulled me along after the Man in Black.

I followed and we moved to the first bed in a row. Nyarlathotep stood on the other side of the bed. He was a face and a front; the rest of him disappeared into the inky black. It was an illusion, a trick of my mind, but I believed I could see him swirling into the darkness. He was the Man in Black, the Midnight Man, the original bump in the night.

A shell of a man lay on the bed between us, wearing striped pajamas stretched over a bulbous, rounded stomach. It jutted in a deformed dome over his midsection. From it extended spindly arms and legs; the pajamas flapped around them like a canvas sack full of sticks. The man looked like the pictures of starving children in Africa that come up on the late night TV screen, except he was adult and all the more horrible for being here in front of me instead of locked away in a digital display.

The skin of his neck was wrinkled, lying in loose folds under his chin; an oxygen mask covered his face. It fogged with moisture from his mechanical breathing, leaving only sunken eyes and lank greasy hair to see. An IV pole stood next to the bed. From it hung bags attached to tubes that ran down and disappeared under the pajama sleeves.

One bag, the size of a large purse, hung half filled with a transparent fluid I guessed was probably saline. A second bag looked purple in the low light, the fluid in it thick and opaque.

Blood? Possibly plasma?

I didn't know. My time in the hospital hadn't made me an expert on medical stuff, but I couldn't think of anything else it could be. I didn't think they gave you blood or plasma except in emergency situations. Again, not an expert.

The third bag on the pole disturbed me. The fluid in it cast a low phosphorus light over the bed. The fluid bubbled and gurgled and glowed a sickly green color inside the bag. I could see small shapes moving in it. Leaning closer, I saw the shapes were tiny things, each one smaller than a grain of rice, swimming in complicated patterns through the liquid. As I watched, one of them rushed at the side of the bag and splayed itself against the plastic. I had a sea monkey colony as a child, and I had loved watching the miniscule shrimp frolic through their water, feeding them, counting them every day to see if they'd made any more minuscule offspring. Then one day I came home from school and found that I had forgotten to move them off the windowsill that morning. The cruel summer sun had boiled them alive, and I found them floating in a mass grave on the top of the aquarium.

This little creature brought back that memory.

Its body was a narrow oval surrounded by hairlike fibrils. The center of the tiny, squirming thing held an orifice filled with what looked like a jagged ring of miniature teeth. It opened and closed, opened and closed, opened and closed.

Chewing at the bag. Trying to get to me.

One by one the other creatures began to plaster themselves against the side of the bag, slapping against it as if they had been thrown there, splaying themselves and chewing, chewing, chewing.

Fighting a shudder, I turned away.

The man on the bed hadn't moved aside from his slow, labored breathing, oblivious to our presence. Large plastic padded cuffs swallowed the lower halves of his arms and legs, shackling him to the bed. They had enough slack that he had turned awkwardly, his knobby knees and elbows pulled into the swollen, distended sack of his stomach. This close he smelled like a bedsore: a moist, musty odor of dead skin and open wound.

"He looks horrible." Daniel said it, but I thought the same thing.

"He is food slowly consumed."

I looked at the Dark God standing on the other side of the bed. "Food for what?"

"Let us find out."

His red right hand came out of the coat pocket holding a long knife, much too long for the pocket it came from. Black iron with a thick spine and trianglular point, it rested delicately between raw, red fingers. The edge gleamed in the low fluorescent light of the ward. It was a plain knife, not one drop of decoration wasted on it. It looked like the knife of someone who *used* it, a tool well cared for and utilized.

Not the knife of the Crawling Chaos.

My eyes were drawn to it, locked on it. I felt the pull of it somewhere deep inside, near the base of my spine. The Mark on my right palm began to tingle, as if electric shocks ran in the lines and whorls carved there. The same tingle ran underneath the heavy iron ring around my neck. It was uncomfortable but not unpleasant, making me *feel* things.

"Why does that knife make me feel weird?"

The Man in Black raised a sharply sculpted eyebrow. He didn't speak for a long moment, studying me. "This is the Aqedah."

"I don't know what that means."

"It is the Knife of Abraham."

"Lincoln?"

"I think he means Abraham from the Bible." Daniel's voice came from the side of his mouth. His eyes were pinned to the knife too.

"That is correct, minion. This is the blade held by the first Israelite when he attempted to slaughter his very own child. He received it from the hand of his father before him who used it to carve idols to Moloch. Abraham stained it with his own blood and the blood of his children by performing their circumcisions with it."

Beside me, Daniel shuddered.

Pulling my eyes from Daniel to the knife I ask, "What does that history have to do with me feeling weird?"

The Man in Black turned the knife in his hand, examining the blade. "It has drawn certain kinds of men to it since it was forged from the meteorite that fell from the edge of the universe. Tsar Peter the Third castrated himself and members of his Skoptsy cult with it. I took it from the hand of a Nazi doctor after his own castration went badly." A look passed over his face, a small smile of fond memory.

"And what are you planning to do with it?"

Please don't say, "Castrate the man on the bed."

I should have known it would be worse than that.

The blade waved over the man's distended stomach. "Minion, undo the buttons on his shirt."

Daniel stretched out his hand, fingers fumbling with a large round button. He pulled it up and the soft cotton, already stretched wide over the highest point of the stomach, slipped over it, popping free. The cloth folded like the skin of an autopsy, caping to either side. I looked away as Daniel undid the rest of the buttons, not wanting to see the revelation of what lay underneath. I knew I would look—I would have no choice—but watching the slow unveiling, button by button, was too disturbing.

My eyes swept over the beds across from us, lining the other wall. They were also segregated in pools of dim light, also occupied by the shapes of contorted humans. In the dim light I could see that they were also shackled to their beds and hooked up to the same three bags of fluid as the man in front of me.

Before I could think about what that might mean, Daniel's voice drew my attention. "It's done."

The man on the bed lay exposed from the waist up. His stomach had looked big under his pajama top; with the covering removed it looked ludicrous. Enormous, it seemed as though it should crush the man beneath it. The skin stretched pale, appearing blanched, the color of chicken boiled too long. Wide red stretch marks radiated from the navel like angry fever lines. Here and there they were pockmarked with pustules, pockets of infection seeping in crusty yellow lines. A network of blue varicose veins throbbed around the bottom and sides of the belly, obscene pipelines of sluggish blood. It was horrible, an anatomy lesson in the grotesque.

The back of my throat burned with stomach acid as nausea swept over me.

The Man in Black put his left hand flat on the man's chest, pinning him to the bed. Softly, almost gently, he laid the edge of the knife against the skin where the man's stomach jutted from his chest at a near ninety-degree angle. He leaned forward, his face low to the man's skin, his arm wrapped around the stomach.

"Wait," I said.

The Man in Black paused.

"You can't kill him."

"I will not."

"That knife is a killing thing."

"One thing has nothing to do with the other, Acolyte."

"Charlie," Daniel said, "there aren't any heart monitors or nurse call buttons here."

He was right. Just the bags, the breathing machine, and the bed over and over and over again.

"I think they might be dead."

"Is this true?" I asked the Man in Black.

"Near enough that you may consider this a mercy." He licked his lips. "Now, may I continue?"

I nodded.

Dark eyes glittered deep in their hollows. "You may want to step back."

I moved at the same time Daniel did. My heart beat against the inside of my rib cage like an animal trapped in a too-small cage. I took another step.

The Man in Black nodded once then drew the knife around in a quick vicious slash.

The skin parted under the edge of the blade. The air filled with the soft whisper-crackle of separating skin, subcutaneous from cutaneous, fat from flesh. A gush of brackish fluid splashed across the edge of the mattress, soaking the bedclothes and splattering on the tile floor. We were suddenly standing in a puddle of something disgusting.

Something that stank of rusty iron, moldy bread, and stagnant water.

My stomach lurched, empty and unable to do anything else.

The Midnight Man grabbed the flap of skin he'd carved out and flipped it back, revealing what lay inside the man's stomach. The man never moved other than to continue his slow, labored breathing behind the mask.

I didn't want to look. I didn't. I tried to turn away, to look somewhere else, to not witness what lay before me.

But I couldn't. I had to look. Driven by a sick fascination I *had* to see what had been revealed.

I had no idea what I was looking at.

I'd taken basic anatomy in school, and none of the charts I had ever seen looked like this. The inside of the man had been turned into a cocoon, the hollow coated with layers of glistening, fibrous threads. They overlapped and crisscrossed each other to form a cushion on all sides. A mass of discolored flesh the size of a small child nestled in the batting. The tumor clung to the spine and rib cage with finger-thick tendrils, fleshy nooses that were wrapped and hung and strung from it, tethering the thing to the bone. It had no symmetry, bulging and protruding out of geometry, disturbing to the eye.

Disturbing to the mind.

Revulsion rippled my esophagus, the lining of my throat closing in disgust that this thing, this malignant mass, this *tumor* could grow inside a fellow human being—stealing his life, devouring his humanity, consuming his body for its own, farrowing cell by cell, molecule by molecule, replacing him with itself.

It was absolutely the most horrifying thing I'd ever seen.

And then it opened its eye.

19

"WHAT THE HELL is that?"

Daniel jumped away from the bed rail. His elbow caught the IV pole, knocking it to the floor with a crash and a clatter. The tubes connecting to the man on the bed stretched and pulled and ripped out. They *thwhip*ped up and around, the sharp silvery needles at their ends slicing the air in a razor-sharp arc.

The air in front of my eyes.

I jerked back, fast enough for the needles to miss, not fast enough to avoid the noxious liquid that slung across my face.

I immediately rubbed my sleeve on it, my skin already crawling with the thought of the little black shapes swimming in the green fluid.

Nyarlathotep looked down at us from across the bed, his voice lashing quickly. "Be more careful, minion. You draw attention to us." Magick tingled in my stomach from the power behind his words.

Attention from whom?

Daniel dropped to his knees, ignoring the puddle of fluid we had been standing in, now soaking into the legs of his jeans. "Forgive me, Master."

"Take your feet and make yourself useful."

Daniel stood, pulling himself up on the bed rails. "What can I do?"

The Man in Black waved the knife over the chest of the man in the bed. "Hold him."

Daniel put his hands on the man's shoulders, pinning him against the mattress. The tumor's eye blinked and rolled, the size of a grapefruit with an egg-yolk iris and a pupil black as an eclipse. Clear aqueous fluid gathered in the corners of folded lids, weeping out with every blink to run and chase down the lumps and pustules that formed the tumor's mass. Waving fibrils ringed around it like eyelashes.

The Man in Black drove his left hand down into the cavity, fingers digging deep into the mass.

He leaned back, pulling. The mass lifted with a wet sucking sound, separating from the walls of its birthing chamber. Nyarlathotep's right hand flashed, red lightning, hacking with the knife. He drove it underneath the thing, the blade slashing through the tendrils anchoring it with a squelch. More dark, brackish fluid gurgled out of them, filling the cavity like dirty dishwater in a used pot. He hacked and slashed until every tendril was severed, spattering himself with sloshing liquid.

Seconds stretched to minutes and felt as if they had stretched to hours by the time he finished. When the last tether had been cut the man on the bed slumped, spindly limbs falling loose beside him. His breathing stopped mid-inhale, dying stillborn in lungs that no longer worked.

"You killed him."

The Man in Black didn't look up at me. "I told you he was dead before we arrived." He waved the knife at the machines around us. "None of these measures were taken to keep him alive." With a jerk of his shoulder he lifted the thing free from its place inside the man. "They were meant to preserve this."

The mass throbbed, wriggling in his grip. Fluid dripped off it, splashing into the puddle inside the empty shell of the man.

Ploop!

Ploop!

Pah-loop!

Realization dawned on me. "Wait. Are you saying that each of these people has one of those things growing inside them?"

He stepped away, coat swirling around his legs. "They will be different pieces of the whole, but yes, they all have something similar incubating in their bodies."

"Can we save them?"

His dark, impassive face stared down at me. "We can only save your world." The knife swept around in his red right hand, indicating the rest of the beds. "These souls are lost."

"You don't sound upset."

He shrugged, holding the tumor with its blinking, rolling eye casually in his hand. "Your kind die, Acolyte. You are fragile, delicate, easily broken, and the entire universe is set against you. The only reason you haven't been snuffed from existence itself is your species's tenacious ability to cling to the merest *flicker* of life wherever you find it."

"You make that sound like a bad thing."

"Not bad. Merely annoying at times."

"Why do you keep trying then? Why are you doing all of this if it's futile?"

He shook his head. "I never called your existence futile. Weak as you are, your kind succeeded in locking mine on the other side of the universe. Your ancestors survived the Deluge in a boat made of gopher wood and pitch built by a drunkard who had never seen the ocean! You have walked away from the seduction of nuclear annihilation and conquered the edge of space outside your world."

He shook the tumor, droplets of fluid spattering the already-wet floor. Leaning over, his voice shifted, rising an octave as he held the tumor like an illustration. "Your kind constantly fouls the plans of beings such as this, a creature so terrible you should wither before it like flowers in a furnace. You fight and you fuck and you carry on with your little lives like a virus the universe cannot shake. You are the *purest* example of chaos I have found in unspeakable eons." The smile that parted his face was so white it was a shock, gleaming jaggedly under his hawkish nose. His voice held the fervent rasp of a believer. "I am the Crawling Chaos. I claim you as my own, and *none* will have you but me."

Daniel fell to his knees, hands in the air, his face beatific.

The conviction of the chaos god echoed over the rhythmic pulse of machinery. I stared at him, looked into those sinister black eyes, and in that moment I had only one thought.

This is our savior?

We are totally screwed.

That's when the overhead lights flickered then flared, breaking my stare and crucifying my eyesight.

20

Blinking against the sensation of ground glass in my eyes I dropped to a crouch, following my training, making myself the smallest target possible. A noise, a crash, the shuffle and thud of many feet spun me on my heel. Things were blurry, my eyes watering as my shocked pupils fought to catch up to the onslaught of now harsh fluorescent light. I found Daniel beside me, feet wide, his hands clenched by his hips. The Man in Black stood where he had before, impassive in his agitated coat.

At the end of the room the two doors had been thrown wide. Four figures stalked toward us. Three of them were nurses, dressed like the guardian who had tried to stop us. They shuddered as they moved, each of them a white shimmy through harsh light that bounced off polished tile and chrome bedrails.

They followed a man dressed in pale green scrubs.

"And so we are welcomed, victims of hospitality

and prey of reception standing meekly in the lair of the beast," the Man in Black said. I could hear the smile on his face even though I wasn't watching him.

No, my clearing eyeballs were locked on the leader of the procession toward us.

He was handsome.

Stunning.

Gorgeous.

Lithe and golden, he moved in a circle of graceful masculinity. Locks of hair flattered a face of planes and angles sculpted by a master. The look in his eyes said he knew my darkest secrets and would gladly help me indulge the most wicked of them. (Only if I wanted to, and, oh God, did I *want*.) He was temptation personified—no, that wasn't right, he was *sin* personified.

And he took my breath away.

His voice rolled through the room, through me, and something low and deep inside *tightened* with a trill of pleasure that nearly made me moan. I bit it back, held it in. The energy, the magick in my belly curled around itself. The golden man's steps slowed as he spoke. "Lord of Chaos, what has brought you here inside these warded walls?"

The Man in Black blinked into the space in front of me, long coat trailing behind him. He appeared without moving, red right hand held back and low, stark scarlet against unrelieved black. Its skinless fingers still casually held the knife point down. The other hand still held the mass, which had stopped wriggling and now hung from his grip, unmoving. I could see the eye, glazed under slack lids. "My power has brought me here, Priest of Yar Shogura."

The golden doctor-priest's eyes slid slowly over to me. (Blue, they were blue, the blue of every peaceful day dream I'd ever had.) "I don't think it was *your* power that brought you this far. It appears you have a very"—he paused, as if looking for just the right word—"*lovely* assistant."

That place deep inside me purred.

The Man in Black stuttered through space, suddenly between me and the golden doctor-priest. The connection between us was cut like a fire dashed with ice water. That deep, low spot inside me went cold and empty, hollow. The magick in me uncurled, flipping from seductive to the low burn of anger it had embodied before.

My head cleared along with the ache behind my navel.

The golden man had made me feel something I'd never felt before, something stolen and destroyed on that night so many years ago. Something that *years* of therapy and living had only let me feel the slightest glimmer of recently.

I looked over at Daniel.

I looked away.

I wasn't ready for this, not yet. Having felt it so real and warm and delicious only for it to be torn away so savagely left me devastated.

Despair clawed at my mind, scrabbling, trying to worm its way in. I *wanted* to sink into it, to let the black wash over me and take me under. I could drop down, fall away, fall apart.

It would be easy.

That was one choice.

If this had happened even a year ago I would have given up; I wouldn't have had the strength to do otherwise.

Now? Here, today?

I *had* to hold it together.

Things were happening. People needed me.

Daniel needed me.

I stood, shaky, but still upright, using my anger as a fuel. Enough of being along for the ride. All night, things had happened *to* me.

No more.

Now, things would happen *because of* me. Right now, I would hold onto the anger.

I could fall apart later.

If I lived through this.

21

Time had passed.

Whether seconds or minutes, I didn't know. Trapped in my own emotions, my own trauma, I looked up and saw that everything had changed.

Daniel fought on the other side of the room, an IV stand in his hands, shoving it into the razor-toothed maw of a transformed nurse. The stainless-steel pole clanged against the spinning, slicing, whirlpool of jagged enamel with a horrible racket. The nurse-thing lunged at him, the top of her now-deformed head flapping up and down, bouncing off what used to be shoulders but were now a misshapen hump. Daniel held her off, but she drove him back step by step, closing the distance between them.

Tightening my grip on the charred stick Nyarlathotep had given me earlier, I started moving toward Daniel. I didn't know what I would do when I got there, but I had to do something.

The Man in Black crouched on the floor, coat swirling around him like dragon wings. The black-bladed sword thrust from his red right hand and the Knife of Abraham from the other. A cut across his cheekbone yawned open, trickling something that wasn't blood. The other two nurses were sprawled away from him, pulling themselves up from the floor at the doctor-priest's feet.

He stood over them, finger pointed at the Man in Black. "You have come here to die, Haunter of the Dark. I am Mason, High Priest of Yar Shogura the Unquenchable, Whoremonger of the Flesh, Masticate of Iniquity, and he shall give me the power of your destruction."

The Man in Black rose. "I hope Yar Shogura's next priest is not so talkative."

"You won't have to listen much longer, Spider God, not after I use your eldritch energy to fuel the transition of my lord into this world."

Nyarlathotep snarled. "Come and try, fool."

Mason pulled an amulet from inside his shirt, a gnarl of thorns on a rope that swirled around something oddly shaped and ivory colored. I couldn't tell what it was from my angle and distance. His mouth moved, and sound came from his throat, but it wasn't words and he didn't speak in a human voice. It blatted across the room and I felt it in my chest, like bass at a rock concert. When the sound ended his hand jerked in a gesture and a bolt of hot-pink energy crackled off his fingers.

The Man in Black spun to the left to avoid the blast.

It wasn't aimed at him.

The magick struck the mass, which he'd dropped to the floor at some point. The lump of flesh began to smoke and hiss. It bubbled, gas stretching flesh to thin blisters that burst in plumes of foulness. Its skin pulled like taffy, puddling and lurching. Drawing into itself, it shrank into a protoplasmic knot that lay on the floor, jittering.

It sat like that for a long, drawn-out second.

Then it exploded.

Strings of flesh were flung through the air, slapping across the Man in Black, a net of stretchy, melted cancer. He jumped, trying to get away, but it caught him, the gooey web sticking to him, clogging his movement like a sheet of tar. He fought and struggled, the tumor-trap tightening around him, wrapping him in liquid shackles. It dragged him to the floor. The two deformed nurses descended on him with gnashing teeth, jackals to a fallen lion.

I stopped, torn for a split second between moving toward Daniel or trying to help the Man in Black.

A sharp tingle started at the base of my skull, an itch of warning.

I turned to find Mason, the doctor-priest, stalking toward me.

"Stay back." I pointed the stick at him.

"Now why in the world would I do that?" His smile *pulled* inside me again. "I would *love* to get to know you better."

I kept backing away. "I don't think so."

"You are an Acolyte. I need an Acolyte." His eyes smoldered. He winked at me. "I swear you would find my yoke so much more . . . *pleasurable* than the one you wear now."

The word *pleasurable* echoed off the hollow below my navel, making me want to stop evading and start squirming.

He had screwed with my head.

I shoved the stick in my hand toward him. "Back *off.* Or I'll use this."

He kept coming.

I tightened my hand around the firebrand. My mind raced, trying to think of how to make it work.

Ignite! Fire! Combust! Flame on! Incendio!

My back hit the wall.

Mason hopped from one foot to the other, capering toward

me. "Nowhere else to go, kitten. I shall have you in just a moment."

I shook the stick frantically.

Work, damn you! Come on!

A thought crashed through my panic. It wasn't my thought; it belonged to the Man in Black, his voice strained but crystal clear in my mind.

Use your Mark.

My Mark? Mason stood only feet away. He'd be on me in a few steps. A dark, cruel look burned in his eyes. I had seen that look before. It didn't matter that it had been on other faces; it was the same, forever burned in my memory. It was the look of a predator who has just found helpless prey.

I lifted my hand to my mouth and licked my palm.

My tongue scraped across the rough lines and swirls incised in the skin.

Magick swirled inside me.

My Sight kicked in with a punch.

Mason went from handsome to soul-searingly beautiful.

Bathed in a golden light, every inch of him had been carved from absolute perfection. Tears ran down my cheeks, hot and quick. I couldn't bear to look upon his terrible beauty—the beauty of consumption, of assimilation, of absorption. The swift, sure beauty that would burn away everything I was and devour me whole.

He would devour me, and it would be okay. Being taken by Mason would make me cry out: *It is well, it is well with my soul.*

I wanted so desperately to be consumed.

"Charlie!"

Daniel's voice. I looked over. He lay on his back, pinned to the floor by a deformed nurse above him. Her skull of teeth chomped the air inches above his face. His arms shook, jerking as the strength in them burned away. He wouldn't be able to fight her off much longer.

And his eyes were pinned to me as he called my name, trying to pull me free from the spell, worry naked on his spittle-spattered face.

Mason reached for me.

I put the stick in my moist right hand.

BURN.

Magick sparked in my chest, rolling down my arm in a hot, wet, ropy jolt. Sharp heat traced the lines incised in my palm and the metal torc around my throat hummed, tingling against my skin. The magick poured down my arm into the firebrand like thick syrup.

Fire roared from the end of the stick like a flamethrower.

It shot out in a jet, flaring at the end, dripping gobbets of liquid fire onto the floor. I felt the heat, but it was shielded, not searing me like it had before. I had control now. Power boiled through my veins like a jolt of adrenaline. My magick ignited and fed the flame. Mine. I felt it in my heart and in my head. It would do as I willed it to.

I was magick.

I was Marked.

I was an Acolyte.

Mason jerked back, nearly falling on his ass. Whipping my arm, I pushed the magick, working by feel, making it up as I went along. The flame slung around, splashing across him like a tide of molten lava. His scrubs ignited, tongues of fire licking across his body in a race to incinerate it all. He rolled away, still clutching his amulet in a burning hand. He screamed words that thrummed against my chest.

Daniel!

I spun.

Oh God, let him still be okay.

I found him, still pinned to the floor by the nurse with the wood-chipper face. She'd pressed even closer, skull clapping open and closed, teeth grinding and gnashing just above him. Quarter-sized droplets of saliva rained down on him, squirting out with each attempted chomp.

I ran, pushing to get to him. I had the flame. I had the magick. I had the power.

I could save him.

I almost made it when his arms gave out.

22

An inhuman sound tore from my throat. A shriek, a growl, a roar that an animal would make. It ripped out of me as I lunged toward Daniel and the nurse monster, and it yanked the magick with it.

A gout of fire jolted from the end of the stick, crashing into the nurse monster like a shotgun blast, driving her off Daniel and into the wall. I kept screaming, kept pouring fire, magick rumbling through my veins in an avalanche. She curled into a ball, trying to hide, but the flame covered her, roiling against her like a blast furnace. Her skin turned black, cracking open as she wailed. Something boiled inside the cracks, bubbling out in hissing clouds of steam as her flesh turned to cinder and crumbled, leaving behind the blackened sticks of a deformed skeleton.

It took seconds. By the time I reached Daniel, the deed had been done.

I hit my knees beside him, ignoring the pain of

kneecaps on hard linoleum, ignoring the puddle of slimy monster spit he lay in. He sprawled on his back, his fingers still locked around the gnarled metal pole he'd used to fend off the nurse, drenched with sweat and saliva, his hair dark and wet with goo. Blood soaked the shoulder of his shirt, but I couldn't see a wound. His skin had gone pale, his lips blue, and even through his closed lids I could see his eyes jittering wildly back and forth. Clenching internally, I cut the magick running to the stick, and it snuffed out with an air-sucking sound. My arm went dead, feeling like a sack overfull with liquid. Shaking it to the side, I reached out to Daniel with the other.

Please let him be okay.

I pulled his head into my lap. His eyes fluttered open.

"Hey, Charlie," he said, his voice hoarse, "you all right?"

His sweaty hair stuck to his forehead. I brushed it back, nodding. "How are you?"

"Tired. My shoulder hurts like hell, but I'm still good to go." His eyes widened, white showing around green irises as he struggled to sit up. "Where's the Master? I have to help him if he needs it."

Pushing him down, I looked around. The Man in Black had freed himself from the liquefied tumor and now faced the two remaining nurse monsters. He pushed off the floor, spinning into an inhuman leap across the room, flying in a swirl of bat-wing black, sword blade licking out like dark lightning. It cleaved deep in a quick line, lopping free the top halves of both monsters' skulls. A geyser of red pulp sprayed up and out, striking the ceiling, soaking into the acoustic tiles. The Crawling Chaos spun his sword in an arc, slinging gore from the edge of the blade. He turned, shark teeth smiling through a mask of runny, scarlet liquid.

"I think he's okay," I told Daniel.

The next second he was beside us. Not kneeling. No, he stood, impossibly tall, his coat whispering around him in tattered tendrils.

I wish he would quit doing that.

"Stand, minion. I am not done yet, and I have need of thee."

"Back off him! He's injured." The snarl hurt my face.

Nyarlathotep's face flushed dark. Magick crackled, dripping off his red right hand. "Acolyte."

I tensed, my body tight with anger, with the desire, the *need,* to protect Daniel. A thought sent a spark of magick down my arm. I felt it as a relief, an ease of pressure in my skin as pent-up energy gushed forward and into the firebrand. It was intuitive, as natural as breathing. My palm hurt, the torc buzzed my throat, and the stick lit like a torch, the flame an eye-searing acetylene blue.

I rose into a crouch, holding my weapon between us. "Back. Off."

"You threaten me, Acolyte?" The Man in Black slid back, his sword held ready to swing. "Bold." Magick dripped off his hand and ran down the sword in trickles of etheric energy, making the sticky gore on the blade sizzle. It spattered onto the ground, eating holes in the tile like acid. "But I *will* teach you your place. There is a price to pay for defiance."

I stayed crouched, making myself a smaller target and reserving power for when I attacked. I fell back on all the years of martial arts I had taken, training relentlessly so I would never be helpless again. Kenpo, jujitsu, tae kwon do, Muay Thai, wushu; I blended all of them to give me the skill set best suited to my physical abilities. Sensei Laura always drilled home: *Run if you can, but sometimes you must fight. If you must fight, then fight to kill.*

Daniel was worth fighting for, even though, deep down, an ice-cold knot of certainty said the Man in Black would kill me for trying. I could make him pay for the privilege, but he would kill me just the same.

We stared at each other. I felt the ripple of heat from the firebrand and Daniel behind me as I looked into the black-pit eyes of a chaos god. He didn't move, save for the sizzle-drop of magick from his sword and the anxious fluttering of his still-living coat. Tension stretched between us.

Who would break the stalemate?

Who would make the first move?

Who would strike first?

Maniacal laughter rang across the room, ending the standoff before we could find out.

The Man in Black looked over my head, past me. "We will finish this at a later time, Acolyte."

I could feel something against my back, a pressure like a hot, dry wind from a gulch of death. It made the back of my scalp itch and crawl as though it were alive. The symbol cut into my palm burned fiercely.

From the corner of my eye, I watched Daniel sit up, facing behind me. He scrambled to his feet, eyes wide. "Charlie, you need to turn around."

I rose and turned and my stomach clenched in a fist of dread.

23

Mason stood in the center of the ward.

Completely naked.

The fire had burned away his scrubs, leaving him bare-skinned and nude except for the amulet that lay on his chest. The fire had also scorched away every hair from every follicle, leaving him bald, slick looking, alien without the markers of hair and eyebrows all humans shared. I looked; I had to, my eyes drawn inexorably downward, pulled the same way they'd been with Ashtoreth.

He wasn't human between his legs.

What hung there was a maze of serpentine appendages, twisted and contorted, a balloon of intestine in the hands of a psychotic clown.

Horror congealed in the pit of my stomach.

A scalpel glittered in Mason's hand. He'd used it to carve his own skin with a sigil that looked eerily like the one on my palm. Blood sheeted down his hairless body, pooling in the hollows and dips, running from the arcane symbol sliced into his chest. Arms out, hips and shoulders loose-jointed, he began to dance in place, eyes wild and swirling in their sockets.

Daniel spoke beside me. "Why is he acting like a marionette in the hands of an epileptic?"

I shrugged and looked over at the Man in Black.

The chaos god also shrugged. "He casts a working."

"You're using words like we know what they mean again," I said.

He sighed. Did I test his patience? If so, good. "The dance he performs will gather magick to power a spell."

I thought about it. "Why can't I feel anything? Ever since you gave me this"—I held up my Mark—"whenever hoodoo voodoo happens, I can feel it inside me. I feel nothing right now."

The Man in Black didn't answer. Instead, he thrust his sword toward Mason.

The magick running down the blade flung itself off, stretching and flying through the air. It crashed against some invisible barrier around the priest in a sputtering of electric blue sorcery. The flash washed my eyesight with the vision of writhing magick, strands of it twisting like a bed of snakes. It lasted only a split second, and then it was gone, marring my ability to see with black, spotty ghost images.

"Well, that failed spectacularly." I didn't try to keep the sarcasm out of my voice.

The Man in Black shrugged. "He is warded. It will open when he finishes the ritual and releases the magick. Then he will be vulnerable once more."

"Can't you break the ward?"

"My coat will not have the strength until it recovers."

I felt the song of the coat tickle the edge of my brain. It felt like the whimper of a beat dog. I shook my head to clear it.

Daniel moved to my left, the side without the still-burning firebrand. He looked over at Nyarlathotep. "What do we do next?"

"We see what spell he is casting, and then we respond accordingly."

Daniel nodded. "I'll find a weapon."

He moved away, and I watched him. His movement had a stilted, halting quality, as if he suffered pain from an old injury. I'd watched him a lot in the last few months as we'd gotten to know each other. Normally, he moved with the grace of a former athlete who still kept in shape, every action fluid and easy. That was broken now. His movements were stiff, slower than they had been.

The rustle of Nyarlathotep's coat as he stepped close drew my eye away from Daniel.

The Man in Black's voice was low, nearly a murmur when he spoke. "I see concern in your eyes for him."

I bristled at his intimate tone. "Yeah, so?"

"It is . . . *interesting* that you care so much for him."

"One of us has to."

One sharply sculpted eyebrow arched. "I care for those who worship me, Acolyte."

Then you must hate me.

What I said was: "He doesn't really worship you. That's just your magick brainwashing. He's a Christian. That's why he stood up to you earlier."

"Oh, Acolyte, you are so naive." His mouth twitched, amusement glittering in those midnight eyes. "He does truly worship the Christ, but he risked my wrath over *you*."

For me?

"What do you mean?"

"His feelings for you are the strength he draws from to slip my yoke."

I said nothing, my eyes sliding over to Daniel. He pulled the bags off another IV pole.

"He will not survive whatever occurs next without my protection. He will be the lamb to this slaughter." The Man in Black's voice slithered into my head, insidiously rubbing across my brain like rough velvet. "Stop fighting me at every turn, and I will grant that protection."

Son of a bitch.

"Send him away, and I'll cooperate without a fuss," I counter-offered.

He chuckled. "And lose my bargaining chip? I think not. Besides, Acolyte, you would not want me to send him anywhere I can take him. The gibbering horrors there would break his mind and flay his soul." He shook his head. "He stays with us and fights, you behave, and he lives through this. That is the only bargain on the table."

I felt just as trapped as I had been before. I had no choice, not really, not one that mattered. I either agreed and kept Daniel safe for now, or I left him on his own.

I felt my lip curl.

Manipulative son of a bitch.

My words came through gritted teeth. "If you let him get hurt, I will turn on you like a rabid dog."

"I would expect nothing less from you, Charlotte Tristan Moore." He smiled. "Nothing less indeed."

"Stop using my full name."

Daniel came back holding a four-foot section of IV pole in his hands. His color had improved, and his movements were steadier. He wasn't back to normal, but he looked better.

His eyes slid from me to the Man in Black and back to me. "What were you two talking about?"

The Man in Black didn't say anything.

"Strategy," I said.

"We have a plan?"

"Not as such. Stay close, and be careful."

He hefted the steel pole, the look on his face determined, brows drawn and his lips set in a hard line. "I'll be right here beside you."

"I can take care of myself. You stay near your Master."

He shook his head, making his shaggy bangs sweep back and forth over his intense green eyes. "*He* can take care of himself. I'll watch your back."

He would get himself killed worrying about me. I needed him to stay close to the Man in Black. I didn't like it, but it was his best chance for surviving whatever came next.

And something *was* coming.

Mason had stopped cutting himself and was now gesturing wildly, gore covered hands jerking through the air. The blood from his body lifted, suspended in front of him. It swirled and congealed into a ball of liquid crimson. The air inside his circle of protection crackled with magick that I could now feel like a pulse against my skin.

We didn't have long.

I pushed Daniel, making him step sideways. "Stay. With. Him."

Before he could protest again, the air around Mason split like a lightning strike, and a rush of magick spilled out into the room.

The spell buzzed in my eyes, and I watched it arc from the ball of blood in front of Mason. It sizzled into the bodies on the beds around the room. They began to thrash, plastic and metal restraints banging against bedrails in a cacophony. Banging and clanging, crashing metal on metal. The beds jittered, skewing sideways like slow-motion car wrecks. The air tasted metallic and sour on the back of my tongue.

I leaned toward Daniel, near shouting over the noise. "Did you see that?"

His eyes were wide. "I see the octopenis man with no clothes and the spinning disco ball of blood. Is that what you're talking about?"

"He does not have the Sight, Acolyte. He only sees the natural." The Man in Black's voice rang clear over the din, more inside my head than out. "Prepare yourself. The moment is almost at hand."

The bodies stopped thrashing as if a plug had been pulled.

An avalanche of silence fell, pulling at my eardrums like a vacuum after the assault of noise a second ago. Then a sound I had never heard before began to build. It was a . . . my mind groped for the right word . . . a *groaning*. The sound of something being pulled to the breaking point. The sound of birthing. It made me look at the people in the beds. They weren't moving, but their stomachs were. Their skin pulsed, undulating like air bladders being inflated and deflated. They expanded, stretching, ripping free of the clothing over them. Each one swelled, road-mapped with throbbing dark blue veins. Every palpitation drew another groan from the body it ripped through, a horrible sound that pulsed through the room, crashing into my mind like an ocean tide. All the patients' stomachs were now the size of young children crouching over their bodies.

Mason whipped his hands apart and stepped through the ball of enchanted blood. It broke like a bubble, splattering across the tile floor. He screamed across the ward at us. "Now you will see the coming of the glory of Yar Shogura. Bask in his presence, join his unholy flesh, and know the peace of consumption!"

The stomachs ruptured in a shower of gore that rained across the room.

24

I TURNED AWAY as hot ichor splattered down on me. It hit like hailstones, striking hard and drenching me from head to toe. My eyes were closed against it, but I sputtered as it ran down my face. I could hear sizzling where it fell on the flame of the firebrand in my hand. I'd stopped concentrating, and the flame had died down to merely a lick of fire, but it still burned, the ichor crackling and popping against it.

It smelled foul: a sour vegetation stink mixed with the meaty scent of decomposition. It clogged my nostrils, shutting them tight. Desperately I wiped my face, trying to clear the goo away.

The sight I opened my eyes to made me forget about the stench.

The tumors had burst free from their belly-prisons and were crawling across the floor.

They stumped along, pulling themselves in trails toward Mason. Some rolled, some lurched, some wriggled, but all of them moved. They were different shapes, different sizes. Here, one with tiny claw-tipped limbs hooked the tile and dragged itself forward. There, one with a row of jagged teeth swirling through its discolored flesh buzzed and hopped. Another trailed a length of hair behind it that spread over the floor like a ratty blanket.

As they met in front of Mason they bumped together, quivering as they rubbed against one another. Two tumors rose, pressing hard against each other until their membranes slipped, allowing the cancerous flesh of one to run and pour into the other. Others joined, metastasizing, growing into a monstrosity. The conjoined masses made a wall of tumorous flesh that throbbed and glistened. The pieces I had seen in the tumors slid through the mass of diseased flesh, swimming into place until they formed a new mass covered in mouths and eyes with two long, slender limbs hooked with claws designed for pulling prey in close. The mouths chewed even though they were empty, a continuous rumination on invisible cud.

"What the hell is that?" Daniel sounded hushed, awestruck.

"That," the Man in Black lifted his sword, "is the thing we have come to kill." He looked over at me. His voice echoed inside my mind.

Remember our bargain, Acolyte.

I nodded sharply and followed the chaos god into battle against the Cancer God.

As we drew near, Mason began to laugh again. It was hard to hear over the wet, squelching, suctioning sound that came from the hideous mass of his god as it shuffled forward. The Man in Black stepped in front of it. The Cancer God towered over him, looming in an avalanche of carcinoma waiting to break and fall in a crushing wave. Nyarlathotep looked up serenely as he swung the sword in an almost lazy arc, the razor edge twinkling in the overhead light.

It took forever for the blade to strike.

It bit deep, the diseased flesh parting in a spill of fluid. The sword slipped straight through like quicksilver, not dragging, pausing, or catching. The flesh of the Cancer God didn't resist, merely parted around the blade and slapped together on the other side like wet lunch meat being stacked.

The Cancer God towered over me. My mind split in two. One part of me felt small, weak, and powerless in the face of such a monstrosity. It was the part that had been damaged so long ago, the broken part that never healed, just got pushed down. She made my knees go weak and my blood run cold with her fear.

The other part of me, her sister born in the same moment, was tired of that feeling. She held a storm of anger, white-hot with wrath. *She* pushed magick down my arm, through the symbol cut into my palm, and into the firebrand.

A four-foot conflagration jolted out of the weapon.

The Cancer God howled at me with dozens of mouths and lunged, falling toward me, wanting to crush me beneath it and absorb me into itself.

Twisting with my hips, I drove the cremation-hot blade of fire *deep* into one of the open mouths.

It slid in, the flesh around the fire bubbling, melting into a boil that spilled out and around the firebrand I held. The other mouths screamed, and the whole mass of Yar Shogura lurched to pull itself away.

My mind went blank, reverting to my training, and I lunged after it, pressing my advantage. I sawed my arm back and forth, swirling the blade inside the Cancer God. I pulled up, leaning into it, dragging the fire-blade through diseased flesh. I managed to cut upward until the flame-sword ripped free, making me stumble, nearly falling on the slime-covered floor.

The Cancer God recoiled. The wound channel didn't close. It

gaped, cauterized and sealed. I had drawn back to strike again when the Man in Black called to me.

"Acolyte."

I looked quickly, not wanting to take my eyes off the retreating Cancer God. The Man in Black had become a blur of darkness. His coat roiled around him, slapping against the Cancer God, holding the monstrosity back while its master wove a web of razor-sharp steel. The Man in Black leaned left, stretching long over his own leg, and sliced viciously.

A piece of Yar Shogura plopped onto the floor.

Daniel darted in, spearing it with the steel pole as it tried to crawl back to its host. A gout of brackish fluid pumped out, through the hollow pole, and over his shoulder. Arms straining, he pulled the chunk of living meat across the floor, dragging it away from the host. It quivered and strained, a fish on a hook, shaking and jerking, trying to free itself.

I ran over. "What do you want me to do?"

"Burn it," Daniel yelled over the sucking noise of the Cancer God moving along the floor. He picked the tumor up with the pole, holding it out like spitted meat to be cooked.

I swung the firebrand, bathing the tumor chunk in flame. The fire crackled along its lumpy surface, and it began to sizzle and pop, releasing a hissing scream. I'd heard that sound before. Lobsters make that sound when dropped live in boiling water. High-pitched and horrible, it made me feel bad.

Then I remembered.

This was cancer.

This *thing* I burned and tried to kill, was the embodiment of the most evil disease I'd ever seen. It had taken the life of a person, its host, using them up as its food. It ate them away a cell at a time, stealing their life in tiny increments. This thing had choked the life out of my grandmother. It haunted me and my mother, waiting in our DNA to bear diseased fruit that would rot our lives away.

It would probably kill my mother one day.

It might kill me.

The flame roared, white hot, a supernova fed by the hatred running wild in my heart for this thing.

Die, you diseased piece of shit!

It shriveled in the crucible of my hate, hardening into a coal-black lump. Burning gobbets of melted fat dropped to the floor, sputtering out in the puddles of ichor at my feet.

"Ow, shit!" Daniel cried, dropping the pole to clang against the tile. The cancer briquette fell, bursting into charcoal dust as it hit the floor. It soaked into sludge in seconds. Daniel shook his hands, blowing on them.

I burned him.

The thought dashed cold water on my anger. The firebrand sputtered out in my hand. Grabbing Daniel's sleeve, I pulled his arm toward me where I could see it. His fist was clenched shut, but the skin I could see was red. "Let me look at it."

"It's fine. I'll be okay."

"Daniel, open your hand and let me see."

Slowly his fingers uncurled. The skin across his palm and the undersides of his fingers had turned bright red, burned slick. It had already begun to bubble, a line of blister where he had gripped the pole.

"I'm sorry," I said.

He shook his head. "It's okay. I should have let go sooner." Reaching up, he pulled his sweatshirt over his head. Wet with fluid, it stuck to his skin. He dragged it off, wrapping it around his hands. I watched the play of his muscles, pulling and bunching smoothly under his skin. The ridges of his stomach twisted as he tied off the sleeve.

In the midst of all the chaos, for one confusing moment all I wanted to do was run my fingers across his skin. To touch him, to brush my nails across the hollow of his hipbone or run them up to his chest.

He looked up, caught me staring, and smiled the full Daniel smile, the sweet one that held a little streak of wild, a little recklessness. It made his green eyes look untamed; they sparkled like the stars in the sky.

They took my breath away.

We were caught in a moment, time suspended around us, and, for that too brief second, nothing else in the world mattered. No Man in Black, no Cancer God, no battle raging just across the room. Nothing but Daniel and me and the look we shared.

Then it all crashed down around us.

25

Mason appeared, just *there* suddenly, standing between Daniel and me. His arm lashed out, a golden blur that crashed against my chest and lifted me off my feet. I flew back and crashed against a bed. Pain, hard and sharp, drove into my back, shoving the air out of my lungs in a clenching spasm as though there weren't enough room inside my body to hold both. I slammed face-first to the floor.

For a second all I could do was lie there, my mind screaming at me:

Get up get UP!

I listened, sliding my hands under me even though it made my bones ache. I pushed myself up. The firebrand was gone, lost in my fall. I didn't look for it. I looked for Daniel.

He hung at the end of Mason's arm, feet dangling off the floor. He fought and kicked, fists pounding against the arm holding him. With a snarl Mason drove him to the floor.

Daniel crashed. He kept his head up, rolling tight from years of wrestling training to keep from getting a concussion, but the slam drove the strength out of him. He fell limply, still struggling weakly as he gasped for air. Mason knelt over him, pressing him down with one arm. The priest was still naked except for the weird amulet that hung swinging from his neck. His free hand reached out and found one of the tumor chunks that the Man in Black had carved off his god.

He raised it over his head, hot-pink magick crackling up his arm and through the mass.

Oh no . . .

Diseased flesh began to run, stretching like obscene Silly Putty in Mason's fingers.

I scrambled, my feet slipping on the wet floor. I wasn't going to make it in time.

Mason's hand fell like judgment, slapping the molten tumor across Daniel's face.

"NO!" I screamed.

The liquefied flesh became a caul, covering Daniel from hairline to neck, blocking his mouth and nose. His hands scrabbled, clawing furrows in the thing on his face, trying to get it off. It molded like wet clay, slipping around his fingers, keeping him smothered.

I screamed in rage as my feet got traction and I started running. Mason turned toward me, smiling widely. His mouth opened, and a word fell out that I couldn't hear but made my eardrums itch like centipedes were inside my ear canals nestling against my eardrums with their trilling, frilled legs. He leapt, crashing against me and driving me to the floor again.

His hands clamped my wrists and I screamed out the only thing I could.

"Master!"

The Man in Black whirled, red right hand still swinging the black-bladed sword at the Cancer God. Chunks of living meat littered the floor, quivering and crawling at his feet. The coat swept around him, pushing them away from their host, keeping them at bay. It was tattered and torn, pieces bitten from it by mouths in the flesh it battled. As my eyes fell on it, I could hear its cries of pain inside my head. The Man in Black had whittled the Cancer God down to his height, but it still stretched around him, trying to fence him in, to capture him, lunging and grasping and biting with masticating protrusions.

Nyarlathotep paused for a blink, a moment, watching as Mason pinned my hands to the floor, his chest pressed across mine in a crushing weight. Panic rose, pounding inside my breast. The Crawling Chaos snarled, face unholy with rage. He would come for me. He would rescue me. I could feel it.

"No!" I shouted as loud as I could, twisting against Mason's grip. "Not me—save Daniel! I hold you to our bargain, Midnight Man! You keep him safe!"

His voice carried across the room even though his mouth did not move. "Damn you, Acolyte."

"Save him first, or I won't fight! I'll die, and you'll have to finish this without me!" I meant it. He had to save Daniel.

"Fight and live, Charlotte Tristan Moore; I will keep our bargain."

He turned, lifting the sword over his head. A roar that shook the room tore from him, and he struck the Cancer God, cleaving the mass to the tile beneath it.

That was all I saw before Mason lunged, trapping me completely underneath him.

26

Panic ran like wildfire inside my head. My body froze as Mason loomed over me, pressed against the length of me. He was between my legs. He was against my chest. His face was near mine. My hands were crushed in his grip against the floor.

OhGodohGodohGod . . .

His teeth were too white as he smiled over me, his voice hushed and intimate. "Why, hello, Charlie. I am so very happy to find you here beneath me."

His hips ground, and I felt him against me, hard and dangerous. Things writhed against my most intimate part, squirming alien and horrible. My eyesight stuttered as my heart lurched and seized, short-circuiting with fear.

It's happening again oh God why is it happening again I can't I can't I can't . . .

The amulet jabbed me, trapped between us, thorns piercing my skin in snakebite-sharp pricks. It swung as he ground himself against me. A small, dissociated corner of my brain saw the ivory thing in the center of the bramble and recognized it.

A child's jawbone.

Mason's face dropped next to mine, features shifting, rearranging themselves until it became tight, like a skin drum stretched over the bones of his skull. His eyes turned to black pits that each sank around something tiny and white, wriggling like a maggot in a grave. His breath exhaled cold, washing my face with the stale, dead smell of my grandmother's hospital room.

He thrust against me. "Do you like the gift my god has granted me? I saw you looking earlier." He ground into me, battering my clothing. "It's much grander than what I had before. I discovered Yar Shogura when I clung to the bitter end of my human life, wasted to nothing by the cancer in my balls. Do you know what it's like to lose the part of you that makes you who you are? To have it cut off to save your miserable life and then find that this effort wasn't enough and you are going to die anyway?"

He chuckled. "I guess you do."

I lay there, trapped.

He kept talking. "Cancer took my manhood. It almost took my life. I prayed to God to be healed." He snarled. "That fucking asshole never answered. I had *days* left when I discovered Yar Shogura lurking in an ancient book bound in diseased skin with pages fashioned from pressed tumors. I called to *him,* and *he* answered." Mason lunged, trying to drive me into the floor. Trying to crush my pelvis. "He replaced my worthless manhood with a piece of himself." That thing squirmed against me.

Terror pinned me to the floor more surely than his hands on my arms.

He leaned closer, dipping his face toward mine.

"I know about you, Charlie." His lips were stretched like worms over his teeth. They moved above mine, shiny and tight, barely an inch away from brushing against my own. "I know what happened to you all those years ago."

The words broke through my panic, turning the boil of my thoughts to a simmer.

He knows? How does he know?

He pushed again, thrusting against me hard enough to bruise. "I know how you lay there and took it like the worthless whore you are."

No, no, I had no choice . . . I wasn't conscious.

His lips touched mine. "Did you think it would ever happen again? I know you want it to."

No.

He whispered, "Did you think you would ever be fucked by a god?"

His mouth dropped against mine, tongue worming its way into my mouth, driving, forcing, pushing its way past my teeth and my tongue. It tasted of black mold and rot, squirming inside my mouth, brushing the back of my throat. My gag reflex kicked and I choked. I couldn't breathe; pain throbbed in my jaw as my throat spasmed.

He pulled his tongue out of my mouth with a harsh jerk.

Air rushed in. I gasped around the pain and burning humiliation.

Mason purred, and it vibrated my chest. "You're a good kisser, Charlie. I think I'll have some more of that."

My mind shut down.

The panic inside me went silent and white and empty.

My body fell limp as my mind closed up, turning into itself for safety. If I wasn't there, it couldn't happen again. I couldn't survive it happening again. I would be destroyed.

I pulled away.

My brain snatched at a word I'd heard in therapy.

Dissociation.

I was inside my body, but it had become a cave I hid in. My body wasn't part of me anymore. It was now something else but not me, something outside of me, something that could take what was about to happen while I hid from it, locked away inside.

Mason gave a sinister smile. "That's more like it. Just lie back and take it. That's what you're here for."

The body didn't move as he pressed against it. It didn't fight as he started to push up the sweatshirt it wore, his hands sliding across its skin, moving up the rib cage.

It wasn't me.

I wasn't there.

I'd gone deep into my mindspace where I would be safe, no matter what happened to the body.

Part of me knew I wouldn't make it back this time.

I would be trapped inside my mind for the rest of my life. *That* I could survive. The body was on its own. *I* would be safe.

A noise rippled across my mindspace. It vibrated the whiteness around me.

I would be alone forever, but I would be safe.

The noise, louder, like distant thunder, rolled through again.

Safe.

The noise cracked, a lightning strike that shook the blank whiteness around me. It became a word.

It became a name.

The noise rumbled toward me. My mindspace shook under my feet.

ACOLYTE.

I turned.

I AM KEEPING OUR BARGAIN. DO THE SAME AND FIGHT.

My eye cracked open to the real world.

The Man in Black crouched over Daniel. The caul of diseased flesh had been ripped away and lay shivering on the floor. Daniel leaned on his elbow, gasping air into his lungs. The coat loomed over them like a shield. The Cancer God reabsorbed its pieces, growing in throbs and pulses. It lapped over the edge of the tattered coat, which cried in pain in its alien, singsong voice as it fought.

Mason had pushed my shirt and bra up to my chin. Cold air ran across my breasts. Panic bubbled at the hard ache the chill brought to my exposed nipples, but I fought it down. The doctor-priest knelt between my legs, jerking at the snap of my jeans.

Nyarlathotep's voice jolted inside my head.

Mason is the anchor. He is the key to this manifestation. As long as he is alive, we will lose this battle. Take this.

I nodded, just barely, willing myself not to fight, not yet. The Man in Black's left hand flicked out, and something long and sharp spun across the floor toward me. It skittered in a dance of reflected light.

The Aqedah.

The Knife of Abraham.

Mason's head jerked up, black-hole eyes narrowing as they flicked over to the spinning knife. It stopped. Too far for me to reach.

He chuckled and went back to pulling at my waistband.

He was a priest to an elder god. He had magick power and inhuman strength.

But in his arrogance he didn't notice that I had come back.

And I brought every ounce of rage I carried in my soul with me.

I jerked to the left, my leg coming up and over his head. It was a move I'd learned in mixed martial arts class, a way to get free from a mounted position. It only worked if your opponent was sloppy, untrained, and not paying attention. Using all the power in my leg, I drove my heel down against Mason's temple, torquing my hips, using the leverage to smash his skull into the floor.

Pushing off with my foot against his shoulder slid me almost a foot away. I rolled over and scrambled toward the knife. My feet slipped on the slick tile. I lunged.

Mason's hand closed on my ankle.

My hand closed on the knife.

His roar of anger shook me as he jerked my leg, pulling me against him. I rolled, and his hand grabbed my shirt, yanking me off the ground. I swung up in his grip, pulled against him.

His fist swung back, ready to fall on me like the hand of doom when I shoved the knife into his chest.

The blade sank deep, slicing through Mason's sternum and skin as though they were air. Dark blood bubbled out, spilling over my hand. Magick sparked and dark energy leaked from the gash in his chest. It ran in streamers of bruise-black, twittering upward, pooling against the ceiling, and rolling into wisps that pulled and thinned and dissipated into the ether. His golden perfection dulled as the dark energy left, his skin turning the color of iron. Blue eyes swam back from the black pits they had become, their eyelids fluttering as his mouth went slack.

I knelt over him as his life drained away, and I watched as he slipped, loose and limp, off the end of the ancient knife in my hand.

27

Someone touched my arm, and I jerked. I looked over and found Daniel kneeling beside me. He smiled. His hand stayed on my arm.

He said something to me that I couldn't hear, but I watched his mouth move.

I blinked at him, my eyelids shuttering down and then up again. His voice sounded muffled, hazy. The whole room sounded that way, as if it had been filled with a light fog. The gap between me and reality was still there, open and raw.

My eyes slid sideways, landing on the corpse cooling in front of me.

I fell back. Scrambled away.

Daniel looked concerned. His mouth moved again. He sounded as if he were underwater.

He didn't get it. He didn't understand. It wasn't the image, the memory, of killing Mason that clawed and scrabbled at the inside of my skull. It wasn't his death that horrified me.

That wasn't it at all.

Back in my body, my mind had to deal with what he'd tried to do. What he'd threatened me with. What he'd almost accomplished. His hands had been on me. He'd *touched* me.

Like *they* had touched me.

The world was too bright. Everything was too close. Too sharp. Too harsh.

Too real.

Daniel reached toward me again.

I jerked away, frantically climbing to my feet.

The Man in Black finished chopping up the leftovers of the Cancer God. He walked up behind Daniel, wiping his sword clean with the end of his coat.

Daniel said my name.

I turned and ran with every ounce of strength I had left.

28

THE NIGHT WAS as bright and clean and sharp as broken glass when I burst through the door and spilled out onto the grass. My lungs hurt as I bellowed air between sobs. A high moon swung bright and full in the velvet sky, ringed in indigo that melted into the pure dark of the void. Stars flared, uncountable eyes watching my frail humanity. Unblinking. Uncaring.

I pulled my legs to my chest and rocked. They hurt from pounding down the stairs. I hadn't been able to wait for the elevator, couldn't be trapped in a box. The pain was good. The pain was clear. The pain was in my legs, not in my head or my heart or my guts.

I still held the bloody knife. I'd tried to fling it away, but my hand had locked down, fused to the handle by a crust of blood dried into glue. Holding the back of the blade, the heavy spine thick in my fingers, I pulled it free from my grip. I wanted to throw it far and wide, to get it away from me.

I don't know why I slid it through my belt.

The handle dug into my stomach.

I was still sitting on the cold, wet grass, rocking back and forth, when Daniel pushed open the door and stepped outside.

I heard him come out. I didn't turn, but I knew it was him. It felt like him.

I listened as he walked through the grass behind me. He stepped around to where I could see him and stood in front of me.

I didn't look up. I didn't do anything but rock and hold myself.

Slowly, carefully, he lowered himself to the ground beside me. He'd put his shirt back on.

That was good.

He needed his shirt.

Sitting cross-legged, he stuck his hands in the pocket of his hoodie.

Seconds passed like hours, him looking at me, me looking at the toes of my shoes.

He made a small noise in his throat, testing the silence to see if it could be penetrated. When he spoke, his voice was soft, easy, as if he were talking to a skittish animal. Maybe that's exactly what he was doing.

"Hey, Charlie. How you doin'?"

I didn't answer.

He bit his lip, trying to think of what to say next. It took him a minute to find it.

"It's okay, what happened. You only did what you had to do. You don't have to feel guilty about it."

"I don't." My voice sounded like I felt: hollow, tinny, and disconnected.

He didn't say anything for a long moment.

"I'd understand if you were upset about it."

I looked away.

You just don't get it.

My eyes felt hot. "I'm not upset about that." I wasn't. Killing Mason sat at the other end of a long, narrow tube. I could see it; it would come up on me one day, and that would be a whole new round of therapy, but that wasn't what made me feel as though my skin had separated from my muscles, as though a thick layer of batting hung between me and the world. That wasn't what made me crumble on the inside, breaking into tiny pieces that tumbled and fell into a cold, bottomless void.

"Are you upset because of me? Because of what happened earlier?"

I rolled my eyes.

Great. Here we go.

"Just leave it alone, Daniel."

His brow creased. "No. You're upset, and I want to help."

"You're not helping."

Oh God, just stop.

"If this is about earlier, I'm sorry, really sorry."

Please stop.

He didn't.

"I didn't mean to move so fast. I just . . . I just think I'm falling for you." He shook his head, bangs swinging back and forth. "No. I love you Charlie." His words were firm, definitive, declarative. A statement. "I'm in love with you."

Tears spilled down my cheeks.

Not this, not now, not after. Can't you see?

I whispered, "You're not in love with me."

He rolled up to his knees, moving closer, still not touching me. "I am. I love you, Charlie. You don't have to feel the same way—it's okay if you don't."

In that moment, somewhere deep inside me, I realized that I did. I did love Daniel. But he was wrong, so wrong. He couldn't love someone like me. Not someone as damaged as me.

My head went ugly, dark thoughts rushing into the black hole that had opened up inside me. Was this some cruel joke? Something he'd been waiting to do since high school? Some sick way to make fun of what had happened to me?

"Screw you. This isn't funny."

Shock crossed his face. "What are you talking about?"

I turned. My mouth felt sharp and feral. "This isn't funny. You know what I've been through. You know why I can't be loved." I jumped to my feet, screaming from my gut. "I'm *damaged goods.* You can't love me. Nobody can love me."

He stood with his hands out, palms up in supplication. "What are you talking about?"

Tears ran hot and salty. The side of my mouth hitched up, making my voice sound strange. "You know *exactly* what I'm talking about. Tyler Woods's party in ninth grade. *I'm* the party favor. *I'm* the girl too stupid to watch herself, the girl who wound up passed around like a two-bit whore. I'm used up and screwed up and no good to anyone anymore."

Confusion swept across his face. "Wait." He blinked, trying to process. "Wait . . ."

I couldn't stop. Not after tonight. Not after earlier with Daniel. Not after Mason. It all spilled out: a wound lanced, a dam burst, a bottle of hurt shattered. My finger jabbed the air toward him. "Don't act like you didn't know! Don't you dare! You chased after me all this time because of it. 'Surely the gangbang girl is easy meat. Surely she puts out. She's an easy mark. She wanted it. She asked for it. She *deserved* it.'"

It spilled out. All the things whispered about me, all the things said behind people's hands, muttered in hushed tones somehow always just loud enough to carry to my ears. Words that cut open wounds that never really healed.

I thought I dealt with all this shit years ago.

More words spilled from me. "You thought it. You *knew* it. The jacked-up Cancer God priest knew it. Everybody knows it!"

I screamed, the pain ripping out in a raw, animal sound of anguish.

Daniel grabbed me by the arms.

"Charlie!"

I screamed in his face, bleeding out the pain, unable to stop.

He shook me. It wasn't hard, just sharp enough to jar me back to reality. We stood there, his hands on my arms, looking at each other. Tears ran down his face, tracing the edge of his jawline, hanging in shaky, silvery droplets before falling.

"I *never* thought those things. I didn't know. I swear to you, Charlie, I didn't know."

"*Liar.*" Pain made my voice ugly, snarling out like a slap.

"I swear."

"*Everybody* back home knew."

He blew out a breath, sharp and hard. "I knew it happened to somebody. It was on the news—but I was fourteen, I didn't watch the news. I had no idea that was you. I promise."

I looked in his eyes. They stared back at me green and bright.

And completely honest.

Dammit.

I believed him.

He *hadn't* known.

The knowledge broke something inside me. A knot of distrust I'd held since the second I'd started talking to him. I'd held back, always waiting for him to do *something,* to hurt me in some way. Maybe he never would.

Maybe the time had come to stop living a half life of doubt and suspicion.

Could I know love?

I stepped into his arms.

Carefully, he put them around my shoulders as I pressed my face against his chest and cried out the pain. He held me and made soft shushing noises of reassurance. A small surge of wild panic started, and I pushed it away. I could trust Daniel.

I could love Daniel.

We stood like that until all the poison had leaked out of me. Until I came up empty and dry. Until all the pain and hurt and betrayal had been spent. I wasn't fixed—the scars were still there and always would be—but now maybe I wouldn't have to bear them alone.

The cold began to set in through our clothes. Pulling away, I wiped the tears from my face. Daniel had a look in his eyes.

"What is it?" I asked.

He shook his head.

"Tell me. No need for secrets now."

He sighed. "I was just thinking about what happened between us. I feel like a complete asshole." He looked away. "I understand now why you reacted like you did. I'm sorry for doing anything to bring back that pain, for making you feel that way again."

I touched his face, turning it so he had to look at me. "Our . . . misunderstanding," I said, searching for the right words to explain, "it made me feel scared and helpless. Angry. It hurt because I thought you knew and just didn't care what I'd been through."

He opened his mouth to speak. I put my fingers over his lips and shook my head. "It's my turn, let me finish."

He nodded.

I continued. "What happened was horrible, the worst thing I can imagine. Not just the physical stuff, but the pain in here." I touched my heart. "And the pain in here." I touched my head. "It destroyed who I was for a long time, and it still messes with my head. It probably always will." My hand moved to his chest. "But what you did was just a mistake, and *nothing* like what happened then. That night, those . . . animals . . . left me feeling as if I had been turned inside out."

I stopped.

If I kept talking, I would cry again. I didn't want that. I wanted to be done crying for the night. Daniel gently pulled me close again.

His voice was soft in my ear. "I am so sorry you had to go through that."

"I am too." I burrowed close, into the safety of his arms. "I just wish those assholes could feel like they made me feel. Especially Tyler—he's one who started it that night, the one who pulled me into that room. He should know what it's like to be ripped apart, to have everything he is turned inside out."

The moment the words left my mouth, I regretted them.

The torc around my neck tightened, constricting in a hard line, bruising the skin of my throat as magick welled up inside me. The warm rain fell against my skin, under my clothes.

What . . .

Ashtoreth's gift struck, and the rain scraped me raw as it jerked us both through time and space. It was different this time. I was pulled, stretched, and dragged into a howling dark void. Vast planets that hated us spun and twirled as we passed, turning their terrible faces to destroy us in their own inexorable rotation. Two moons were locked in orbit, each plotting the other's demise.

Things gibbered by, skritching and tearing at us, constructed with a strange geometry that made the blood in my body run cold. My eyes slammed shut, but it didn't help. The horrors still seared through them as if my lids had been made transparent in the face of unimaginable iniquity. Things never human swept by. A malevolent entity of only colour, incomprehensible to our tiny human minds, swirled toward us as we narrowly missed the edge of it, barely skimming past, and I knew, I *knew* that if we had even brushed against that, that, that *colour* we would have been obliterated, snuffed from existence.

Madness acid-washed my mind, welling up, trying to drown my soul. I was very nearly lost when we crashed back into our reality, nowhere near where we had been before.

29

NOISE PRESSED ALL around me, constricting me. I was on my hands and knees, the world gone black, my eyes squeezed tightly shut as if they'd been nailed together. I didn't want to open them. Nothing good would be there when I opened them.

What the hell was that?

My brain scrambled, turning in circles, trying to re-orient itself—make sense of what happened.

Think. One thing at a time.

What do you feel?

Something rough under my hands, not gritty, not hard, just firm and . . . textured. And warm. Sticky.

What do you smell?

I breathed, pulling the air into my mouth, tasting it on the back of my tongue. The smell of a playground—metal monkey bars, to be exact. Iron left out and heated in the sun.

What do you hear?

I clamped down, concentrated, pushing out of my head the echo of the howl in the void. There were noises, all around me. They started separating, pulling apart as I concentrated. A rhythmic sound welled up, a noise that came and went, sweeping in and out like a tide. A wet sound, harsh and raw.

Someone's throwing up.

I could hear shouting.

How many voices?

Three voices. I recognized one as Daniel's. The other two were male: one rough and raspy, the other shrill, undercut with a brittle edge of panic. They jumbled, running over each other. "What the fuck!" "Who are you?" "What the hell just happened to Tyler?"

Good. You did good.

Now what do you see?

I opened my eyes. I knelt on red carpet.

Red, *shiny* carpet.

Red, shiny, *wet* carpet.

The carpet was saturated.

With blood.

I recoiled in horror, scrambling backward. My eyes jerked around the room, trying to take it all in, trying to see everything at once.

I was in a room. A bedroom.

Familiarity pushed against my brain. The walls were the same color, the dresser the same dark-stained wood, the shelf crowded with trophies bunched together like a fake gold and imitation silver mob—just like they had all those years ago. Some details were different, but I *recognized* this room.

This was the room where my life had ended.

Daniel stood a few feet away, hands knotted around a tie worn by a tall man hunched over, pulled down to Daniel's level. The tall man's hair had been clipped short to hide the fact that it had started thinning, his angular face clean shaven instead of wearing a scraggly goatee as he had before. Ten years had carved lines around them, but I recognized the man's rodent eyes.

The last time I had seen them, one had winked as he strolled past me, leaving the courtroom with an acquittal and a clear record.

The time before that, they'd been dark and sharp with merciless cruelty as he used my hair to hold me to the bed.

Brad Curson.

My eyes jerked away, finding two men on the other side of the room; one was standing, the other sitting in a puddle of sick.

Dark jeans over heavy black boots covered the squat, bowed legs of the man who stood. A black T-shirt, stretched over his expansive stomach, bore the cover art to an album by a band I didn't recognize. His hard dark hair came from a box, lighter over his ears where it tried to cover gray, gelled up and back in a pompadour. He had an air of desperation, as if he were trying to hold on to something he had already lost. His face looked different, a bust someone had coated in lumps of clay to resculpt, covered but still recognizable.

The last time I had seen him, he'd held my face in his hands, squeezing my skull hard enough that I could feel the bones shift, their edges grinding against each other as he pushed my jaw out of its socket, forcing me to look at him while he tore his way inside me.

Donnie Zito.

The man on the floor wiped sick from his mouth, scrawny hand clapped in place. Narrow trails and trickles ran down his ratty chest in beaded dribbles. The pants he wore were frayed, worn through in places, the denim stiff with old paint. His baby face and boyish body had been whittled down and worn away, his sharp nose a raw red, cheeks pitted with scars from sores that had been picked at with addict fingers. The eyes I had last seen clenched tight over mine almost a decade ago were now pulled wide, strung back with wires and staring at something on the floor between us.

Jimmy Deets.

Slowly, I dropped my gaze, pulling it away from one of the people responsible for over ten years of brittle, broken existence to look at the thing on the floor between us.

My eyes locked on it.

I stared at something I didn't recognize.

It lay on the carpet in a patch of vermillion, the edges creeping away, wicking from one fiber to the next, the stain marching steadily across the face of the carpet.

There were shapes and colors. An oblong geometry that branched in two even parts on one end and three uneven parts on the other. It was nearly, but not exactly, the same color as the stain it lay in: lighter, carmine over burgundy, a topographical map done in 3D, the main part dotted and layered with abstract shapes. There were two pale-pink harbors in the center, an ivory mountain range that twisted and curled below them all connected and similar, the whole thing covered in a tracery of blue streams and rivers that originated and culminated in the fist-sized peak lying between the two rose-colored harbors. My eyes traveled the length of it, taking in the artistry, the colors that stood stark and those that blended like brushed chalk powder.

This thing was foreign to me. Alien. Weird.

But familiar.

My gaze landed on the upper right branch, the end of the shape as it stretched out in front of me.

There at the end, I discovered a pair of colors not found anywhere else, an object that was different from the rest.

A knot of burnished gold wrapped around a hard, faceted emerald.

My head buzzed as I stared at that thing, chewing on the image.

I'd seen that thing last on the hand that broke my fingers.

A ring.

A ring handed down from father to son.

The Woods family ring.

The room swam as my mind stopped trying to keep me from seeing what was right in front of me.

I was looking at Tyler Woods.

The one who started it all that night. The one who pulled me into this room so long ago. The one who hurt me first.

The one who hurt me the worst.

Tyler Woods.

He'd been turned inside out.

30

"CHARLIE."

I turned, my head buzzing with numb horror. Daniel was talking to me. He held Brad Curson in a half nelson, twisting his arm up behind him. Curson's face turned purple, a knot of pain as he arched backward, keeping the pressure off so his arm didn't break.

Something dark and ugly curled inside me.

"Charlie."

I looked past him to Daniel. Curson was taller, but Daniel had complete control, using the skills and strength he still held from high school.

Curson jerked and pulled. "Let go of me, asshole!"

Daniel leaned back, putting pressure on the taller man's arm.

Break it, the dark, ugly thing inside me growled.

"Shut up," Daniel snarled at the man in his grip. Curson quit talking and just stood there, sucking breath against the pain in his arm. Daniel looked at me. "Charlie, what's going on?"

The metal circle around my neck sat cold and heavy. "I made a wish."

"You made a . . ." Realization crept into his eyes. "Does that mean these are the guys who . . . ?"

I nodded.

His face flushed dark. A vein throbbed along his temple.

And with a small, almost casual move of his shoulders, he snapped Brad Curson's arm with wet crack.

That dark, ugly thing inside me thrilled.

Curson screamed, high pitched and thin, leaking the pain out in a howl that threaded through the room. Daniel let go, and Curson crumpled at his feet, arm turned the wrong way. The scream continued, muffled and slightly smothered as Curson rolled into a fetal position around his ruined arm.

Daniel looked down, his hands shaking. He took a swaying step back.

I reached toward him. "Are you okay?"

He nodded, still looking down. "I'm okay. I'm all right." His voice buzzed tightly. He looked up at me. His eyes widened, and he jerked toward me. "Charlie, look out!"

The words were barely out of his mouth when jagged, sharp pain cut from the back of my skull to my eyeballs in a black-red bolt.

31

Donnie Zito stood over me, an ugly look on his ugly face.

He clutched a small, mean revolver in his hand like a captured rattlesnake. A thick droplet of blood—my blood—hung under the snub-nosed barrel from where he'd pistol-whipped me. It swayed like a pendulum, threatening to break and fall as the pistol swung between me and Daniel.

"Somebody better tell me what the *fuck* is going on, and they better start telling me right fucking *now*," Donnie said.

The only answer he got was Brad Curson's moan of pain.

Donnie shook the gun, slinging the droplet free. My eyes lost it as it tumbled through space. He scowled. "Do I look like someone who is fucking around right now? You, chickie"—he pointed the gun at me—"answer the fucking question."

I looked at him. The dark, ugly thing curled inside me again, and I realized something with the cold, hard clarity of universal truth. Something so fundamental that it shifted reality around me and, I knew, would alter my every interaction great and small for the rest of my life.

I realized that Donnie Zito could kill me, but he would never be able to hurt me again.

The thought made magick hum from the center of my chest and run tingling down to the Mark incised in my palm.

I got to my feet.

"I made a wish, Donnie. I made a wish and turned your friend Tyler inside out."

He stepped back. "My friend Tyler?" Beefy eyebrows pulled together. His eyes darted inside their pockets of flesh, moving around the room. They came back to me narrowed and lit with suspicion. "Wait a fuggin minute. Is this Tyler Woods's room?"

I nodded. A sinister grin pulled at the corners of my lips. I felt a little buzzy, a little disconnected. I felt invulnerable.

"I ain't seen Tyler since . . ." He looked me up and down. Sweat rolled from his hairline, zigzagging down his jowls. "Wait a minute . . ." His eyes narrowed. "Does that mean you're . . ."

I nodded.

He thrust the gun at me again. "You need to explain how the hell I got here. I was at a club in LA. How the *fuck* did I get in Tyler's bedroom?" Fear stink wafted off him. I could smell it, metallic and sour, mixed with the salt of his sweat. It made my head swim. I breathed it in deeply, and magick flared inside me, brushing against the inside of my rib cage, sweeping upward and clearing my head.

"I told you, Donnie. I made a wish." I raised my hand, my right hand, and held it out to him. It pulsed, the symbol cut there glowing with malevolent red energy. I took a step toward him and smiled. "I'm magick."

"You're a crazy bitch, is what you are."

"I am what you made me, Donnie."

The dark, ugly thing spoke in my mind. My hand fell to the Knife of Abraham, still tucked through my belt. Slowly pulling it out, I took a step toward him. The iron blade was dark, but the point still gleamed wicked sharp. I smiled. "I am the angel of vengeance come to collect what's owed."

I felt Daniel move behind me. I didn't turn, my eyes pinned on Donnie Zito.

Daniel's voice spoke. "Charlie, are you sure this is a good idea?"

I ignored him and took another step. Donnie Zito moved back.

"Careful, Donnie." I pointed the knife at him. The magick inside me spilled out of my Mark, trickling and sparking off the iron blade. "You're going to step in Tyler if you don't watch out." I giggled, and it cut through the room, sending chills up my own spine. Donnie flinched.

He jerked and looked down, his booted foot squelching in the soaked carpet. He shouted and danced to get out of it. I turned, keeping him in my sight. The gun in his hand swung toward me, his face dark with anger and fear.

"Bitch, I'm gonna gut-shoot you if you don't get me out of here."

"You can't hurt me, Donnie."

His lip curled into a snarl, pulling up as though he'd been fishhooked. "I hurt you before. I hurt you real good." His voice dropped into a mean, intimate tone. "I still think about it when I whack off."

Rage crept slowly up my spine, inching along, crawling its way into my brain.

His smile was an ugly, twisted thing. "Oh yeah. I still think about our time together. I always wanted us to have another date."

"It wasn't a date, you bastard." The words hurt leaving my mouth.

"Call it what you want, cupcake. I don't care. It was good times."

I said nothing. The fuse burned.

Daniel moved. I saw it out of the corner of my eye. Donnie Zito swung the gun around toward him. "Ah, ah, ah . . . settle down, boy." Daniel stopped moving, stood glaring. Donnie kept the gun pointed at Daniel but looked at me. "Yes indeed, you were a good piece of ass. Tell you what—you drop that knife or I'm gonna shoot this asshole in the face."

Magick sparked like electricity along the metal around my neck, crackling under my chin. It felt as if someone shoved me forward as Ashtoreth's gift kicked in. My mind jolted, and I was inside Donnie Zito's mind, seeing what he desired most of all.

My brain swirled around a dark image of me pinned to the bed, a gun held to my head by a naked, grunting Donnie Zito while Daniel lay bleeding on the floor.

Everything swirled again, and I blinked, back in my own body. I looked up. Donnie Zito smiled at me. He raised the pistol in his hand and pointed it at Daniel. I felt his desire spike as his finger squeezed the trigger.

I lunged, slashing with the Aqedah. The blade flashed in my hand, crimson magick trailing in a shower of sparks. It struck deep, slicing through the meat and bone of Donnie Zito's arm as if it were made of cheese. The gun bucked as it fired, jerking his arm, the blade embedded in it, my hand clenched tight on the handle. Hot blood sprayed in a fine mist across my face, and someone screamed.

32

Donnie Zito staggered, fat fingers clamped around his bleeding arm in a sorry tourniquet. He crumpled to the floor, landing on the pistol that had fallen from his useless hand. The wound still pumped blood, welling around the exposed bone. It didn't even look real.

Dread pinned me there, watching him lie on the floor. I didn't want to turn. Didn't want to see Daniel laying dead from a gunshot wound. I couldn't take seeing that. Looking at a fat rapist bleeding out on the floor was bad enough. Seeing Daniel dead would destroy me.

I slid the knife back through my belt.

I didn't know what else to do with it.

My ears were shut, the world muffled in the aftermath of the gunshot. I could still hear screaming, but it was far, far away. I wanted to be far, far away. The torc around my neck tingled, and I opened my mouth to wish when something clamped on my arm.

I turned and found Daniel standing there holding my arm.

What?

He said something. I saw his mouth move. He stared at me and said it again, slower, his lips moving wide as he enunciated. Concentrating, I made out: *Car zoo smoky.*

What the hell?

I shook my head. He said it again, leaning in, putting his mouth close to my ear. "Are you okay?"

Am I okay?

It took a long second for me to make sense of the question. I *was* okay, and I wasn't anywhere close to being okay.

Wait.

Daniel wasn't dead. Wasn't shot.

My eyes slid around him. Curson lay on the floor in a slowly widening stain of dark blood. He wasn't moving. He wasn't breathing.

Donnie's bullet had found a home.

"Charlie?"

"I'm all right," I said.

I'm not, but what else can I say?

Relief washed over his face.

"Who's screaming?"

His mouth pulled into a hard line. Lifting his hand, he pointed. I turned. It took me a second to see him pulled in on himself, a spider dropped down a line of silk into an open flame. Bony knees hugged high to his chest, his hand scrabbling at his mouth, trying to stuff his screams back inside.

I'd forgotten about Jimmy Deets.

His eyes jumped, flinging themselves around the room from the inside-out man on the floor in front of him, to Donnie Zito's bleeding bulk, to Brad Curson's cooling corpse. They flicked up and locked with mine. The longer we stared at each other, the wider his eyes got, until I thought the skin would actually peel away, letting them roll out to bounce across the floor like those crazy balls that come from fifty-cent novelty machines.

I shoved the thought out of my mind before it could take hold of the magick that still hummed and vibrated in my veins.

Daniel touched my arm. "We should maybe get out of here."

It was hard to pull my eyes away from Jimmy's—it felt like they were actually tethered to his—but I did it.

I sighed, and it took me by surprise, pulling deep from the bottoms of my lungs and rushing clean out my nose. "You're right. I'll wish us away."

I had started thinking of where in the world we could go when Jimmy Deets stopped screaming and started moving.

He rolled up on his knees and began crawling toward us. He was thin, so thin I could see every jerk and jut of his shoulder blades, spine, and ribs. In high school he had been in ROTC. He'd been fit and healthy. Looking at him now was like watching a hairless, starved rat crawl to you on its last bit of strength. He scurried around the mess of Tyler Woods and hit his knees at my feet.

He looked up and I looked down. Splinter-nailed hands reached but didn't touch me, hovering in front of my waist in supplication. Tears streamed from red-rimmed eyes, racing down hollow cheeks, skimming around the sores in their way.

His mouth opened then closed, a white gummy substance in the corners of his lips. They opened again, and his voice came out choked. "Please . . ."

The word shocked me.

He swallowed, a tiny sob breaking at the end. "Please . . . " he repeated.

"Please what?"

"Please forgive me."

The dark, ugly thing inside me curled up, rubbing against the pity being born, blossoming in my heart.

His head dropped, muffling his words, but this close I could still hear him. "I am so sorry. I know what we did to you was horrible. I . . . I can't imagine what it was like."

"No. You can't."

"I can't stop remembering it."

The dark, ugly thing lashed my spine.

"I bet you can't."

His face flew up, horror painted there. "No! No! Not like that, never like that. God, I wish I could scrub it out of my head. I've tried. I've tried so hard. Crank, pills, drinking . . . but it never works. The memory is always there. I can't clear it out of my brain."

Twist.

I snarled. "Maybe you should have used a bullet."

His head fell. "I tried." Scrawny shoulders shook with silent sobs. "I couldn't do it." His fist beat against his leg. "I was too weak. Just like that night . . . I couldn't stand up to Tyler, and you . . ."

He choked, an ugly noise shaking his ridged chest like a palsy. "I'm so sorry for what I did, for what I let happen."

Ragged fingertips moved to his temples, rubbing in circles. "It's been horrible. I can't hold a job. I haven't ever been able to find someone to love. I live off disability and painting houses." His fingers curled into fists. They beat on the sides of his head. "I barely sleep, I only eat enough to live, and I'm alone, so damn miserable no one wants to be around me."

The dark, ugly thing inside me came out in my voice.

"I feel really sorry for you. I'm sure it's been tough." I fought the urge to spit on him.

He broke, his spine folding until he huddled, compressed over his knees, rail-thin body shaking as he cried.

Daniel touched my arm. I looked at him. He ran his fingers through his hair, not looking at me.

"What?"

It took him a second to speak. "Listen to me, Charlie. Hear me out. I'm not saying he deserves it, but maybe you should forgive him."

"Forgive him?"

His hands went up between us, warding off the anger in my voice. "Not for his sake, but for yours. I'm watching you right now, and I can *feel* the anger, the hate . . . hell, the *magick* rolling off your skin. I don't think it's good for you."

I looked at Daniel's face. The dark, ugly thing curled inside.

Screw him. He doesn't know what this animal did to me.

The look on his face cut through that ugliness. It wasn't anger. It wasn't pity for me. It wasn't self-righteousness.

It was a look of care.

A look of love.

It shone in his oh-so-green eyes. He loved me. He asked me to forgive Jimmy Deets because he could see what the anger and hatred were doing to me. The look in his eyes made things clear in a click.

I could feel the hatred inside me, stoking the fire of the magick, eating away my resistance to its siren call. I could let it go. I could drop that burden.

I wouldn't absolve Jimmy Deets of his sin. I wouldn't make it okay in any way. I would just let go of the anger *I* was carrying. The rage. The pain.

I could be free.

Not healed, but closer.

"Stand up," I said to Jimmy. He looked up at me, scrambled to his feet, and stood in front of me.

I took a deep breath. My heart pounded in my chest. It throbbed at the edges of my vision, making the room seem darker.

Jimmy looked at me expectantly, fear on his face.

I couldn't do this.

Not after what he did.

My head hurt. The room grew darker still.

Daniel's fingers found my shoulder. I could feel the strength and support in his soft, reassuring touch.

"I . . ."

The words stuck in my throat.

I swallowed and tried again.

"I forgive you."

The air in the room grew thick like syrup.

A smile broke Jimmy's face open, fresh tears streaming. "Thank you. Thank you. I don't deserve it."

The room dimmed as though a lamp had been turned off. A shadow moved behind Jimmy. It swirled and coalesced then strode over, a naked sword in its red right hand.

Daniel saw it too. "What the . . . ?" was all he had a chance to say.

The sword rose then fell like lightning, splitting Jimmy Deets from the crown of his head to the bottom of his crotch. He stood there, a shocked look on his face until his left knee buckled and both halves of him fell apart.

"No one gets to harm my Acolyte." The Man in Black stepped through the bloody mist, dropping the sword into the eldritch depths of his coat. "Not even ten years ago."

33

My hand slid across the mirror, wiping away condensation in a smear. The shower ran behind me, hot water rolling steam into the bathroom. My bathroom. I stared at my reflection.

I look like shit.

A fine layer of grime covered my face, turning my eyes into black holes. My eyes are dark—it's part of my heritage—but now they looked painted, Cimmerian circles around both as though I'd been awake for days. The skin over the right one was discolored. It hurt to touch, a deep soreness under my fingers. It also felt mushy, swollen.

It's from when your face got slammed into the door.

All the way back at the beginning of this night. God, that felt like weeks ago, but it had only been a few hours.

Damn.

I turned my head slowly. I didn't want to, but I had to. I looked at my right ear.

It wasn't as bad as I had thought it would be. It looked a little weird, but I couldn't really see it. Using a finger, I moved the hair curling over the top rim of cartilage. The curl of hair was stiff, hard with dried blood that cracked and crumbled under my touch. It stuck to the torn flesh like a hard-packed bandage. I took a deep breath and pulled it away.

It didn't hurt—I couldn't feel it at all because of whatever Nyarlathotep had done earlier—but I still had to grab the sink to keep from falling down.

My ear was ruined.

Taking a deep breath, I pulled together my resolve and looked again.

The ear looked perfectly normal on the bottom half. The lobe still curved delicately to my jaw, and it still bore the diamond earring given to me by my dad as a graduation present. But the top half . . . the top half was destroyed. It had been torn into four jagged sections, and a piece was missing. I could see white cartilage in the rips. It didn't look like an ear. It looked like mangled meat.

How will you explain what happened when people see this?

This would be out there, out where the world would see it forever. Maybe a doctor could fix it, but I couldn't afford that. What would I do? Wear scarves or hats? Grow my hair out?

The thought made my stomach hurt.

I had short hair.

I'd cut it short the day I got out of the hospital and had kept it short since. The thought of growing it long tripped the ugly old feelings. It dragged my mind off my ear and shoved it toward what had happened earlier.

I'd killed someone earlier.

No. You killed three *people.*

Mason, Donnie Zito, and Tyler Woods.

Brad Curson and Jimmy Deets were dead because of me too. I hadn't stuck a knife in them or used magick . . . *I still couldn't believe I used magick at all* . . . to *turn them INSIDE OUT.*

That thought made my stomach lurch. I bent at the waist, aiming for the trashcan, but nothing came up. I stood there, bent over, with the room spinning lazily. The air grew hot, the shower steaming up the tiny bathroom. That didn't help.

Pull it together.

Reaching deep inside, I forced my mind to think clearly. I stepped outside myself so I could look at the feelings inside me without being caught up in them. It was a trick I had learned on my own, and I could only do it by myself when I was someplace safe.

My therapist hated it, always worried that the dissociation might cause a hard split in my personality, so I didn't tell her about still doing it. I could see her reason for concern, but it worked, so I did it when things pushed my issues too far. Tonight had definitely pushed my issues all the way over the edge.

In seconds, my mind cleared and my heart slowed down.

You killed Mason.

I had. It was self-defense, and he'd been a monster. Did I feel bad about it? No. I didn't. I should.

I thought I should.

The whole thing felt surreal, a nightmare that almost didn't feel like it had happened at all. The image of him, of his face as the knife sank into his chest, swam up in my mind. My body had the memory of the knife sliding in, stopping when the hilt hit his sternum, his weight pulling down on my arm as he slid to the floor, and the jerk upward as the weight fell off. I could feel all these things as though they were happening at that very moment.

But I didn't feel bad about them.

What about Tyler Woods?

The image of Tyler reduced to a mound of meat smeared across my mind. It blared, filling my mindspace with lurid colors and grisly shapes, a geometry of gruesomeness. It was a disgusting picture that I could feel would come back on me, in nightmares and flashbacks, anytime my mental defenses drop it would appear. I would see it for a long time, maybe even the rest of my life. My nose filled with the wet-hot scent of raw flesh dredged from memory.

It repulsed me.

But I didn't feel guilty about it.

I hadn't done that to Tyler Woods. I hadn't actually wanted that to happen to him. It was an accident of my magick. Magick that I didn't want. What was I doing with the ability to cast spells? How did I have the power to do something like that with just a casual wish?

I looked down at the symbol in my hand, the open cuts now turned to raised red lines of angry flesh. They'd sealed over and lay stark across the plane of my palm. Looking at the symbol made it tingle. I rubbed it across the front of my hoodie. My mind went back to the fact that I hadn't done anything to Tyler on purpose. It had been the magick's fault, not mine.

But did you try to wish him back to life?

Guilt panged across the dissociation, echoing hollowly in the space between me and my feelings.

No, I hadn't tried. I should have. I should have wished for him to not be turned inside out. It might have worked.

Even as I had this thought, something inside me knew it wouldn't have.

Donnie Zito shot Brad Curson because you *stabbed him.*

The gap I'd made inside myself narrowed, squeezed in by the truth. I hadn't meant it, but it had happened that way.

And the Man in Black killed Jimmy Deets because of you.

He did.

The gap slammed shut, dissociation crumbling as my feelings swarmed into my mind.

I hadn't wanted any of it to happen.

I had wanted all of it to happen.

They all deserved it after what they did.

I hadn't tried to kill any of them.

But they're still dead.

I stumbled, my knees suddenly unhinged, and slid down to the floor. The weight of all that had happened pushed me down. It crushed my chest under its weight.

God, please forgive me.

The tile was cold under my face as I wept.

34

DANIEL TURNED AS I stepped into the kitchen, clean and solid once more. He swallowed the spoonful of soup he'd just taken.

"Wow. You look . . ."

I stopped. What? What did I look like? Crap?

He finished: ". . . tough."

I don't know how long I laid on that floor—long enough to cry out all the guilt over what I'd done and what had been done for me. Long enough to reconcile the part of me that was glad about what had happened to those four animals. Long enough for the water to be ice cold by the time I dragged myself into the shower. It still cleared my head and washed away the dirt and dried blood.

I'd dressed in clean clothes—another a pair of jeans and a long-sleeved shirt—but this time I wore sturdy hiking boots and a watch cap that covered my ruined ear. The torc from Ashtoreth still lay around my neck, and the Knife of Abraham jutted from my belt. It somehow felt right there, laid over my hip and close at hand.

I looked tough?

I could own that. I *felt* tough.

I was compartmentalized and reconciled enough to have a talk with the Man in Black.

Alone.

He sat at the table across from Daniel, sipping what I assumed was coffee from the same George Takei mug as earlier. He looked exactly the same as he had at the beginning of the night. Even the coat had mended itself and was whole as it hung off him, rustling slightly and murmuring softly in the corner of my mind. Nothing we had been through in the last few hours had affected him at all. The benefit of being a chaos god, I supposed.

Daniel, on the other hand, looked terrible.

He slouched over in his chair, hair hanging lank across his forehead. I'd sat and talked with him a lot over the last few months, and I'd watched him carefully. Daniel didn't slouch. He had almost impeccable posture, sitting with his spine straight and his shoulders wide every time. Even once our talks moved to his apartment, he would slide down, head on the back of the couch and legs stretched out before him as we discussed everything under the sun; even then he still didn't slouch. I'm a sloucher. I always have been, but being around him made me sit straighter, made me pay attention to my posture.

To see him bent nearly double over a bowl of soup drove home how hard a night he'd had.

I walked over to him. He smiled, reaching for me. His hand stopped before touching, and his eyes went to the knife on my hip. Its edge gleamed wickedly in the kitchen light. He wasn't sure where to put his hand now. I took it to solve his problem. His skin was clammy against mine, so cold his fingers felt wet. His face was pale, purple-black smudges crouched under his eyes, and his lips were colorless. His oh-so-green eyes were bright and glassy, over-shining with something like a fever. He looked like someone who should be in a hospital receiving fluids.

"Are you okay?" I didn't know why I whispered it.

He nodded, turned in his chair. "I'm fine. The soup helped."

"Where'd the soup come from?"

His head tilted toward the Man in Black. "He found it in the pantry."

I looked over. "You made him soup?"

A dark smile twitched Nyarlathotep's face. He raised his mug. "He did not want coffee."

Daniel didn't drink coffee. Whenever we'd gone to the coffee shop he'd always ordered juice or green tea. The thought of the Crawling Chaos opening a can of soup and working the microwave with his red right hand flashed in my head.

It was weird.

And damn creepy.

Daniel shifted. "I know now isn't the time, but you smell really good."

I laughed, and it caught me by surprise. "Thank you." My fingers found his hair, the wayward cowlick behind his ear that he couldn't control. I'd always wanted to touch it. "It's called soap, and there's more upstairs in the shower if you want to use it."

He was just as filthy as I'd been. When I'd taken off my clothes to get in the shower and caught a glimpse of myself in the mirror, the grime had been like a mask and gloves, my body pale and near gleaming where my clothes had covered it.

His eyes slid sideways. "Are you okay being left alone here?"

The concern touched me, breaking loose something inside. I felt a surge of . . . love, it *was* love, for Daniel. It trilled through me, a delicious, dreadful ache. I touched his face with my other hand. "I'm good. Go take a shower, it'll make you feel better."

He nodded and stood slowly, using the table and the chair to push himself up. I moved to help him, but he held up his hand in a STOP motion. "I got it. I can do this. If I can't, I'm no good to you."

I stepped back and watched him find his balance. He took a second, swaying on his feet, before straightening and walking out of the room. The Man in Black and I watched him leave. I kept looking at the doorway until I heard him go up the stairs. When I turned, the Man in Black set his coffee cup on the table. Amusement twinkled deep in his obsidian eyes.

"Well, Acolyte, have a seat and tell me what is on your mind. I cannot wait to hear what you are so eager to say."

I sat, sliding the chair close to the table. The leftovers of Daniel's soup sat in front of me. Chicken noodle. I pushed it aside so I wouldn't have to watch it congeal. My fingers slid across the checkered tablecloth as I worked up the courage to talk. A soft whispering sounded under the table and something brushed the fronts of my shins. I didn't look down, sure it was the coat. For some reason its caress reassured me. The Man in Black spoke before I got the nerve.

"Would you like some coffee?"

The question surprised me. I shook my head. "What is it with you and the coffee?"

"It is one of the things I enjoy about your world. Nothing like it exists anywhere else in the universe."

A chaos god on a caffeine bender. Excellent. My eyes found the spot on the tablecloth where his finger had burned a hole through it earlier. It looked like someone had put out a cigar, the charred wood of the table visible beneath the marred checkered print.

Shasta's going to be pissed about that.

He leaned forward, the skinless fingertips of his red right hand gently stroking the rim of his coffee cup. Something twinkled in the shadow of his chest, drawing my eye. A gemstone the size of my fist hung around his neck. Its surface gleamed, faceted like a piece of quartz, long straight planes and sharp creased angles that formed a strange geometric shape. Color pulsed, shifting inside the gem, transitioning from harsh magenta to an indigo that almost disappeared against the darkness of the chaos god, then bursting with putrescent yellow and chartreuse chasing into crimson.

"Where'd you get the necklace?"

"It is the essence of Yar Shogura imprisoned." The raw-muscled fingers of his red right hand stroked across the surface of the gem. The colors ran from his touch, roiling back and pushing against the other side of their gem prison. The movement of it caused a weird ripple inside me, as if some tiny creature with too many legs had run across my small intestine. "I collected it while you were . . . reconnecting with past acquaintances."

"What are you going to do with that?"

His fingers slipped away from the gem. "Stop playing games, Charlotte Tristan Moore. I do not believe you want to discuss the remains or fate of the Unholy Masticate."

"You're right." I wasn't quite ready though. "Answer one more thing."

He nodded.

"What is it with you and all the titles and full names? Why can't you just call me Charlie?"

His fingers tapped the table. "Names have power. They define a thing. If you know a thing's name, you can own that aspect of them. There are . . ." He held up his finger, dark eyes sliding up and to the left. ". . . 866,578 humans named Charlotte on this continent, but only one Charlotte Tristan Moore. Only one who can be my Acolyte."

"Was that flattery?"

"You may take it as such."

I rolled it around in my mind. Since I'd met him, he'd mostly been the Man in Black to me. That name defined him in my head, but at different times I'd thought of him as the Crawling Chaos, the Midnight Man, and even Nyarlathotep, all of them at times when those names applied. It wasn't intentional on my part, but it held true to what he just told me.

I filed the information away.

Time to get to it.

I took a deep breath. "I want you to let Daniel go."

His lips twitched. He said nothing.

I pushed on. "You've got me with the magick wishing collar and the Mark, so you don't need him anymore."

"Oh, but we do need him. He is a key part of what is occurring."

"How?"

"That does not matter. All you need know is that it is necessary for him to remain near us."

I looked at him through narrow eyes. "That's not a reason."

He took a sip of coffee.

I leaned forward. "We did enough tonight. We helped you kill the Cancer God."

"There is another. You Saw it with your gift." He placed the coffee mug on the table. "I must imprison it also."

"Yar shogun-what's-his-name isn't dead?"

He shook his head. "We merely destroyed his avatar here in this reality. It will be a long time, possibly centuries, before the Whoremonger of the Flesh gathers the strength to try again."

"And we have to do this to the next one?"

He nodded.

"Then let Daniel go, or you can find it on your own." I sat back and crossed my arms. "And good luck with that."

"It is your world that will be destroyed, Acolyte."

"You know what? I thought about it while I was in the shower, and I don't believe you."

A sculpted eyebrow arched sharply over an obsidian eye. "What do you mean?"

"I think you've underestimated the human race." I put my elbows on the table. "I saw that thing we killed, imprisoned, whatever. It was scary." An image of the Cancer God rising over me in all his tumor-ridden horribleness sent a shiver across my spine. "But I think the military or even the local police could have handled it. They've got heavy firepower. And you"—I shifted, pointing my finger to indicate him—"you're scary, but I don't think you could destroy the world."

He gave a long, slow blink. "Do you not?"

I shook my head.

The Man in Black leaned forward.

Black-pit eyes stared into mine, starless light sucking voids set deep in their sockets. A minuscule comet cut its fiery trail across their depths, racing and rushing and flying to decimate some microscopic planet that lay in those pitch-black vacuums. His hand, his terrible red right hand, lifted delicately, the fingers hanging lackadaisically from loose joints of raw meat. Slowly, deliberately, he slipped the middle one, the longest one, over the rim of the cup before him. It looked obscene, and something deep inside me squirmed in reaction. The digit caressed up and then down, stirring the coffee, troubling the caffinated water as if it were an elixir being mixed, measured, and tested. The finger lifted, glistening with fresh alchemy, droplets slipping from the tip, transmogrified by the insertion of that skinless digit. It became the seed of Onan or the blood of Eliezer indebted to the Sodomite.

Either.

Neither.

Both.

Laden with magick, it was more, so much more than coffee now.

I couldn't look away. The Midnight Man coughed up a word

not meant to be formed by a human throat. It crackled in my eardrums, brittle glass rubbing edge to edge. The finger turned, then curled, then flicked, becoming an unholy aspergillum.

The transformed liquid arced across the table, an echo of the comet in his eyes. I watched it, unable to move, unable to dodge, unable to avoid the splash. It struck me across the chin and lips and cheek as though baptizing me. The not-coffee brushed my mouth. The magick inside me convulsed to life.

Then it tried to rip me apart.

35

THE WORLD TILTED, sliding sideways in a languid twirl. Everything washed across my eyes like the hand of God wiping the condensation of the world away from His mirror. I blinked and found myself standing in the center of a field of ash and embers.

I could still feel my body. Distant, disconnected, still sitting in the chair in my kitchen while my . . . mind? . . . soul? . . . stood on the edge of hell itself.

A night sky stretched over my head. All the stars had been ripped down and flung to earth in spiraling trails of poisonous cinder. The firmament sat empty and void except for the moon, which hung low and full, the color of fresh-shed blood, casting ruddy light like arterial spray. I looked around, the place where I stood both alien and familiar. The ground was hot under my feet, baking up through the soles of my boots.

A fence ran to my left, ash covering the chain links like gray, used snow. The fence followed a road beside a drainage ditch clogged with soot-stained corpses. I stepped over, looking. The bodies were jumbled, discarded and jigsawed together, some whole and some in pieces. Their blood had turned to grime, mixed with ash and black in the ruddy moonlight. One of the dead lay face up. Eyes that had been struck open in death stared at me upside down, and realization dawned in the midst of growing horror.

I knew her.

Mrs. Mickelson.

Mrs. Mickelson, my senior-year Lit teacher. Mrs. Mickelson, who always smiled when she talked about the classics and smelled like sugar cookies when she leaned over me to discuss my work. Mrs. Mickelson, who lived down the street from my parents in a bright-yellow split-level and drove a Hyundai Accent the color of a ripe tomato.

Her plump face snarled now, contorted and locked by death in a grimace that looked like a mask. The skin had been cut and peeled from her throat down to her chest, a wallpaper of flesh whose glue had failed. I pulled my eyes from her death stare, looking down the fence line.

I saw the small house on fire in the distance and realized where I was.

That was my parents' house. The house we moved to after I got out of the hospital. The house where they still lived.

I started running.

Smoke curled, rising to disappear into the empty sky. I ran harder, screaming, just screaming out to the world. The house had become a blackened stick skeleton skinned over with lurid red flames.

In front of the inferno, strung by tendons ripped out of his calves from the lowest branch of the great shady oak tree where we once had a tire swing, I found my father.

He'd been split and splayed like prepared game, everything

inside spilled out on the wet ground, and his ribs stuck out like narrow teeth in a raw mouth. His hair, worn too long since his midlife crisis, was a wet sheet that hung down, pointing at hell. The fire roared hot, throwing his shadow far out into the yard and roasting my face. The noise of it cracked open my blocked ears, letting in the chaotic choir of screaming that filled the air around me.

A sob lodged in my throat, choking me. I turned. Other houses were on fire, crackling against the blackness. Shapes moved in front of them. Inhuman shapes. Multi-jointed legs swung from bulbous bodies and contorted carapaces. Monstrous demons and things undreamed that had not walked the earth in a millennia danced and wheeled, scooping up smaller, human shapes.

The things the creatures were doing to them . . .

I turned away.

My mother. My brother.

They were here somewhere.

I had to find them.

I stumbled away, my foot slipping in the red mud that stretched under my father's hanging form. I moved toward the house, skirting around the wall of heat radiating off the inferno. It beat against my skin, pulling it tight against my face like jerky, blasting away moisture. I ran with my head turned away lest my eyes shrivel like raisins.

Ten steps later, I found half my mother in the curled and charred hydrangea bushes she'd planted the summer I turned fifteen.

I knew it was her by the sparrow tattoo on her ankle, which she'd gotten long before settling down with my father, long before I'd been born. The lines were dark, thick with age, and the colors faded to a pale, watercolor version of their former glory. I knew it was hers by the two bright stars under it, one pink and one blue, added when I and then my brother were born. Her legs stuck up from a hole, twisted and bent, the tattoo almost eye level with me. I carefully touched her leg and found it as cold and hard as clay under my fingertips.

Nausea made me turn and I kept moving.

Jackson! I have to find Jacks. He needs me.

I found him around the corner.

He lay limp and loose across the stomach of a monster, limbs spilled out as if he'd been disjointed. His face was blank and serene, his blond hair sweeping across his forehead the way it always had. It bothered him, but he never wanted it cut. Wearing superhero pajamas in blue and webbed red, he looked like he merely slept sweetly, dreaming of spring days and warm cookies. The monster holding him sprawled on spindly legs, enormous balloon stomach hanging like a loincloth between them. Its jagged teeth, like broken glass in a windowpane, were peeling skin from bone on Jackson's leg. Webbed hands held my brother's frail body while wings of tattered sailcloth slowly beat the air.

I screamed at the bloated horror squatting in the firelight of my childhood home. It goggled at me with blank orbs like peeled eggs gone rotten and continued to munch and chew, mulchy grinding noises leaking from its gaping maw. It shifted and let loose a blast of intestinal wind before settling back to its chewing.

I was taking a step toward it when something clamped on my shoulder and jerked me around in a swirl of absolute darkness.

36

THE REAL WORLD smashed into me like the fist of God. I found myself sprawling on the linoleum of my kitchen, feeling as though someone had beaten me. My throat was raw and so was my mind; the images of what I had seen were flash-burned across the theater of my brain like the afterimages of a strobe effect. My stomach twisted, trying to tie itself into a knot, acid boiling rapidly.

I looked up. The Man in Black was on his feet, staring down at me. The coat unfurled at the bottom, slinking across the floor to lightly brush my arm. I shook it off before it could start singing in my brain.

"What. The *hell*. Was that?"

"That is what your world will be if we do not stop my kith and kin from crossing over." He knelt, coat flaring out around him. "Once an elder god fully manifests in this realm, they will bring their offspring and their allies. The martial strength of the human race will be the flailing of infants before lions, and you will be destroyed."

Pushing off the floor, I scrambled to my feet. My knees shook, and so did my hands. At least I was standing. "Why did you show me that?"

He rose in a column of ebony. "That was your gift at work. You Saw what was necessary for you to understand the enormity of the task at hand."

"Do you have any idea what just went through my brain?" Anger flared as echoes of the images I had seen bounced behind my eyes.

"It was only a pale sliver of the horror that will be visited on this world if we do not finish our task." He flickered, a filmstrip hitting a snag, and then he was sitting back in the chair, coffee cup in his red right hand. I didn't see him move. One second he stood in front of me, the next he sat across the room. He indicated the empty chair with a flourish of his normal hand. "Sit, Acolyte. I have one more thing we should discuss."

Anger hummed inside me. My hand fell to the handle of the Aqedah stuck through my belt. It felt right and natural for the handle to be in my palm. "If you try anything like that again, I'll pull this knife and take my chances. I'm sick of you just demanding and casting spells to make me do what you want. It ends now."

I expected him to get angry, to rise in a roll of black coat and sorcerous wrath and have it out with me there in the kitchen. I was ready for it, hand on the magick knife, body tense, my own magick pumping through my veins and riding a flash flood of adrenaline. My teeth hurt as I snarled. I was ready to fight and ready to die.

The Man in Black chuckled.

"This is why I have fallen in love with your race. Given an

inkling of power, you go instantly to war. You are perfect instruments of chaos, ready to take life, the thing you hold most precious in yourself, from another. You ruin the world that gives you sustenance and believe yourselves immortal while fearing your own death every moment. I could not have created you more perfectly myself. It warms my heart." He smiled, sharp-pointed and wide. "All of them."

I wasn't expecting humor. It took me by surprise, and I faltered, taking a step back.

He motioned to the chair again. "Sit. I have no threats and no incantations, simply an offer that you need to hear, Charlotte Tristan Moore."

My fury fell away, slipping off like scales, but I wasn't ready to simply take the chair and parley. I kept my feet, and I kept my hand on the knife. "First, tell me why you won't let Daniel go. I need a reason."

I loved him. I had to try.

"You are familiar with the concept that gods gain power from their worshipers."

He didn't phrase it as a question, but I answered anyway. "Yeah, Neil Gaiman covered that idea. A lot."

"The concept holds true in this case. Your magick is inside you, but it needs a catalyst, an outside power source for you to use it. His feelings for you make him that catalyst."

An image of Daniel outside the hospital earlier filled my head. He had been sick and weak. My mind flashed forward to him after teleporting to that room, the room with those animals. In my memory he was pale, his skin washed out and his hands shaking. Flash forward again to him here at the table, unable to sit up straight, looking like death warmed over.

It all fell into place, crashing inside me like Tetris played with twelve-ton stones.

"You bastard." My voice was low and harsh. "Every time I use magick, it steals some of his life. You knew, and you waited until now to tell me?" My hand tightened on the knife.

"It is the way magick works, Acolyte."

"Not anymore. Not him." The knife slid out of my belt. "Let. Him. *Go*."

The Man in Black set down his coffee cup, red right hand slipping under the flap of his coat. "You should hear my offer before you do something rash."

"Let him go."

He stood. "I can free you from the memory of what happened, Charlotte Tristan Moore. I can wipe it from your mind as if it never occurred."

I said nothing, just stared at him. His coat rustled, but he was motionless, as if he had been carved from obsidian and sandalwood.

He continued. "You need never again flash back to that night. You can be free of the fear, the anger, the pain you have carried with you for a decade now, and it will require only one thing of you."

We stared at each other. I didn't know what my face looked like, but his was perfectly blank, Semitic features closed and dark.

Free.

He offered me freedom from a prison I'd been locked in for nearly half my life. Somewhere deep in my heart a yearning for that sprang up. To not spend my entire life worrying about every man I met, to not have nights when I couldn't sleep in the bed because of the feel of the mattress underneath me. To not have every ache or pain, every headache, be an instant reminder of how I'd been hurt so long ago.

And I would only have to sacrifice Daniel for it.

. . .

It was too much.

I opened my mouth, not sure what I would say. Daniel's voice cut me off before I could speak.

"Name your price, and we'll pay it." He stepped into the room. "Master."

The Man in Black smiled.

Oh, Daniel, what did you just do?

37

My bedroom door shut with a loud *click.* I stood, my hand on the knob, not turning around, not moving, just standing there facing the white painted wood.

The Man in Black had left us downstairs in a swirl of coat, saying he had to prepare for our next encounter. The pale light of a coming dawn pressed against the window. The Man in Black said his spell would end then, meaning my roommates would wake up, so we were waiting in my room, out of sight and away from any questions they might have. It'd been a silent walk up the stairs. We hadn't said a word to each other since Daniel's declaration in the kitchen. I could feel he wanted to speak, but I didn't know what to say. My thoughts and feelings swirled in a maelstrom of confusion.

"Charlie." Daniel's voice came from behind me. "Talk to me. Please."

I didn't turn around. "I just need a second, Daniel. Give it to me."

He didn't say anything else. I felt him step close to me, stop, and then step back.

He doesn't know. He can't.

I took a deep breath and held it, letting it sit in my lungs. The pressure built and I still held it, kept it until it began to burn, held it hostage until my heart began to beat harder, until my pulse pounded in my chest and temples.

Black spots speckled the edge of my vision.

I let the breath out slowly, allowing it to carry away my anger and leave behind a hard shell of calm.

I turned around.

Daniel stood looking at my bookcase, leaning in and reading titles off the spines. It was a cheap thing made of particleboard and laminate. I'd bought it at a box store and kept it for years. It had made two moves it wasn't designed to endure, once to college and once here. Because of this, and the amount of books I'd shoved on it, it leaned to the left and had to be propped up with folded cardboard to retain its upright position. Books of all kinds hung off the edges of the shelves. They jutted and jumbled, haphazard and threatening to fall for lack of space. Hardbacks, paperbacks, graphic novels; some new, most old and used; in double-stacked rows organized only by size and how they would fit on the shelf. I read everything and anything, judging each book and each writer on their own merits but keeping almost everything I consumed. In each book I found something—its language, its imagery, a character, the plot—to be worth retaining.

I don't loan my books. Don't even ask. I'd loan you my kidneys first.

Daniel realized I was watching him. He half turned. "You said you were a reader. I had no idea it was . . ."

"How much did you hear?"

The question stopped him short. For a long moment he didn't say anything.

"You heard why he won't let you go." I didn't make it a question. "You understood the part where every time I use magick it kills you a little bit."

He nodded.

"Then why in the world would you agree to keep helping him?"

He stepped forward. "Because I was in the room tonight with those sons of bitches who hurt you. I saw your pain because of what they did, and if the fucking God of Nightmares can take that away then I'll pay the price. Gladly." His brows pulled together, mouth set in a straight line of determination, but he was still so very pale, eyes still buried in dark hollows.

"I'm touched." I put my hand on his arm so he would know I wasn't just saying it. "I really am. But you can't."

"I'm the only one who can."

"*I* can't let you do that."

"Why not?"

I looked away, pulling my hand back.

He grabbed it, holding it fiercely. "Why not, Charlie?"

"Because I love you, dammit."

There. I said it.

We both froze. The words hung between us, locking us in that moment. A small part of me was more afraid right then than I'd been all night, with all the terrors I'd been through. Afraid he would push me away. Afraid he would laugh at my love.

Afraid he would use it to hurt me.

His hand slipped from my fingers, moving up my arm, then warm against my neck. He cupped my face and gently turned it toward his. His eyes were bright, intense. The look in them burned into my soul, lighting me from the inside.

"I love you too, Charlotte Tristan Moore."

He kissed me, and the world went away.

38

JERKED FROM A dreamless sleep, I awoke in a tangle of covers and clothes. Sunlight slanted in from the blinds on the window. Late afternoon. The sun came up on the opposite side of the building in the mornings. Daniel lay beside me, out cold, a thin sheen of sweat across his forehead. It was stuffy in the small room, the air thick and still. We'd fallen asleep. I hadn't meant to fall asleep.

I'd never slept with a man before.

Sitting there in the overbright room, I realized I wasn't panicked. I wasn't scared. It somehow felt right. Different. A little strange . . . but *right* to be inches from Daniel's sleeping form. He stretched on his back across one side of the mattress, both arms laid over his head, his stomach exposed where his shirt had ridden up.

Isaac on the altar.

The thought made my eyes drift to the Aqedah. The ancient knife sat on my bedside table beside the dog-eared, thrift-store copy of *The Wasteland and Other Writings* by T. S. Eliot, highlighted red by the cheap alarm clock.

Something shrilled under the covers. My phone. My phone was ringing. Throwing the comforter aside, I dug it out of my pocket, reading the display to see who was calling before putting it to my ear.

"Mom?"

My mother's voice came across the line. It sounded hollow, echoing lightly, like the connection was off. "Charlie, are you okay?"

It was a strange question, and she didn't sound right. "I'm fine." I sat up and shook my head to clear it. "What's going on? Is everything all right?"

Please don't say Dad's heart, please don't say Dad's heart.

She cleared her throat on the other end of the phone call. "Well, dear, there's been . . . I don't know how to . . ." She took a deep breath. "Something's happened."

Oh, God.

My finger joints ached around the phone. I couldn't talk. I couldn't speak the words into existence. I took my own deep breath and forced myself to go on. "Is it Dad?"

"What? No, why would you ask that?"

"Mom, just tell me what's going on."

"Something happened to the four boys . . . to the four boys who hurt you." Her voice trailed off.

Her words were a cold jolt down my spine, and numbness spread along my ribcage. Swinging my legs off the bed, I stood and walked over to the window, trying to think.

"Are you there, dear? Did you hear what I said?"

"I heard you." I didn't know what to say. "I don't know what to say."

"Do you want to know what happened?"

I know what happened.

"What happened?"

"They're . . . dead. All of them."

I know that. I was the one who killed them, but I can't tell you that.

The thought was cold, already compartmentalized away from my core. It had been dealt with and filed away. I needed to respond to my mom, to tell her something. Silence boomed on the phone. I said what I thought I would have said if I'd had no foreknowledge, if I hadn't played a hand in the men's deaths.

"Good."

My mom took in a sharp jerk of breath.

"What else do you want, Mom? You know what they did to me. I don't feel sad for them, not at all."

"I know, Charlie. I know. It's just that—"

A voice broke in, cutting her off.

A man's voice. "Hang up, Mrs. Moore."

The bad connection wasn't a bad connection at all.

My mom's voice wavered. "I'm sorry, dear. They made me call."

"It's all right, Mom. I'll talk to him."

"I can call our lawyer."

"Mrs. Moore, clear the line. Right now." The man's voice was sharp, commanding. Used to being listened to.

"Mom, you should go. I don't think I need a lawyer."

"I love you." I could hear the start of tears in her voice. I'd heard that same catch a thousand times before.

"I love you too. Kiss Dad for me."

She didn't say anything else, but I could feel her leave the line. I didn't speak, waiting to let whoever was there go first. That felt safer, smarter. I didn't know how to do this. I'd have to lie.

I didn't have to wait long.

"Miss Moore, I'm Special Agent Bronson. May I ask you a few questions?" The voice was quiet—not speaking quietly, but quiet of its own nature. It didn't sound like a voice that ever yelled at the game on TV or screamed at the dog. It was a voice that spoke little and only once, and if you weren't listening it wouldn't repeat itself.

I pushed the phone harder against my ear. "Okay."

"Have you left your city of residence in the last twenty-four hours?"

Tyler Woods's house was in my parents' city, in the same district where I had gone to high school. Five and a half hours away from where I lived now.

"No," I lied.

"You have not flown or driven from your home in the last twenty-four hours?"

"I went to work and then to a friend's apartment, but that's all." Lie.

"Thank you, Miss Moore. That will be all for now."

"Wait, what? That's all you want to know?" Silence echoed. I wasn't sure he was still there. "Mr. Bronson?"

"Special Agent Bronson," he corrected. "There is one more thing."

"Yes?"

"Miss Moore, do you own a sword?"

39

I STARED AT the phone in my hand as though it had turned into a poisonous snake. I'd answered *No,* and Bronson had said, *Good-bye, Miss Moore,* and hung up.

He knew.

I didn't know how he knew, but he knew I'd been there.

I looked at the phone. The time read five fifteen. The slaughter at Tyler's house had happened before dawn. Not much before, maybe about four a.m.

Nearly thirteen hours ago. Long enough to fly there, kill them, and fly back.

Panic swept over me, hot and moist, making my skin tingle everywhere it touched. My armpits, my elbows, the backs of my knees: all of them were set alight with a buzzing, electric jolt sensation.

There's no record of a flight, because you didn't fly.

Relief fell on me, driving me down into the chair I kept by the desk in the corner. A bubble rolled inside my chest. Laughter. Ridiculous, hysterical laughter. It twittered behind my breastbone like a caged hummingbird, trying to take wing and fly free from my voice box. I swallowed it, sniggering instead.

It was okay. I was going to be okay.

Daniel moved, his legs sweeping the covers off him to fall and tumble in a bundle to the floor. His head twisted, and he began to murmur.

Daniel's going to be okay.

The moment the thought was complete, he convulsed, jerking off the mattress as if a string had been hooked to his spine and yanked sharply upward. Arms and legs stiff, he vibrated on the bed as though a hundred thousand volts of electricity were coursing through him.

I grabbed his arm. His skin burned my fingers with fever. "Daniel!" I screamed, trying to wake him, drag him back to this reality.

His voice stuttered from his throat, jerking past clenched jaw muscles, coming out low and animal-like. Foam boiled through lips pulled thin and tight over his teeth, a symptom of rabid dreams rampaging through him. His skin purpled as he failed to squeeze air into the lungs trapped inside his constricted chest.

He choked, suffocating on a nightmare. I tried to jam my fingers into his mouth, to pry it apart, but they bounced off his teeth, shut like a portcullis.

Think. THINK!

Shoving my hands against his chest, I tried to push him down on the mattress. He was made of case-hardened steel, unmovable, unbendable. Pressing with all of my weight made no difference at all. His face darkened, gallows-black creeping down his neck as arteries throbbed like living things trapped under his skin.

Desperate panic clawed at my mind. Without thinking, I shoved my hand under the edge of his shirt and touched my Mark to the sweaty, fever hot skin over his heart. The cut lines in my palm lit like a brand against his perspiration, making me cry out. Pushing through the pain, I commanded the magick inside me.

Show me.

The steel circlet convulsed around my throat, a cold metal clench that sent shivers up my spine. The magick sputtered to life, flickering inside me, a hand shaking off droplets of water, and my mind's eye fluttered open. My vision slewed sideways into a weird, grainy tone, as if the room had switched to a cheap black and white film.

Daniel looked hollow, a near empty chalice, slicksided with the remnants and the dregs of a slow-draining pool of his life force. The energy gathered in the low places of his body. Some of it flowed through our connection, a thin tributary running from his chest into my arm, feeding the magick that connected us. The rest turned in a slow-moving whirlpool, corkscrewing away into a sinister spot nestled by his spine.

I pulled my hand away, breaking the connection. The real world slapped me in eye-searing color. Leaning over, I grabbed Daniel's arm and pulled. His body slid a few inches on the sheets. He was too stiff, too heavy. I couldn't flip him over.

Changing tactics, I shoved, pushing him off the edge of the bed to roll onto the floor.

Scrambling, I found him face down on the floor, spine still arched, making his feet hang in the air—but that's not what I saw, not what my eyes locked on.

His shirt had ridden up in the fall off the bed, gathering around his chest, under his armpits.

A fist-sized chunk of tumor blinked up at me from the small of his back.

40

THE THING STARED at me, its sulfur-yellow iris leering at me. It pulsed, black veins running into Daniel's skin, melted and fused to the bottom of the ugly, malignant mass. Prickly waves of angry magick radiated from it.

Daniel's muscles gave out in a chain reaction that left him spent and loose on the floor.

Do something, do something, DO something.

I slid off the bed and crouched beside him. My hand fell on the Knife of Abraham, sliding it off the table.

The tumor's eye widened.

I shoved my thumb into it.

The surface was slimy and firm, resisting, fighting the intrusion of my digit, then suddenly bursting around my nail and opening to my knuckle in a squelch of egg yolk, runny and aqueous. My hand became a claw. I dug in and pulled up, stretching the diseased parcel against its mooring. The thing felt rubbery, slick with its own fluid. Daniel made a noise, a grinding, choking moan from the back of his clenched throat.

Stomach churning, I laid the gleaming edge of the knife on the seam of corrupted flesh. The edges of the lids around my thumb turned sharp, the eyelashes turning into needles. They jabbed my skin, stabbing through to pierce tendon and bone. The eye gnawed at my thumb as I screamed and pulled the knife *hard*. Flesh parted like water against the razor edge, a brackish jelly leaking from the wound and filling the air with the stench of meat gone spoiled. I yanked on the tumor, hacked with the knife, and peeled the rotten nodule from Daniel's body.

As the last tendril split under the knife edge, his jaw unlocked, releasing the howl of suffering held captive in his mouth. Though it only lasted a second, it was the worst sound I had ever heard.

The tumor acted like a landed fish in my hand, flopping and flapping, trying to slip the hook. Needle-lashes raked my thumb in diabolical acupuncture as the lids chewed and sucked. Dripping jelly hung in strings from the cut end, solidifying, skin forming over their length, turning them into grasping tentacles that wrapped my wrist in clammy wet circles. Stretching and contracting, it tried to pull itself over my hand, the evil essence of the thing trying to bond with me, skin to diseased skin and bone to jelly.

I don't think so, you little bastard.

Magick rushed from below my stomach, from the pit of my pelvis, sweeping in a twisted whirl through my body, a tornado of energy up and out to my hand.

BURN.

The remnant of Yar Shogura began to sizzle in my palm.

I felt no heat, no flame, but my hand began to glow, sunset orange like the electric eye of a stove, and smoke curled off the scrap of elder god as it shook. The purple-gray membrane that covered it like a decomposing sausage began to fissure, miniature flames *flickering*, licking along its surface in a wildfire chain reaction.

In seconds it was reduced to a handful of ash.

I shook it off, wiping my palm on my pants and turning to Daniel.

He was pale as a ghost, skin so cold tiny wisps of white curled from it to dissipate into the warmth of the room. The patch where I had excised the tumor was raw and bloody, the meat of him exposed to my eyes. I touched him just to make sure he was still breathing.

He was.

Barely.

My heart locked, frozen between one beat and the next.

No. No, I can't *lose him. I'll do anything.*

Anything.

And I meant it.

Carefully, as gently as I could, I pressed the symbol on my palm against the bloody patch on his back.

41

MAGICK CRACKLED THROUGH every fiber of me, arcing along nerve endings, spitting from cell membrane to cell membrane. It filled me, all of me, swelling my insides shut and turning my bones to heavy, polished alabaster.

I pushed through it, fighting to clear my head.

My eyes were closed, and I forced them open. My magick-soaked vision painted Daniel in alien color. I could see through him, as if he'd been transformed into glass. His heart beat in slow, heavy *thumps*, a wounded animal trying to drag itself away. I could see the blood in his veins lurch with each throb.

He was dying in tiny ebbs and flows.

I can save him.

The sure knowledge became a stone in my mind, immovable, irresistible.

I began to draw energy to me. The room dimmed as I pulled, sinking low in the fabric of the world, making a depression where all the magick around me would pool and soak into me. I was a magnet, a sinkhole, a dwarf star.

The room darkened further.

Outside, a bird fell dead from the withering branch 'neath its tiny, clawed feet.

Multi-legged creatures lodged in the structure of the house stopped moving, a slaughter of microscopic lives.

It all fed into me, into my magick.

Inside me the magick roiled. I felt like a pot, overfull and on high heat. The mystical energy in my stomach simmered through my limbs. I had life. I had more life than I knew what to do with, and my head swam with the power.

I pushed the magick through my Mark.

It spooled out in a ribbon of pleasure that reached me deeper than just my arm. This was creation. I gave life, and it was glorious. I watched the energy pour from me into Daniel, filling him, making him whole in my eyes.

Making him real.

Making him *mine*.

Ecstasy rolled through the deepest part of me as our connection grew. Our skinsong sang across time and space. My mind was a lotus flower that opened to his, and I *knew* him. I could see his life laid like a tapestry before me, the texture of memory woven into who he was: a man of honor, still growing into his own skin but close, so close to the man he would be forever. He had no stain of guile, no taint of deception in him. My eyes followed a golden vein that ran from his heart, a crack of ore in a mountainside. As I watched, it widened, spilling energy into the magick I poured into him. The two mixed. The golden energy began to suffuse through my magick, running along the channel. It hunted, seeking the source of magick.

It found my Mark and slammed into me, and Daniel and I became one flesh.

I was overwhelmed. My essence and his slowly revolved around each other, a key turning until the tumblers in the lock set. I fell back, my hand sliding off the now-healed slick spot on his back. Daniel turned in one swift motion, fingers curling around my wrist, catching me before I crashed.

His eyes were bright, glittery, and a brilliant shade of sea-foam green. He gave me his boyish grin, the one that made his dimple so deep you could lose yourself in it. "Thank you . . . Mistress."

Oh, damn.

Darkness swirled in the corner of the room, reality bending along curved lines. The Man in Black stepped through the gloom. He looked down at us for a long moment.

"What have you done?"

42

The asphalt was dirty under our feet, littered with trash and oil and grime. I knew because I looked down at it when we popped through the skein of reality. My own skin burned with fire, and my head spun, but I thought I was getting used to this transdimensional travel.

Daniel pulled away, staggering a few steps until he reached the brick wall of the alley we were in. The sound of him being sick made me turn. His shoulders heaved and jerked.

I turned away to give him privacy.

The Man in Black glared at me, nearly disappearing in the gloom of the alley, black coat rustling uneasily around him. He loomed in the shadows, his brows furrowed, his mouth drawn into a sneer.

He was pissed at me.

Screw him.

He wasn't my favorite person . . . elder god . . . whatever . . . either.

Apparently, when I saved Daniel's life I cut the Man in Black's hold on him. I'd done what I wanted and set him free from the chaos god, which was great, but now he was tied even more tightly to my magick.

I could *feel* him in the corner of my mind. Like a thing you can't quite remember, a specter of consciousness that haunts the hallways of your mind, a memory you can't put down, the wallpaper of your brain that you can't peel off or paint over. It wasn't unpleasant; in fact I found it comforting. Comforting but weird.

Daniel came over, wiping his mouth.

"You okay?"

He nodded. "Better now."

I studied him. He still looked healthy—a little flushed from throwing up, but okay. Not weak and near collapse like before. My eyes shifted, the muscles behind them twitching as my vision changed and I Saw Daniel through my magick. He still appeared to be full of the gold-infused energy from before. I blinked, and the world came back into focus.

The more I used the magick inside me, the easier it came.

I'd have to be very careful.

Noise wrapped around us, coming in from the alley opening, a hum and buzz of people and vehicles, the hustle and bustle of a metropolis. People stood in a line stretched across the alley between the buildings that rose on either side of us. Only a handful of them looked over at us. Most looked ahead, or down, or were engaged by their phone or other electronic device. Jacked in, constantly connected through social media to people they never saw in real life, they read instant updates about every little thing that happened to distant friends, all the while ignoring people standing less than a foot away.

The blank looks on their faces, even on the few who turned to see what we were doing, reminded me of the people in line at Ashtoreth's hotel.

Daniel leaned in toward me, speaking from the side of his mouth. "Creepy."

Creepy indeed.

I nodded.

"Do you know what city we're in?" he asked.

I shrugged and looked over at the Man in Black. He said nothing. I looked back at Daniel. "I don't suppose it really matters."

"No, I guess not." His eyes slid past me, moving up and over my shoulder to look deeper in the alley. "Hold on."

He moved away from me, taking four steps and picking up a discarded chunk of rock or metal. His hand covered it almost completely, so I couldn't see what it was. The words to ask what he was doing were on my lips when he pulled his arm back and slung the thing into the alleyway. My eyes tracked it as it flew fast and true toward a low-slung shape crouching beside a Dumpster.

The skinhound.

It jerked back, nimbly dodging Daniel's missile. Whatever he had thrown clanged loudly against the side of the metal Dumpster where the skinhound's head had just been. The devil dog's muzzle cracked in a grin that would have given a rabid jackal the creeps, and it stared at us with its one baleful yellow eye. The other one, the one I had injured, was a stark, empty socket that sat black on its skinless face.

Daniel stomped his foot and waved his arms. "Get the hell outta here!"

The skinhound simply crouched lower, nearly disappearing into the shadow of the Dumpster.

The Man in Black raised his red right hand. It sat on the end of his arm, an unlit torch, a treacherous signal fire yet to be struck. His fingers twitched, the middle one touching and then snapping across the thumb in a *SNAP!* that sounded like a lightning strike.

The skinhound's face jerked up, its eyes wide as it studied us. After a long moment the Man in Black swept his hand in a dismissive motion. The skinhound turned tail, disappearing into the shadows.

Daniel grunted. "That was the next thing I was going to try."

I leaned in. "I didn't even see it down there. Why is it here?"

He shrugged. "I don't know, but I saw it back at the hospital too, when we were outside. I was going to shoo it away, but then we did the disappearing trick and I got sidetracked."

I didn't think we'd seen the last of that thing, but I didn't say it out loud.

The Man in Black began walking toward the front of the alley. He didn't turn to see if we were following him.

Temptation weighed on me to stay there. Let him fight this thing. Why should Daniel and I risk ourselves anymore? *He* was the elder god, not me; let him handle this.

But I started walking.

I needed to make sure, to see this through. I'd come this far, and I knew what would happen if we didn't end this. I'd been given magick, and, dammit, that obligated me to do something with it even if I hated the one I had to help.

Daniel followed me, staying close to my side and just slightly behind. The Aqedah pressed hard against my hip, the flat edge of the black iron blade between my belt and my jeans. The shirt I'd thrown on used to be my dad's and worked as a jacket, so it mostly covered everything, but I still felt tense walking into a group of people with a foot-long magick knife at my side.

Nyarlathotep didn't slow as he approached the people stretched across the alleyway. He walked as if he owned the entire city, coat flaring around him like bat wings. His red right hand pulsed with crimson energy. It left a color trail in my vision, but that could have been my magick making my eyes go weird again. The people stepped aside as he reached them, parting like water. He stepped through, and they shuffled back into place.

Blocking me and Daniel.

I didn't slow, just kept walking. I drew near, and coldness crept up my legs as if I were walking through a chill fog.

I stopped an arm's length from the line. In front of me stood a man in a blazer and a pair of slacks. He looked older than my dad but held himself like someone my age. He slouched casually in line, exuding a cool "I don't give a damn" attitude, fingers moving rapidly around a small touch screen in his hand. He didn't look over at us.

"Excuse me."

The man's fingers moved. He still stared at the screen he held.

Anger burned. "Let us through."

He turned his head.

His eyes were dilated, the pupils painting over the irises. His lips parted; the gums inside were stained dark as if he'd just drunk squid ink, teeth gray in their notches. It wasn't a smile, it was a snarl.

Behind me, Daniel said, "Holy shit."

My hand drifted to the knife under my jacket.

The man stepped aside. His head fell as his eyes swept down to the device in his hand, fingers on the move once more.

"C'mon," I said to Daniel. I twisted through the narrow opening, not wanting to touch the man with the black gums. I knew deep down that if I did, this would go bad quickly.

And it would be bad soon enough.

43

THE LINE STRETCHED down the entire block.

The sidewalk we were on was wide: ten feet or more separated us from a street teeming with cars that flew helter-skelter past, the roar of engines cut only by horns that honked in a discordant symphony. I could see the Man in Black ahead of us, taller than everyone else on the sidewalk. People moved out of his way, crushing against each other as he passed.

One lady darted out of his way and into the street, her fingers pulling hair from her scalp as she ran. Her voice was a loud warble of meaningless babble. A taxi slammed on its brakes, the car's rear rising on its shocks as black smoke boiled from its tires. She didn't notice, just continued to wail as she ran down the lane past us. The cabbie followed behind her, head and arm out the window, screaming curses that were a mix of three languages.

The Man in Black turned the corner, disappearing from my sight.

I reached out, grabbed Daniel's hand, and began to hurry.

We were in a city. A big one. All the buildings stretched high in the night sky. Lights shone everywhere: streetlights, signs, traffic lights, headlights, even just the ambient light of thousands of windows along buildings lit from the inside. Everything seemed to glow in a thousand colors that blended into a dull, blanched white. Light pollution bounced off everything.

All I could see were the shadows.

They clawed up the sides of buildings and lay in pools underneath everything. I could feel things inside them watching me. Maybe even the shadows themselves had taken on some malevolent sentience, some hostility to human life that made them watch and hate and lie in wait for someone to slip into their trap, to fall prey to their patience.

It would have sounded stupid yesterday.

Tonight I knew it could be true.

Nerves jittering, I moved faster, my steps hurrying into a run. Daniel ran beside me, his hand in mine, unquestioning, following my lead. We pelted toward the corner, pushing through people on the sidewalk.

Rounding the corner, we nearly ran headlong into the Man in Black.

He turned. "Rushing into the maw of the lion, Acolyte? How unlike you."

"I'm here to finish this."

"So you are." The gemstone around his neck pulsed in the shadowed depth of his coat. People stepped around us as we stood in a pool of neon light. The Man in Black's coat fluttered out, tattered tendrils licking the ankles and feet of passersby.

Daniel made a noise in his throat. His hand tugged mine, and

I looked over at him. He stared with wide eyes over the Man in Black's head.

I followed his gaze.

We stood in front of a temple dragged from some ancient time and wrapped in bars of neon lights. The stones that formed its bulk were green like jade and cut in odd shapes that shouldn't have fit together but did, held in alien geometry by some arcane masonry. The lines of the building hurt my eyes, dragging my sight in too many directions to follow without discomfort. The roof curved deeply like a Shinto temple of Asia, made of sodium-yellow tiles laid like scales on a lizard's back: overlapping, interlocking, and conjoined. They formed lines that pointed to the heavens, where the peak of the temple disappeared into a murky shadow. Garish tubes of neon light traced every corner, every crease, and every edge, blaring out into the street where we stood. The words *R'yleh Wok 'N' Roll* pulsed across the front in bloodred neon flashes like the ponderous heartbeat of some great beast lying in wait. The line of people we'd run by shuffled and shambled up wide concrete steps that led to a pair of doors yawning open beneath the flashing words.

Lambs to the slaughter.

Daniel spoke. "So that's where we're going?"

The Man in Black nodded, once down then up.

Daniel grunted. "Looks like a sushi joint designed by a nut job."

The Man in Black turned, looking up at the building. "It is a juncture, a temple folded from lost history." Dark eyes glittered. "They once served as feasting boards for my kind."

Daniel's eyebrow rose in an arch. "So we should steer clear of the California roll then?"

44

WE PASSED THROUGH the entrance by the people lined up to get inside. The doors were tall, made of dark mahogany, and carved in intricate patterns. I looked carefully as we passed, my eye picking out details in the artwork. Human faces melted into one another, forming a cascade of agonized expressions from top to bottom. They'd been carved by the hands of a master, each one as unique as a snowflake, their expressions locked in a moment of despair and anguish.

It made me shiver. I kept walking.

Inside the doors, the lobby ceiling soared away and out of sight. I'd seen the outside of the building, which stood only a story tall. The ceilings should not have disappeared like that.

But they did.

Daniel leaned in. "It's bigger on the inside."

"Someone should have painted it blue," I said.

He nodded.

The Man in Black walked until a maître d' in a white jacket stepped in front of him.

Holding a menu in his hand as a stop sign, he looked ridiculous compared to the elder god who stood before him. He was shorter than me and soft in the middle. His pudgy hand clutched the laminated pages of the menu. Lank but glossy black hair hung across his forehead, shadowing almond-shaped eyes. His voice came out lightly accented: a spice, not the meal.

His lips formed words. *"Aa'sahh shaema my'ialalake-um."*

As the words left, his lips rippled, exposing ink-stained teeth, wide and opalescent gray like the man in line by the alley.

Visions of the nurse guardian at the hospital flashed in my head.

I let go of Daniel's hand, reaching for the knife at my hip.

The Man in Black lifted his red right hand, reaching for the face of the maître d'. The hand pulsed with dark crimson energy, casting magenta highlights on the smooth planes of the man's face. The maître d's jaw slung down, mouth hanging lax and loose as he stared at the skinless appendage.

The Man in Black spat a word, his raw, red fingers twisting into an arcane symbol. As they rubbed together, a fat pink spark of energy popped off, arcing into the man's open mouth.

The maître d' stopped moving as though he'd been flash frozen. He didn't breathe or blink, and no tremor disturbed his skin.

"Is he dead?" I asked.

"His kind do not die easily as long as they retain their heads."

I looked around. The people in line continued to shuffle forward until they were met by another maître d' who could have been a clone of the one standing before us. He handed out menus, then turned and walked away. The people followed him into the dining area that stretched before us. The back of the room disappeared in the shadows of dull light provided by a combination of muted neon and guttering candles. The line shuffled forward, and within seconds another clone appeared to take a small group away.

I watched diners at tables in twos and threes and fours, all of them smiling and laughing and talking. Forks and chopsticks dipped and lifted morsels of sushi during breaks in conversation. It looked like any busy metropolitan restaurant full of hip diners enjoying an evening meal with friends and family.

So why did the skin creep across the back of my neck?

Realization fell on me like a ton of bricks.

It was absolutely silent.

The number of people I looked upon should have produced a dull roar of white noise: voices mingling and meshing, laughter boiling over the top of it, the underscore provided by the clink of fork on plate, the muffled thud of cup on tablecloth, the creak and breath of chairs, even the rustle of cloth as people moved and reached and lived.

There was none of that.

The only sounds in the pin-drop silence were the shuffle of feet to my left, the whisper of Nyarlathotep's coat rustling around his feet, and Daniel's rhythmic breathing beside me.

And the sound of my own heartbeat in my ears.

Daniel leaned in, his voice close to my ear. "It's like a silent movie."

The Man in Black turned. "We have very little time before our entrance is noted. Use your Mark. Find our prey."

I hesitated, not wanting to use my magick, not with the cost of it coming from Daniel. My eyes quickly slid over to Daniel. His hand found mine again. It felt warm. Solid.

He leaned toward me. "It's okay. I didn't feel it when you did it before. It's the teleporting that takes it out of me."

The magick inside me buzzed to life at his touch, murmuring along the skin of my hand. I closed my eyes and let it go.

My mind slipped sideways, disjointing itself as my mind's eye opened. Prickles of pain rushed in from the edges, but I ignored it, concentrating on finding what I needed. The metal circlet around my neck crackled, its temperature plummeting until it grew so cold it frost-seared the skin underneath. The room blossomed in my mind like an unfolding flower, each person's desire a petal.

They all pointed toward a thing I could barely discern. It was close but indistinct except for its hunger to assimilate, to mate and marry and meld with each person who fell under its influence.

My stomach growled, low and angry.

My eyelids fluttered open, and the magick sloughed away, falling to a low simmer. I could still feel the pull of the thing, but now it had distance. It was fuzzy, less immediate. But I knew where it was.

"It's in the back of the restaurant."

The Man in Black gave a slight bow and a flourish of his red right hand. "Lead the way, Charlotte Tristan Moore."

I pulled the Knife of Abraham from my belt, holding it point down along my forearm like I'd been trained to do.

I had a bad feeling, but I stepped into the dining room anyway.

45

We crossed the room, moving quickly. Daniel was pressed close behind me, the Man in Black sweeping along behind him, both of them following me as I followed the tug of magick in my stomach. None of the diners looked up at us. They continued their silent meals and their wordless conversations, and we passed them by like wind through the grass.

My eyes kept sliding to the left and the right, staring as I passed. One lady lifted a pair of chopsticks, holding a piece of squid nigiri at its end. She drew it to her mouth, lips painted nearly neon pink parting as the morsel drew near, teeth opening to accept the bite.

It *squirmed*.

Tiny tentacles zipped out, stretching into her mouth, minuscule suckers latching on the soft flesh inside her lips and cheeks. The miniature kraken heaved and pulled, lurching off the chopsticks and into her open mouth. Her lips closed around one tiny suckered appendage that slithered in after the rest of the creature with a slurp. Her eyelids fluttered as she chewed. Black ink trickled from the corners of her lips, running down her chin to hang in a fat droplet off her jaw. Her date lifted a finger and caught it.

I kept walking as he drew the finger to his own lips.

Daniel's voice came low behind me, but it broke the unnatural silence like a gunshot. "I didn't think we would ever find a place creepier than the last one. I underestimated us."

At the sound of his voice the room stopped moving.

Every one of the diners froze like a movie on pause: utensils in midair, mouths open to speak.

As one they all turned in our direction.

ACOLYTE, WE NEED TO GET PAST THIS ROOM.

The Man in Black's voice rolled through my mind. I picked up my pace, stepping quicker. In front of me were two swinging doors that looked as if they would lead to the kitchen if this were a restaurant instead of a nightmare temple. The magick inside me pulled toward them, the urgency to get *out* of this room riding hard on my back.

The diners were rising from their seats as I hit the doors, shoving them apart in front of me. Daniel and I fell in. The Man in Black stepped through and turned, grabbing one door in each hand. I could see under the arm of his coat, through the doorway. The diners were all up, stalking toward us with hands full of knives, forks, and sharpened chopsticks. Eyes rolled back in their sockets, they peered out through fish-belly-white skeins, blind as glaucoma patients. Runny black liquid drooled from open mouths, smearing lips and chins. Nestled in some of their throats were tiny kraken, spindly suckered appendages waving over their hosts' blackened tongues. At their feet squirmed a carpet of the tiny tentacled creatures, dinners that had crawled from their plates and now lurched toward us on roiling, rubbery limbs.

The chaos god jerked the doors closed and held them shut with his red right hand. His head dropped, and his voice rose in a guttural mutter that burned across my eardrums.

The coat began to jerk and twitch around him.

A sizzle cut the sound of his voice, an electric buzz of nova flame on metal. Smoke curled around his red right hand where it pressed against the metal swinging doors, glowing a dull orange red like the coals of a long banked fire. He pulled it away as something thumped hard against the other side.

The door held.

Where his hand lifted away, it left behind a black scorched outline and a smooth patch of newly welded metal.

He turned in a flair of ebony coat and smiled a sharp-toothed smile. "That should be entertaining to pass through when I leave."

"Will they go back to normal when we stop this . . ." I didn't know exactly what we were dealing with. A god? A monster? Both? So I went with, ". . . thing?"

He shook his head. "Their minds will never be the same. Madness will take them, and they will end their lives as gibbering idiots."

"So, serving you guys has a really shitty retirement package." Daniel shook his head. "Glad I got out of *that* rat race." His hand found mine.

"The night is still young, Daniel Alexander Langford."

The Knife of Abraham spun in my fingers, blade swinging around so that I held the handle in my fist, back and low, ready to rip up, to strike, to gut a chaos god. "Is that a threat?"

Nyarlathotep looked down at me, red right hand hidden in the folds of his coat. "I have no need to threaten him, Acolyte."

"Then what the hell are you doing?"

"Telling the truth."

"I don't believe you."

"I always speak the truth."

The edge of sarcasm cut into my voice. "And you wouldn't lie about that."

"I am the Crawling Chaos. I have no need to lie." One sleek eyebrow arched up. "Have you not found truth to be the most chaotic force in your world?"

I stopped cold.

He was right. Truth could injure. Truth could maim. Truth could *destroy.* My mind flashed backward, moving through time. Their lawyers had told the truth. I *did* have a drink that night. I had worn a skirt. I never said *no.*

They didn't care that my drink had been one mouthful of beer tried and spit out as disgusting, that my skirt hem had hit my ankles, or that I had screamed *stop* and *don't.*

The Crawling Chaos was right.

Truth was absolutely destructive.

46

THE DOORS RATTLED with a hard *THUD!* that brought me out of my head. A series of wet slaps and metallic scratches followed the loud noise as the people on the other side tried to get through.

Daniel eyed the doors suspiciously. "Are those going to hold?"

The Man in Black shrugged. "We should continue on our way."

The magick inside me tugged, drawing me forward to follow it. We were in a dim room with enough light to see, but not enough to see well. It was narrow and bare, almost a hallway. The walls were tiled in pale greenish limestone, the cracks between them filled with some kind of dark grout that showed black in the low light. Shapes and sigils twisted across the surface, finger-painted by lunatics. They worked around clumps of luminescent fungi spilling out of damp cracks in bulbous loam and fanned ridges like dully pulsating lamps spaced along our path. The floor was uneven under my feet, rolling slightly up and down. Thick moisture gathered in crevices and shallow pools, giving the air a musty, salty, fishy smell.

I walked carefully, knife out, ready to cut anything that might leap from the shadows.

The hallway twisted and turned, narrowing into a true tunnel. Openings appeared randomly, pitch-black gaps in the wall that blew cold, damp air across the path as we passed as if we were inside the lung of a sleeping creature. Each step increased the tension along my spine in a slowly tightening ratchet. The magick inside me pulsed harder and harder, faster and faster, like a second heartbeat that crashed and lurched inside my stomach as we moved down the hallway. A slow ache crawled across my temples.

It was maddening.

I looked over my shoulder, checking to make sure Daniel and the Man in Black were still behind me. They were, Daniel watching me closely, brows drawn together. He smiled as our gazes met, making his dimple appear. It made me feel better.

Then my eyes slid past him.

The Man in Black loomed behind him, filling the space, his Semitic features pulled into a tight sneer. Black eyes glittered in the caves of their sockets as he scowled at me. The coat fluttered around him, soaking into the gloom of the tunnel, barely a flicker to differentiate it from the shadows. The look on his face had turned predatory. Feral. It was the look a restless lion gives to a rabbit.

He winked at me.

I stumbled, my fingers tight on the handle of the knife, the ancient hardwood making me aware of each raised line that formed my Mark. Daniel's hand shot out, latching onto my arm, jerking me short. The knife moved before I caught myself and stopped it.

He pointed past me. “Careful.”

Eyes following his finger, I turned and looked. The floor dropped away into a set of stairs that led down into the gloom.

“Thanks,” I said. “I could’ve broken my neck.”

“I wouldn’t want that. I don’t mind if you’re head over heels for me, but not literally.”

I smiled but didn’t answer. Turning back, I looked at the stairs. The magick inside me called.

Down.

I took a deep breath and a first step and headed down the damned stairs.

47

The stairs were wide and too tall to walk down easily, oddly spaced and staggered as if they were carved for something other than humans to move up and down them. Daniel and I held the wall as we descended.

The Man in Black had no trouble at all, walking as if he were on flat ground.

The wall under my hand curved as we spiraled down. The limestone was porous, rough and wet under my palm like sandpaper dipped in baby oil. The stone under our feet ate the sound of our footsteps and air closed around my head, silence pressing in like a shroud. The tunnel grew darker and darker as the lumpy fungi became sparser and sparser, the clumps smaller and smaller. The dim light began playing tricks on my eyes, which were glued open, the lids spread wide and stuck to my cheeks and brow trying to see. Weird light globs and jagged shadows began to dance across my strained retinas. Sweat trickled down my spine despite the chill air. My nose ruffled at the heavy iron and salt smell that wafted up from below us. It climbed into my sinuses and curled there in olfactory clots.

We passed a section of darkness so complete I could *feel* it press against my skin. A hand touched my shoulder.

"Daniel?"

"It's me. I just don't want to get separated." His voice was hushed, dampened by the dark.

A chuckle looped around us.

I wanted to move faster, to hurry, to run, and that feeling wrestled with the pressing need to turn and dash up the stairs and back to the light. It was a prey instinct, an urge nestled in the base of my brain, the lizard part that sought safety and survival and self-preservation. It hitched my stomach with each step, but I kept going. I wasn't a slave to my fear. I'd worked too hard to not be, so one step after the other I kept going.

Gradually, so softly I thought my mind was playing tricks on my eyes, the stairway brightened. The light that spilled around the curve of the wall was orange and flickery, growing brighter like the dawn of a polluted sky. Soon my shadow stretched behind me, lying up the uneven, inhuman stairs like a deflated skin.

A low, rhythmic sound began to pulse up the stairs, growing louder with each step.

I stepped down one last step. The stairway ended and a cavern yawned open before us.

"Holy frickin' fish tank," Daniel whispered.

The floor of the cavern spread before us, littered with stalagmites that jutted like rotten teeth and broken stalactites that had fallen from the ceiling above, shattering into boulders and gravel. From the stairs a pathway had been cleared, rubble pushed aside, smaller limestone spikes sheared off into stumps of sedimentary stone. It led to a man in a crimson robe and a white chef's hat behind an altar of limestone slabs. He held a knife, the sharp edge of the wavy blade glinting in the orange glow of a massive iron-and-glass tank that rose from floor to ceiling behind him.

A syrupy, orange-yellow liquid filled the tank. Bubbles drifted slowly from the bottom, packets of gas the size of me roiling and tumbling five stories to the top of the tank like a gigantic, obscene lava lamp.

A monster floated inside the liquid.

It curled around itself, thickly muscled arms wrapping knotted legs in the fetal position. A swollen, bulbous head lay tucked into its barnacled knees, and one indolent eye revealed itself between lids that parted in a crimson slash. Black wings pressed between its bulk and the glass of the tank, trapped and pinned in place, crumpled and crinkled against the decomposing-pine-tree green of its skin. Seaweed waved around the thing like tendrils of flesh pulling away in strips, and tiny tentacled shapes swirled around its form like schools of fish.

Slowly, as if the effort caused it great pain, the creature lifted its head. The crimson eye shut for a long moment then jerked wide, its slitted pupil dilating to glare at me.

I couldn't imagine something so enormous being alive, being real, but it was—it was horribly, terribly alive. Its mind pressed against mine, weighing against me like an ocean of alien thought, incomprehensible, dispassionate, and inhuman. I shivered as its presence slipped across the magick inside me, sliding, seeking a foothold. It made things low in my body tighten, tension building until my skin wanted to crawl off my bones. Finally the creature's mind bumped against the place it sought and my magick surged, connecting to the presence like a key slipping into a lock.

I couldn't tell which of us was the lock and which was the key.

"Come." A voice singsonged across the cavern, drawing my attention but not breaking the connection between me and the giant creature. "Come closer."

The Sushi Priest waved us over, the knife gleaming in his hand.

Daniel spoke. "This is probably a bad idea."

The Man in Black's coat rustled in agreement.

I thirded the statement.

The Man in Black shrugged. "We do as we must." Black-pit eyes glittered with excitement.

If the chaos god looked forward to this, it was a really, really bad idea.

48

THE SUSHI PRIEST made sushi.

Arrayed across the top slab of the altar were ceramic plates covered in rectangles of sticky rice, lidded dishes, and piles of squirming, wriggling things in high-sided clear bowls.

Intent on his task, he didn't look up as we approached. "Dishonorable Nyarlathotep-san, allow me a moment. The timing of this is crucial for plating."

I looked over at the Man in Black. He nodded.

I guess we were waiting.

The Sushi Priest drew the knife in his hand through a slab of meat on a cutting board in front of him. The blade sliced smoothly through the flesh, parting the dark, slick skin on top to reveal the meat underneath. Color exploded from the cut, the light from the tank behind him causing an oil-sheen rainbow. None of the colors were the orange-yellow of the tank; instead they were a riot of purples, magentas, greens, and black swirling around one another. I had eaten a lot of sushi, and I'd never seen fish that looked like that. Staring at it hurt my eyes.

The Sushi Priest kept working, cutting and slicing, not looking up as we watched. The robe he wore hung on his shoulders and pulled tight across his stomach, the fabric of it a stark red, trimmed in black embroidery. The designs running along the edges were alien, squiggles and angles and swirls. The Mark on my hand tingled as I looked at them. They blurred, making me blink away the strain of watching them morph and change. When I looked again I could read them.

Ph'nglui mglw'nafh Cthulhu R'lyeh Wgah'nagl fhtan.

I couldn't understand them.

Blinking them out of my vision, I looked at the Sushi Priest's face. He'd finished slicing the meat and now placed a small cutlet on each tiny bed of rice. Reaching into the high-sided bowl, he snagged a wriggling thing with his fingers. My stomach lurched as he pulled it out of the squirming mass. It was one of the little kraken from the dining room. Suckered arms slapped at his hand as he swung it over the plate of sushi. Fingers tightening, he squeezed viciously, and the creature gave a thin hissing squeal. Black ink squirted from the nest of tentacles, and the Sushi Priest drizzled this over the plate with a wave of his hand. He tossed the deflated kraken over his shoulder into the gloom of a shadow. It landed with a wet plop as he spooned a lump of bright green wasabi onto the rim of the plate. Using chopsticks, he laid a pile of shredded ginger beside the spicy horseradish garnish.

Sorrow crashed into my mind. It rained down from above me, through the connection I still had with the creature in the tank. I looked up. It had shifted its head, the red eye now turned down, staring at the spot where the crushed kraken lay. The schools of black shapes around it swam, agitated, zipping back and forth. This close, the creature was too massive for words. The sadness radiating off it crushed me, pressing like stones on my shoulders.

My eyes traveled up its form, and I saw that chunks of the creature were missing. Holes gaped in its slick green skin, the wounds a raw rainbow of colors.

As if someone had been cutting slabs off it.

The Sushi Priest looked up.

Our eyes met, and he smiled.

My chest tightened with bubbling anger and magick.

He looked away, pushing the plate forward on the altar. "I apologize for keeping you waiting. Please, help yourselves."

"I don't think so." My voice came through clenched teeth.

"Yeah, I'll pass," Daniel said.

The Man in Black reached forward with his red right hand.

I looked at him. "Surely you're not."

Skinless fingers closed on a piece of elder god sushi. He lifted it. Black ink had stained the rice gray under the meat. Like the teeth of the people in the dining room and the line outside.

"I have always wondered what another of my kind would taste like." The Man in Black's lips parted, and he popped the entire piece into his mouth. He chewed with his eyes closed, savoring the morsel. Small sounds came from his throat, jerking their way out and spilling from his lips. They made my skin feel dirty. Finally, he swallowed.

The Sushi Priest looked up expectantly. "Your verdict, Nyarlathotep-san?"

"Earthy. His flesh is rich, if a touch gamey, with a nice flavoring of brine." He gestured with a flourish. "My compliments. He is delicious."

I shook my head. "I can't believe you just did that."

"You should try new things, Acolyte." He frowned at me, his voice grave. "Do you not know that life is about new experiences? When will this chance come to you again?"

"Never, I hope."

"Not to interrupt," Daniel said, moving closer to my side, "but don't we have something to do here?"

The Sushi Priest smiled at us. His teeth were a brilliant white. I'd expected them to be stained gray but they weren't. The sight of them gleaming disturbed me. "Ah, yes, the reason for your visit to my little eatery." He gestured to the tank behind him. "Have you come to free your brother god? I am afraid I cannot allow it if you have."

"We are not here to free him," the Man in Black said.

The Sushi Priest made a face of mock surprise. "You don't intend to share this world with him? To rule the land and air while Great Cthulhu rules the sea? No, that cannot be your game. Whatever could you want, Nyarlathotep-san?"

"He must be destroyed. It is necessary."

Slender fingers stroked the Sushi Priest's razor-thin mustache as he considered this. "Hmm." He shook his head. "No. I simply can't allow it."

"It is not your decision, priest."

Daniel elbowed me, drawing my attention. He lifted his chin as he looked over my head. I turned.

Behind us stood a line of black-eyed waiters. With gills.

There were four of them cut from the same cloth, all wearing peg-legged black slacks, white button-front shirts tucked in with the sleeves rolled up, and skinny black ties. Shaggy bangs fell over wide foreheads on moon faces, their features soft, almost mushy. All their eyes were large, teardrop-shaped baby-seal eyes set far apart, as if their faces were melting from the middle out. Their gills flapped up then down in unison as they breathed with a wet snuffling sound.

My hand tightened on the knife. This was not good.

I turned so I could keep one eye on the fish-men waiters and one eye on the Man in Black and one eye on the Sushi Priest.

I had no more eyes to spare.

The Sushi Priest laughed. "You are in *my* place of power."

The Man in Black shrugged. "Your power is nothing to me."

"And *that,* arrogance of that nature, is what landed the mighty Cthulhu in my net."

"He had slept for eons when you snared him." The chaos god snarled. "You will find me fully awake."

"You underestimate me at your peril, O Prince of Darkness."

"Does a shoggoth underestimate a titmouse? Your reach exceeds your grasp, puny mortal. You have no power to harm me."

"I have no intention of *harming* you, Nyarlathotep-san." The Sushi Priest smiled. "But you *will* be a delicious addition to my menu." His hand moved from behind the altar, holding out a medallion on an iron chain. Metal swirled in a cage around a glass sphere filled with liquid. Inside it floated an eyeball.

The eye bulged, an uneven, jaundiced globe trailing pink optic nerve from its backside like an obscene jellyfish. The pupil and iris shone with energy, lighting the sphere like a lantern with violet light. Slowly the eyeball turned to look at us, using the fluttering optic nerve like the fins on a beta fish, a rudder of dangling flesh.

The magick inside me throbbed.

"Surely you recognize this?" the Sushi Priest asked.

"I have seen the Eye of Omens before, priest. Now I know how you took the mighty Cthulhu."

"With it in my grasp, I can hold two just as easily as I hold one."

He pointed his hand at the Man in Black, vomited out a chunk of green magick, and the situation went to hell in the blink of an eye.

49

VERDANT MAGICK BLASTED over the altar stone in front of the Sushi Priest, sizzling toward us. The air filled with the stink of burnt calamari as the tiny krakens piled in the bowls caught fire. The Man in Black lifted his red right hand, its raw fingers knotted together, and a shield of ruby-colored magick cupped around him. The green energy slammed into it, driving the Man in Black back a step, gobbets of magick spattering off to each side.

The force of the impact rushed across me like a runaway train careening through a station platform. I stumbled from the brunt of it, falling to one knee.

Daniel howled and dove to the ground as some of the excess green magick splashed across his legs. Rolling to a stop, he sat up, beating out tiny flickers of flame that speckled his jeans.

I moved to help him.

"I got it, I got it!" he yelled, pointing with his free hand. "Watch them!"

I spun and found the waiters walking toward me.

They chanted, their voices combined in a quartet of creepy lockstep like a Deadite version of a show choir. Every one of them now held a box-cutter with short, wicked razor blades extended.

I moved the Knife of Abraham in front of me, holding it tight. Mine was longer, but there were four of them. Not good odds. The words of Sensei Laura blasted into my mind.

If your opponent has a knife, run. *If you fight someone with a knife you* are *going to get cut. Better to run than bleed.*

Trapped between them and the sorcery battle, I had nowhere to run.

Daniel stepped next to me. He smelled burnt and limped as he moved. He hefted a chunk of stalactite and leaned toward me, pointing. "What are they doing?"

I looked, and the waiters were still closing in with short, shuffling steps. They had crossed their arms, laying the blades of the box-cutters against the insides of their elbows. Their chanting intensified, beating against my eardrums.

In his tank, Cthulhu stirred, agitated, pressing against the glass. Pressing against my mind. Pressing against my magick.

Free me.

From the corner of my eye, I saw the Man in Black lean forward and sling crimson magick at the Sushi Priest.

The inhuman waiters pushed the short, sharp blades into their flesh and dragged them down their own arms, splitting the skin in wide seams. The chanting never stopped as their skin unzipped beneath the cutting blades, yawning wide. Things moved in the wounds, writhing and squirming, and as blades reached wrists, the things burst out in a mass of slimy, flapping tentacles.

"Damn," Daniel said.

Then they were on us.

50

I SLASHED UP with the knife as Daniel swung his stone club. The edge of the Aqedah bit into a mass of rubbery tentacles, snagging and pulling in my hand. Black ink spurted in high arcs from the cut, splashing up my arm and across my face in thin, cold streams. Chunks of tentacle fell to the cavern floor, severed by my knife. They squirmed and squiggled under my feet.

The waiter gave no indication of pain, his moon face blank, wide mouth gaping up and down, still chanting. The skin of his arm lurched, and *more* tentacles spilled out in a bouquet of writhing, clicking flesh.

In his tank, Cthulhu pulsed at my mind. I could *feel* him trying to communicate with me, trying to get my attention.

Something grabbed my left arm.

Two fat tubes of mottled gray-green flesh wrapped my arm, squeezing tightly as they constricted. Sharp pain dotted underneath it as the suckers began to bite.

The waiter attached to the tentacles stepped closer. More reached for me.

I jerked back, the tentacles wrapping my arm tighter. Pain pulled up my arm. Slicing down, I cut myself free and stumbled. Falling.

My back hit something solid.

Daniel.

He spun, trying to grab me, to keep me from hitting the ground, turning his back to the monstrous waiters he fought.

I pushed away, trying to say I was okay, to tell him to keep fighting.

I couldn't get the words out before a mass of tentacles slithered across Daniel's face, covering his mouth and jerking him off his feet.

I screamed as he fell, both of his waiters latching on and dragging him toward them.

I took a step in their direction.

Something wrapped around my waist, yanking me backward.

I spun, slashing blindly, desperation clawing at my mind, magick pulsing in my stomach. The Knife of Abraham cut across a waiter's stomach, parting the white shirt and the skin beneath like water. Black ink spurted, coating me in a slimy sheet of icy liquid. Tentacles burst out, more tentacles than should have fit inside the waiter. They spilled onto the floor, thigh-thick and python-long, lying limp for a moment before they rose into the air, tips swinging to and fro, hounds scenting for prey.

The waiter giggled as his clone stepped close to him, giggling in perfect unity.

The clone's mouth split at the corners, ink running from the rips. His wide throat convulsed once, then again, and a fat-tipped slug of alien flesh came up and out of his mouth. It slithered out, rolling and undulating down his chest. Two smaller tendrils pushed his baby-seal eyes from their sockets, twisting and curling down his cheeks as they waved beside his moon face, the eyeballs unblinking on the ends of their stalks.

I stepped back, swallowing hard against the sickness that wanted to happen.

Cthulhu sloshed in his tank.

Free me.

My Mark burned as the words pulsed in my mind.

Daniel fell, wrapped in the grip of the two waiters he fought. They knelt over him as he struggled, holding him down, masking his face with a pile of writhing tentacles.

My eyes found the Man in Black.

He crouched on the ground, pressed down by a cage of green magick. I could hear his coat screaming as it smoldered where the corruption of magick touched it. The Sushi Priest stood on the altar, holding the Eye of Omens high, face pulled in a wide smile as he cast his spell over the chaos god.

I looked for a way out, an escape, a way to go.

A wave of tentacles crashed into me, slapping around my body, dragging me to the ground. They squeezed, tightening, cutting off my air. Black spots swam across my vision, and my head throbbed.

The knife fell from my numb fingers.

FREE ME.

The waiters loomed over me, one smiling like a lunatic, the other's face a flaccid sack around the three tentacles waving from the stump of its neck.

I couldn't breathe.

FREE ME AND I WILL SAVE YOU.

My chest collapsed, crushed by the weight of the tentacles constricting around me. I gasped, trying to pull air into crushed lungs.

Daniel, I'm sorry. I failed.

The world began to go black.

Cthulhu moved in his tank.

Everything grew dark, so very dark.

Before I went under, I made a wish.

51

THUNDER FELL IN the middle of the cavern as Cthulhu crashed to the floor, freed by my magick.

He crouched, massive, enormous, gigantic; filling the space with his size, his presence. Syrupy fluid sluiced off him, splashing to the cavern floor and racing to fill uneven divots and crevasses in an amniotic rush. Out of his tank, he pressed against the walls of my mind with the weight of a titan.

"No!" the Sushi Priest shouted, magick crackling off his skin, rolling down the folds of his robe, fed by his anger. He still held the Eye of Omens, streaming magick from it to keep the Man in Black pinned to the ground.

The Great One shifted, turning at the sound of his captor's voice. He spoke, words crashing through my mindspace, turning me into a butterfly in a hurricane.

THE TIDES TURN, LITTLE MAN. NOW YOU SHALL PAY.

The Sushi Priest screamed out a spell and flung his free arm in an arc of sorcery that cut across the space, striking the sea god in the face. The magick sizzled against inhuman flesh, smoke billowing as Cthulhu screamed inside my mind.

The tentacles around me loosened, slipping away. Air, sweet air, rushed into my lungs, painful and cold. The waiters pulled away, moving to help their master. Gibbering, they shambled toward Cthulhu. They were joined by their brothers, who'd let go of Daniel. Rolling on my side, I pushed up, looking for him.

I found him lying on the cavern floor.

He looked dead.

Oh God, no.

I scrambled toward him.

An explosion rocked the cavern with a *BOOM!* that shook the ground, throwing me down. My face hit the limestone, and a line of pain shot across my cheekbone. Chunks of rock rained down from the ceiling, stalactites falling in spears of crushing stone. I looked and found the source.

Cthulhu had slammed his gigantic fist down on the gill-throated waiters.

He shifted, lifting massive, barnacled knuckles from the ground. Pulp stained black with ink stretched from cavern floor to sea-god fist in a torn net of gore. The waiters had been crushed, reduced to paste and amputated tentacles that wriggled and twitched in the stain.

Cthulhu turned toward the Sushi Priest as he flung more magick at him.

I hurried to Daniel, pushing aside the thought that there were gods and a sorcerer Sushi Priest fighting behind me. I couldn't do anything but get to Daniel; the rest of it was too much to deal with.

Propped on one elbow, he rubbed his forehead with the fingers of his other hand. Relief flooded over me to see him alive.

He was filthy, slime and blood mixed with rock dust and ink to form a layer of grime from the top of his head to the bottoms of his feet. I touched his chest and saw that my hand was coated in a layer of the same grime.

"Are you okay?" he asked.

I nodded. "Are you?"

"As I can be." His eyes looked over my head. "Oh, damn, that can't be good."

I glanced behind me. Daniel stared at Cthulhu advancing, moving step by step toward the Sushi Priest, batting aside spells as he did with webbed hands the size of treetops. I turned to Daniel. "I think he's on our side."

"None of them are on our side."

He was right. "On our side more than most," I said.

"Go, go, Godzilla then." He shivered. "How did he get out of the fishbowl?"

"I did it. I didn't see another way out."

He nodded. "No wonder I feel so crappy."

I'd used magick. Dammit.

He grabbed my arm. "Hey." He shook me, not hard, just enough to get me to look at him. "Get that look off your face. You only did what you had to. I'll be okay."

"No more magick." I meant it.

"No more magick *tomorrow*." He let go of my arm. "Today we have stuff to get done, and magick is required."

I didn't agree, but I didn't argue.

"Here's your knife. You'll need that too." He held out the Aqedah, handle first. I took it, and he tried to stand.

I grabbed him before he collapsed.

He sat on the ground, face twisted in pain. "Maybe I'll sit here for a minute."

"Does it hurt?"

"A little."

Sweat cut trails through the dirt and grime on his face, skin showing waxy underneath. His breathing sounded ragged, and his hands shook, twittering and trembling as he held his legs, curled around himself. He was hurting. A lot. I let my eyes shift, sliding my focus like I had before, calling my magick up to See through.

In my vision, Daniel became a clear vessel. The golden energy had been drained to almost half. It lay inside him, sloshing through his body with a lot of room to spare. Turning, I blinked the magick away.

"As soon as you can stand, I'm getting you out of here."

He shook his head. "No. We've got to finish this."

"Screw *this*. Let the world burn. All I want is you to be safe, to stop being hurt." I moved closer, my hand on his face. "The rest of the world can go to hell."

He grinned. It was weak, but it was there, dimples and all. "We have to save the world. I need it to be here tomorrow, and the next day, and the next, and all the days after those." His trembling hands pulled me closer. "I need them, because I want to spend all of them with you."

My heart swelled in my chest. It was hard to breathe.

His voice was soft, his mouth close to mine. "So we fight. Till the bitter end."

"Till the bitter end," I echoed.

A wave of magick knocked us sideways before we could kiss.

52

Daniel's arms wrapped around me, keeping me from tumbling across the floor. Pinned against him, I felt us slide nearly a foot across the gravel-strewn floor. The magick washed off us with a crackling snap like a fire whip. Daniel groaned, his arms falling away from me

I moved, scrambling to take my weight off him. He sat up, and blood spotted his hoodie where the gravel on the floor had torn through it and the skin beneath. My hands touched his arms and chest, avoiding his injuries. "Are you okay?"

"It hurts, but I will be." He shook his head, making his shaggy bangs fall over his eyes. "What was that?"

I pointed.

The Sushi Priest now stood on the limestone altar. A tendril of vile sorcery from the talisman in his hand still pinned the Man in Black to the ground, but the priest was surrounded by a crackling orb of chartreuse magick. Cthulhu's tremendous hand cupped over it, squeezing, sea-god flesh sizzling as the etheric energy scorched and sparked between webbed fingers the size of the Sushi Priest himself. I could feel the pain in Cthulhu's hand; it echoed down the connection between us, making the Mark on my own hand grow hot, the lines burning across my palm. I looked down. The swirled and whorled scars glowed a dull red-orange. Rubbing it on my pants made little wisps of gray smoke. I looked back at the fight between elder gods and sorcerer.

The Sushi Priest's spell cast Cthulhu in lime-green highlights, flashing and popping like a strobe, making the elder god look like a special effect in a movie as he loomed in the darkness. His back brushed the ceiling of the cavern, crushing stalactites into a rain of dust.

Cthulhu leaned on the sphere, pressing harder. The limestone slab under the Sushi Priest's feet broke in half with a *CRACK!* that resounded across the stone-littered floor. The Sushi Priest screamed and swung the Eye of Omens up, adding its magick to his own. The sphere around him doubled in size, intensifying, pushing Cthulhu back. The energy flared so bright I had to squint just to look, the sparks and crackles shooting little pains across my retinas. Inside my mind Cthulhu howled his agony, but he pressed on.

The Man in Black, free from his prison, rose off the ground in a fury, his coat flaring dragon-wing wide around him. The black-bladed sword gleamed in his red right hand, naked and wicked and iniquity-sharp. His hand pulsed with crimson energy like the still-beating heart of some cursed creature. It dripped gobbets of magick, spilling scarlet-black down the blade. His dark face twisted with raw anger and naked wrath, his black, glittering eyes slit-staring at the Sushi Priest.

He lashed out, slamming the sword through the sphere of energy. It struck the Sushi Priest at the knees, shearing through flesh and bone like black-bladed lightning.

The Sushi Priest screamed once as his protective spell crumbled. The scream still echoed as Cthulhu's hand snapped shut around him, plucking him upward and leaving his legs from the knees down to stand on the broken limestone altar.

53

THE TWO ELDER gods stood facing each other across the severed stumps perched on the limestone altar. Blood soaked the white-green stone, turning it dark as they glared at each other. Cthulhu loomed from floor to ceiling, hunched over gigantic knees, his colossal, stone-crushing knuckles cracking the rock underneath him. He breathed through gills the size of ship sails under a tangled nest of wriggling tentacles where a mouth should have been, and it moved the air inside the entire chamber in dank, lagoon-moist drafts.

The Man in Black looked like a wisp in comparison, a tiny slip of a figure next to the massive sea god. He stood in his fluttering coat, thin blade in his red right hand.

Then he *shifted,* and everything changed.

The Man in Black looked the same, but suddenly he was different. His presence expanded between one eye blink and the next, growing into something that pressed against the magick under my skin. He was the Heart of Darkness, the Lord of Nightmares, the original Suicide King.

He was the Crawling Chaos in all his terrible glory.

Daniel scurried next to me. His voice was still thready with pain. "What do we do?"

"Be very, very quiet," I whispered.

"'Cause we're hunting wabbits?"

I shook my head. "We are the rabbits."

"Good point."

Cthulhu shifted, and more of the ceiling crumbled against his winged back, dust falling across shoulders like mountains, sticking to damp, sea-god skin. His voice was the sounding of cloister bells inside my head, loud but hollow, warning of danger.

NEPHEW.

"Uncle." The Man in Black gave a small nod, lips pulled into a grin.

WHERE DO WE GO FROM HERE?

"You are free from your prison, Lord of R'lyeh."

BECAUSE OF YOUR ACOLYTE.

The Man in Black tilted his head. "You are welcome. Indebted, but welcome."

Cthulhu shifted.

IT WAS NOT AT YOUR HAND.

"She is my hand. She bears *my* Mark."

The symbol in my palm flared hotter as he said it. I bristled inside but stayed quiet.

Cthulhu shook his head, and the cavern vibrated.

HER POWER IS HER OWN. NO DEBT IS OWED TO YOU.

His massive head turned slightly, red orb of an eye looking directly at me. Under his gaze, my magick began to bubble and boil. My skin flushed fever-hot, and it took every ounce of control to not squirm, to not turn away and hide from the weight of that awful, crimson eye.

The Man in Black lunged forward, coat flaring around him with a snap, his saturnine face pulled into a snarl exposing long, jagged shark teeth. "She is my Acolyte. What is hers is mine by right of possession."

The implication of that struck me like a fist. My hand reached back, falling on Daniel's leg. He was mine. No one else's.

Mine and mine alone.

Cthulhu turned toward the Man in Black.

SHE ONLY FOLLOWS YOU BECAUSE SHE DOES NOT KNOW THE TRUTH.

"My truth is her truth, Deep Dweller," he spat.

NOT FOR LONG, PRINCE OF LIES.

Cthulhu didn't move as his mind crashed into mine like a tsunami, sweeping me under and washing me away into a riptide of darkness.

54

I WAS BACK.

Back in the vision of a blood-black future where the moon hung low and red in a tattered and falling sky, and the world burned and bled, and the stench of torn gut and violent death threatened to choke the air from my lungs. It all closed around me like a fist.

Squeezing.

Constricting.

Oppressing.

I blinked rapidly, trying to clear the tears that welled in my eyes, burning from the soot that hung in the air. Movement in front of me caught my eye.

I stood behind a monster, the monster I'd seen earlier, the one that held my little brother, Jacks. The one eating my little brother, Jacks, with jagged, gnashing teeth. I could just see my brother's tiny socked foot around slowly flapping wings of stretched membrane.

My stomach clenched.

"Don't move, Charlie. You can't save him. That's not why I brought you here."

The voice came from behind me. It carried over my shoulder, a pleasant tenor with a muted accent that was vaguely Bostonian. I turned.

A man stood just a few feet away.

He was dressed in dark jeans with folded cuffs, a brown leather jacket over a skin-tight black T-shirt, and motorcycle boots, and his dark hair was greased into a pseudo-pompadour; he looked like a seventies version of someone from the fifties.

He had kind brown eyes and a large nose.

"Who are you?" I asked. "Really?"

"You know me, Charlie."

"I don't."

He opened his mouth and spoke something in a language I could not understand, one made of feelings and urges instead of language and sound.

The moment he said the word, knowledge poured on me like boiling oil. He pushed against the magick inside me, sweeping back and forth like the tides. He felt immense, bottomless, near infinite.

I breathed his name.

"Cthulhu."

He nodded, warm eyes twinkling.

"What are we doing?" This made no sense.

"We are having a conversation in a possible apocalypse."

"Wait, why aren't we in the cave?"

"We are."

I shook my head. I didn't understand.

"We are both avatars of ourselves. You are still beneath the Temple of Ba'althune next to your paramour. I am still in the golden city of R'yleh, *and* I still fight your master in the same temple where you are. All of these things are true. I splintered us and took a portion of each to the moment you chose your path, the moment *you* chose *this* future."

"I didn't want any of this."

"You chose to help Nyarlathotep achieve his goals."

"To *stop* this."

He shook his head sadly, then lifted his chin, indicating the scene in front of us. "Watch closely."

I turned to look. We'd shifted, now looking at the event from the side. I saw myself.

I looked terrible. Other Charlie looked like a child compared to the squatting monstrosity she faced. I watched myself scream in rage, face purple and knotted. The creature leaned to the left and broke wind, my brother's body sliding on its bloated stomach.

"Watch," Cthulhu said. Other Charlie took a step, her hands clenched in fists of rage, and then the night swirled behind her and coalesced into the form of a man.

The Man in Black.

He looked different now, his coat flaring off him in spikes and blades of inky black energy, his skull swollen and malformed around a shark's maw of triple-rowed teeth. His eyes glowed crimson, pulsing in syncopated rhythm with his red right claw. He reached out, razor talons clamping on Other Charlie's shoulder, spinning her around. He grabbed her, snatching her off her feet and lifting her into the air. Blood burst where his talons pierced her body, tearing a scream from her throat that cut into my bones, going on and on and on in an undulating wave of agony that stole her words away.

He grew, expanding and swelling, his shark maw swinging wide and vicious. She tried to fight, legs kicking, her hands moving. I could feel her try to use her magick like an echo inside my chest. The Crawling Chaos smiled around his slung-open jaw, arm-thick tongue slithering out, whipping the air. A guttural bark blew Other Charlie's hair as he laughed at her futile effort.

Her tears fell, splashing against rows of jagged, jutting enamel.

Then he shoved her face first down his throat.

Cthulhu's hand clamped on my arm, stopping me from running to save her. I jerked hard against his grip, but he kept his fingers closed.

A small part of my mind noticed they were webbed to the second knuckle.

"Let me *go*!"

"It would do no good."

I pulled harder, jerking with all my body weight. "What's happening?"

He let go of my arm, and I stumbled. "You were only shown a portion of this future. You were manipulated into using your power to guide reality to this future. Your choices have been tumblers in a lock, one by one falling into place until this future cannot be undone. It is almost too late. This is the reality if you allow the Son of Azathoth to win."

I looked at the scene with Other Charlie and the Crawling Chaos. They were perfectly still, time-locked; everything around us was frozen in place. Her legs hung in a mist of blood freeze-framed around the monstrous countenance of Nyarlathotep. It was gruesome and gory, and the fact that I was looking at another version of myself made the horror even more surreal. It scratched at my eyeballs, picking away at the edge of my sanity.

I turned away, back to Cthulhu. He stood there as if he were innocent, the kindly old guy who would buy you beer but never ever try to feel you up after you drank it. It was a lie, and I recognized it. "Oh, and you want me to throw in with you?"

He shrugged. "It would be better."

"I doubt that."

"All I want is a home for my star-spawn. They swim the aeons of space, skirting through the Void without form, without a home. It . . ." A tear trickled from a watery brown eye. ". . . *pains* me to be separated from them."

Loss struck me like a fist, blasting into my gut, leaving me scooped out. I felt as though part of me, part of who I am, had been trapped a million miles away, and I couldn't get to it, couldn't be whole, would never be whole again.

I felt like I did when I'd woken up so many years ago.

Cthulhu moved closer, his webbed hands moving to my arms, gentle this time. "Charlie, you have to understand, *he* is the Great Destroyer! *He* is the Ravening Lion. You are food to him and his kind. If he has his way, your world will be a feasting board. All I want is a home for me and mine. My children will come and bring everlasting life to this planet. No more death. No more illness. No more war. Just peace and plenty and an endless, pleasant dream." His hand swept over his hair, coming away shiny. Before I could flinch, he swiped it across my face. My eyes slammed shut as they were anointed with a thin sheen of oil from an elder god.

When I opened them, I was flying through space, and I wasn't human anymore.

55

We huddle close, but it does no good; the cold still cuts through us, slicing its way to our cores. Bits of dust and debris, detritus from planets smashed long ago into pieces, whiz past, scouring my skin. I am filleted in a thousand micro-tears.

My brother next to me isn't as fortunate. He is reduced to a shred of flesh and a cloud of fluid that the ones behind fly through, blinking him away from their single open eyes.

He is gone.

One less of us.

The loss of him is a sharp pain throughout our shared mind.

We huddle closer.

Filling in the gap.

A sun goes nova as we sail by, flaring into a bright purple burst, unleashing gamma rays that cold-scorch the flank of our school.

I feel their nerve endings burn and curl as if they were my own.

Hundreds fall away, drifting into space, becoming detritus themselves.

Flotsam.

Jetsam.

Still, we swim on.

The hole inside me hurts. I need. There is something out there that can heal me.

I just have to find it.

We just have to find it.

Father, help us.

Please just call us home.

56

I'D BEEN TORN from the outskirts of space and flung to the ground like a bird plucked from the sky by the hand of God. Tumbling across the ash-covered ground of the nightmare future, I rolled to a stop. I couldn't breathe. Fine gray soot filled my nose, coating the inside of my throat, closing it down so air couldn't squeeze through.

This is the ash of everything I love.

I scrambled to my feet, coughing and choking.

Swallowing over and over again, gulping air, I finally managed to catch my breath. I held my chest, trying to keep my heart from pounding out of it.

Blinking through streaming tears, my eyes found Cthulhu in his human guise.

He'd fallen to his knees, the Crawling Chaos looming around him with deadly spikes of ebon energy. His face turned toward me, eyes filled with saltwater. He spoke into my mind as the first stabbing talon reached him.

YOU MUST STOP HIM. I AM TOO WEAK AFTER MY CAPTIVITY.

"I can't." The words hurt coming out.

YOU MUST.

His voice pitched up an octave, smoothing out, soothing against my ears.

THREE TO BREAK THE SEAL.

THREE TO TURN THE WHEEL.

THREE TO LOOSE AZATHOTH.

THREE AND ALL HOPE IS LOST.

The words meant nothing to me. Azathoth. Azathoth was bad. I knew that, and the fact that he was tied to the Man in Black. Before I could ask what Cthulhu meant, the Crawling Chaos surged, swallowing him into the darkness of his coat. The dark god's back was to me, the soot-and-ink blackness of the coat struggling to consume the body of Cthulhu. Shapes moved on the surface of the coat, bulging here and there in misshapen forms, the sea god trying to punch his way free. Nyarlathotep's distorted face loomed above the collar, his hands, red and dark-skinned, both clutching the coat together as it screamed and screamed and screamed in my mind, its voice joining the voice of Cthulhu himself, a duet of glass-edged pain as one drove to consume and one fought to keep from being consumed. The clarion skrill of their agony crushed me to the ground.

I screamed, joining them.

Slowly, at a bone-grinding pace, the cries of Cthulhu faded, drifting into oblivion, and the coat fell to a whimpering that I echoed as the Man in Black shuddered and shifted, sliding back into his human skin.

One last shiver and he snapped back into place.

Slowly he turned, his dead white chaotic gaze falling on me.

57

"CHARLIE, MOVE!"

Daniel's arm hooked around my waist, dragging me to the side as a chunk of limestone the size of a small car crashed to the ground where I'd been standing. It exploded in a rain of dust and a shower of white stone. Daniel grunted as a fist-sized chunk slammed into his back so hard I felt it through the other side of his body as he wrapped himself protectively around me.

The world crashed, falling to pieces.

Daniel sucked in air and continued to pull me, dragging me away to safety.

I shook my head, tearing through the confusion of the alternate reality I'd just left like a rotten spider web, and poked my face over his shoulder, looking for the engine of all this destruction.

The Man in Black swung his red right hand back, flinging globules of crackling magick that bounced along the cavern floor behind him, scorching the limestone black where they landed. His hand clenched in a fist, surrounded by a nimbus of crimson lightning. It flared cornea-searingly bright, flinging the shadow of both elder gods toward us like a falling eclipse. Stark shadows cut the Man in Black's face into a strobe-lit mask of fury, and the sea god's back disappeared into the darkness of the ceiling.

Cthulhu's massive webbed hand fell, dropping like an avalanche toward the chaos god. It looked slow, ponderous, because of the sheer mass of it, dropping inches instead of feet at a time. It had so far to fall it seemed to hang suspended in the air.

Nyarlathotep lunged, flinging the spell in his red right hand.

It flew, smashing into Cthulhu's chest like a nuclear missile.

Magick exploded, filing the cave with a red blast. My eyes slammed shut, but it still seared through my eyelids, spiking pain through them and into the back of my eye sockets. Rocks and dust fell like snow from the concussion of the impact. Silence rushed in as my ears shut from the *BOOM!*

I tore my eyes open. I had to see.

Cthulhu's chest had been blown open.

Mold-green skin yawned apart, strange and alien shapes smoking where the crimson magick had scorched them to charcoal. I gagged as a stench blasted over me, smelling like a sewage treatment plant on fire. Daniel jerked the collar of his hoodie up over his face.

Cthulhu fell to his hands and knees. The ground shuddered under my feet. Wings like tattered sails on a sinking ship hung limply off his mountainous back. The tentacles around his mouth dragged through the dust, limp and flaccid, no movement to them at all. Those giant red orbs were shut tight, and his rounded head hung low between massive shoulders.

The Man in Black leapt, the coat around him pushing him like a springboard into the air. He landed on Cthulhu's face, just above the nest of tentacles that served as a mouth, and scrambled up him, arms and legs digging into the gigantic sea god's mottled greenish skin. His coat flared around him, its tendrils becoming spikes and digging in to help pull him up. He looked like a black-carapaced beetle climbing a corpse.

Maybe he was. Cthulhu had disappeared from my mind. I couldn't feel him anymore, just the lack of him like a vacuum in my soul.

The butchered god didn't move, didn't even shrug to shake the other elder god off. He just knelt there, head low as the Man in Black scaled his skull. Reaching the top, Nyarlathotep stood triumphant in a maelstrom of swirling darkness, the only color on him the gleam of too-sharp teeth and the lurching crimson pulse of his red right hand.

Out came his sword, sliding from the depths of the coat. Something inside me slid into place, like a joint going back into socket with a sick, wet *POP,* and I could feel the pounding of the cries from the coat as it struggled against its wearer.

Nyarlathotep ignored it.

Shifting to a crouch, he raised the black-bladed sword over his head.

A scream lodged in my throat, stuck against my trachea.

He leapt, spinning delicately like a dancer, blade cutting the air around him.

The sword fell like lightning, splitting the skull of Cthulhu in a tidal wave of gore.

"NOOOOOOOOO!" Daniel screamed beside me, too little, too late.

Black liquid poured across the limestone floor, rushing around stalagmite stumps, knocking over the altar, lifting the bodies of the Sushi Priest and his squid waiters in a dead man's float.

The Man in Black grabbed the edge of the sundered skull of his brother god, swinging himself up to perch at the crest of Cthulhu's head. He leaned into the gap, his arm sinking into the fissure he'd carved, stretching into the gash, disappearing as it rooted around.

The sensation came down the thin connection between me and Cthulhu, a faint echo of what the sea god experienced. It felt as if my brain was being stirred with a blender that had been set on fire.

I fell to my knees, soaking to my waist in the tide pool of Cthulhu's brain juice.

Daniel grabbed me, lifting me before I could collapse completely and fall face first into the brackish slime.

Cthulhu's eye cracked open, just a slit, and our connection jolted across my nerve endings. I felt that gaze bore into my soul.

STOP HIM BEFORE HE GETS A THIRD.

The Man in Black gave a cry of triumph and pulled his arm out with a moist *schlurp*. He lifted a shining crystal that pulsed with energy, roiling from teal to putrid yellow to hot magenta.

Cthulhu fell, crashing to the ground in a riptide of his own fluid.

He was gone from my brain.

58

The Man in Black stepped off the giant skull of his dead uncle god. He pranced toward us, puddles of gore splish-splashing around his feet. A smile cut his face in half, and he rubbed the crystal on his coat like an apple he planned to take a bite from.

A mad gleam shone in his eye.

I stepped closer to Daniel, and he stepped closer to me until our hands found each other. It felt like we were circling the wagons.

The Man in Black stopped in front of us. He stretched like a cat, arms up, back arched, on his tippy-toes with his head tilted at an odd angle. He moaned as a series of quiet cracks ran in a chain from inside him.

He dropped down, flat-footed.

"Well, that was almost too easy." His eyebrow arched sharply as he looked at me. "It was as if he were distracted."

Daniel's hand tightened on mine. "Why would you say that?"

"Oh, I do not know, the Lord of R'yleh may have been many things"—his fingers stroked the air as if looking for these things—"dull, single-minded, sentimental . . ." He ticked them off one by one on his left hand, the human one. ". . . but he was not a . . . what is your human word? Oh yes, he was not a bitch, and he should not have gone down like one."

"Does it matter how you stopped him?"

"It matters if my Acolyte has designs to turn against me because of something she was told."

My heart stopped beating.

He knows.

Daniel tensed, moving just slightly forward, between me and the Man in Black. "They didn't talk. He didn't say anything to her, and she didn't say anything to him."

"You know nothing." Nyarlathotep plucked at a tattered piece on the edge of his coat, capturing it between two red, skinless fingers. He pulled it slowly, tearing it from the rest of the coat in one long, drawn-out rip.

I felt its pain as a faint echo in my head.

Laying the strip of coat against the jewel in his hand, he began to wind it around, stretching it as he went. He didn't look when he spoke, but his words were aimed at me. "What did he tell you?"

"Nothing," I said.

Pulling the strip into a loop, he hung the jewel around his neck beside the one from the Cancer God. They rubbed against each other, the crystalline planes and corners chinking and squeaking in protest. The colors in each of them whipped into a frenzy, rushing toward the other jewel and then darting away, like living, liquid energy trapped in a prism of quartz.

"Liar, liar pants on fire." He stopped. "Well, not literally. Not yet."

"We fulfilled our part of this deal. Let us walk away now."

His tongue clucked the roof of his mouth. "Tut-tut-tut, Acolyte. That was not the bargain struck."

"Yes, it was."

Dark eyes glowed. He licked his lips. When he opened his mouth his voice had changed. Daniel's voice came from the Man in Black's throat. *"Name your price, and we'll pay it."*

Oh no.

"I name my price, Daniel Alexander Langford." The Man in Black's smile widened, teeth gleaming in the dim luminescence of the cave. "That price is your life."

Before I could move, he fell on Daniel in a swirl of black coat. In a blink, they were gone.

I screamed, the only person left alive in that dank, subterranean pit.

59

I HAD TO find them. Seconds ticked by as my mind scrambled for a solution. Seconds Daniel didn't have. I'd seen the Man in Black kill. Daniel might not even be alive now.

The thought stabbed through me, dropping me to my knees.

I needed to find them to save him to stop this to find him to save him. The wish inside me screamed out, desperate to be fulfilled.

Nothing happened.

What?

Horrible realization dawned. Daniel was gone. My magick had no fuel. It lay quiet and still inside me. Small. Smaller than it had ever felt since being sparked. I could feel it like a shallow pool deep inside me, a nearly dry well.

No. No. Not now. Not when I *needed* it most.

That I could fail Daniel when he needed me most felt like a knife in my guts.

Knife.

Wait.

My brain turned slowly, rotating around something the Man in Black had said to me earlier.

When you need your magick it can be activated by touching your Mark with any bodily fluid. Blood is the strongest.

Shifting the Aqedah to my left hand, I laid the edge of the blade against my wrist. It sat next to the line already there, the scar straight and thin. The surgeon had done a great job sewing it up. Just a thin white line of hard tissue was the only sign that anything had ever happened.

I used it as a guide.

Across the street, not down the river.

Not unless you're serious.

The magick knife didn't drag at all, slipping through my skin as though it were water. Crimson welled in its path, a furrow of my own making filling with my life blood. It spilled down my palm in a thick trickle, following the crease of my lifeline, running toward my Mark.

It hit the red, raised scar tissue of the Mark, and the magick inside me tried to push itself out of my skin like needle-hairs through every pore.

The blood pooled in my palm, making a little puddle.

I closed my eyes, seeing Daniel's face in my mind. His green eyes, his dimple, the way his hair kept falling into his eyes.

I kept him there and thought one simple thing.

Take me to him.

I felt no pain this time. There was a sharp tug that felt as though my spine were being yanked through my belly button, but no pain. I stumbled forward, stepping from where I had just stood to where I wanted to be in a swoosh of passing reality.

I left the close, dank darkness of the cave with its mottled stink of limestone and sea-god brain juice and stepped into the cold, clear, open darkness of a moonless night.

Pinprick stars lay their light upon me, making the world shine. I stood on a hill. There was grass under my feet. The air felt frosty, my breath hanging in a cloud with each exhale. My hand felt warm.

And wet.

I looked down to find it sheeted in red, a thick claret of life-blood dripping off the ends of my fingertips.

Shit. I cut too deep.

My stomach lurched, and warm prickles danced from my scalp down to my shoulders like a hundred drunken centipedes crawling through my hair. I didn't have long before I'd need to find medical attention. Using sticky fingers, I cut a strip off my shirt with the Aqedah and tied it around the cut. My mouth tasted of old iron as I knotted it closed with my teeth. It would help, but wouldn't hold for long. I tried to spit the taste from my mouth and took a jerky step, lifting my eyes to look for Daniel.

I found him immediately. I saw what was happening and began to run.

A group of standing stones surrounded a flat spot in the vale of the hill. They jutted toward the sky in a semicircle, thick granite fingers in a grasping reach. Moonlight pooled inside their guard, painting the scene inside with a quicksilver glow.

A cracked altar, a flat slab of stone stained with the blood of sacrifice, stood in the center. Daniel lay across it, feet hanging from the end, head lolling to the side, too big for a place designed to lay children on.

The Man in Black hung between the standing stones on a tattered net of stringy darkness like a fat, black *thing* of dripping venom and murderous teeth. He hung over Daniel, looming inches above him.

Long, spindly legs strummed along the netted darkness as he had become a double-segmented arachnid, no longer in human guise, no longer pretending. He had become every spider from every arachnophobe's hellish nightmares—a shining, unrelieved black, shifting slightly side to side on herky-jerky joints.

He'd changed, transformed and altered into the Spider God: Lord of Illusion and Nightmares, the Eater of Iniquity.

And, my God, I could *feel* the connection between my Mark and the pulsating, crimson handprint emblazoned on his distended, bulbous stomach as he ate the sanity from Daniel's mind.

60

ECTOPLASM, SEMISOLID AND shiny-slick, leaked from Daniel's eye sockets, his nostrils, and his silent-screaming mouth. It curled through the moonlight, twisting upward and sashaying its way into Nyarlathotep's open maw. Long, spindly legs worked, rolling the ethereal substance into a ball like cotton candy, feeding it between grasping pincer mandibles. The round head of this grotesque still looked like the Man in Black, his features slipped and twisted on a sphere of a head. The mandible mouth still held his shark-toothed grin, now sunken deep inside, gnashing and chewing Daniel's essence. The black-cosmos eyes had slid around and now sat on the outside of the skin, socket-less and bulging, ringed about with replicas of themselves until they formed an all-seeing crown of unblinking, moist orbs.

Thick hairs like splinters of volcanic glass prickled off the many-jointed legs plucking the web of darkness he squatted on, the strands pressed tightly against his hard carapace, highlighted in crimson as the handprint on his abdomen beat like a heart. The rest of him formed an unrelieved spot of eternal darkness, a black hole eating the glare of the moon above as he drank down Daniel.

My feet pounded the grassy hillside, heels slipping in the midnight dew that coated each blade, threatening to twist my ankles, working against me, trying to trip me down the hill to crack my fragile, human skull against one of the stones.

The hill leveled as I reached the standing stones, still running with all my strength, still running to save Daniel.

Still running to save my love.

I crossed the threshold of the stone circle and *leapt*.

I pushed with all I had, all the power in my legs and all the magick inside me. The collar around my throat burned ice cold against my skin as it tightened. The ground fell away, my stomach turning over. I rose, stretching toward the hanging black tatters strung between the stones, my fingers desperately clawing out to grab something, anything I could use to pull myself up.

And knew I wasn't going to make it.

My wish sprang from desperation.

Take me there.

Etheric energy burst inside me as the wish whipped my magick into a frenzy. It pushed out under my shoulder blades in a sweep of ache, unfurling behind me.

Pull.

Drag.

Lift.

Wings of eldritch energy bore me through the air. I rose in a jerk, between the strands of the web. The tatters of it fluttered up, stretching, reaching for me, not to pull me back but to brush my skin in comfort.

The web was the coat, the still-living skin of an archangel shredded and mangled and torn to appease the will of its master.

It barely touched me as I passed through it, the tattered tips just a whisper against my skin. Even through the thrilling wonder of flight, its alien singsong broke through, making a connection.

The coat wanted me.

The song faded to an echo as I swept through the night, still lightly hollow in my head.

I had just enough time to think one discordant thought:

This is absolutely amazing.

My feet touched down on the web, and the coat latched on, wrapping my ankles in tendrils until I stabilized, standing as if on level ground.

The Spider God swung up, skittering to face me, then he spun, lowered himself, and pounced.

He fell in a blur of ebon lightning, crashing into me, spider legs clutching my body. The magick of my wings shredded and we fell to earth with a flash and a crash like a pair of meteors locked together. He drove me to the ground, and pain blasted me from heel to crown in one hardpan slap.

My eyes were locked open. I could see, but I couldn't move, every muscle clenched around my spasming diaphragm. It cramped inside me, struggling to make my abdomen move, to expand my chest, desperately trying to draw oxygen into my empty, deflated lungs.

The Spider God swayed above me, arachnid legs shoved into the ground all around me, arachnid abdomen thrusting, thrusting, thrusting toward me like a wasp trying to plant its stinger, arachnid mouth clicking and clacking and dripping greenish spider saliva across my chest, my throat, my lips.

My lungs hitched. Once. Twice. Trying to kick over, to catch, to start.

Hard-edged, brittle oxygen ripped into them as the Spider

God pushed himself back, stretching upward as he transformed, transmuted, transmogrified into the Man in Black. Spider legs shortened and thickened, becoming arms; black spiky hairs pulled into the hard shell of the exoskeleton with long, creaking squeaks of glass rubbing glass. His swollen abdomen deflated like a burst bladder, collapsing into itself to hang flaccid and folded in disarray around his now-human body, before drawing up and withering into the shape of sleek muscles. His chest, his perfectly carved sternum, split like an unstitched seam and let slip out the two gemstones containing the essences of the gods we'd defeated earlier. They hung around his neck like two brightly colored nooses. The globe of his head broke, denting and creasing into the shape of a face. The skin holding his features side-slipped around, twisting into place like latex across a greased surface. Black orb eyes popped back into their sockets, and he blinked rapidly, lids fluttering.

Holding his hands out to his sides, one dusky-skinned and perfect, one skinless, red, and raw, he stood in sinister, naked glory.

My muscles broke their mortal lock, turning liquid and movable as he settled into his form.

I scrambled backward.

He opened his eyes and smiled.

61

"You are too late, Acolyte. The deed is done."

My eyes shot to Daniel. He lay as still as the flat, gray stone underneath him. Not moving. Not that I could see.

My heart stopped.

All the strength ran from my legs like water.

I stumbled.

Oh God, please no. Please don't let this be true.

Pushing from within, I sent my magick down the line between us, the connection I'd established earlier. It felt like swimming through sludge, the air thick with resistance to my magick. I shoved, the effort tearing something loose deep inside me, looking for him at the other end.

buh-bump

.

buh-bump

.

There.

Faint, nearly indistinguishable from the rush of blood in my ears, I found his heartbeat. It threaded into my hearing, a tiny pitter-pat of hope. I clutched at it, dragging it to me as I tried to push magick down the line to it, to send mystical strength from me to him. My soul breathed out:

Live.

The collar clenched, cutting into my trachea in a hard, bruising line. I ignored it, pushing.

The heartbeat grew stronger, steadier, even if it sounded hollow in my ears, as if it were trapped in an empty house.

The Man in Black stepped between me and Daniel. My magick crashed against him, breaking and spilling to the side, as ineffectual as saltwater.

I cleared my throat and lifted my face. "He's still alive."

"For the moment." He raised his hand, his human one, to his face. His stomach rolled and he began to retch and heave, his throat jerking in time with the hitch of his navel. A sound like flesh ripping tore itself out of his mouth, his jaw dropping to spit something hard and glistening into his hand. Rolling it across his palm, he caught it and held it between two fingers.

It was a ring. A gold circle holding a chartreuse gemstone that cast a faint lime colored highlight on the yellow metal.

He smiled. "However, I hold what truly makes him human." He slipped the ring onto the third finger of his red right hand. "Without this essence, the substance of his . . . *personality* . . . he will fade into the eternal night where I will wait to reap him. I will cast him into the land of Nightmare, and he will dwell in the house of this Lord forever and ever. Amen."

"Give. That. Back." Pain shot through my jaw, my teeth clenched hard enough to grind in my ears.

He stepped back, his arms falling wide and to his sides. "Come. Take it if you can, Acolyte."

I stepped forward, pushing my magick to call the Aqedah to my hand. The knife slapped into my palm, flying from wherever it had landed when Nyarlathotep drove me into the ground. The connection clicked immediately, punching my magick like a closed fist. I realized the knife had a measure of magick imbedded in its ancient iron. It hummed against my Mark, and I *pulled,* drawing the magick out and into myself. Shockwaves of power rippled through me, riding on my anger. It spread inside me, settling into a flat, hard place in my mind, the same flat, hard place I had found in my training.

I knew how to fight, and for Daniel's life I would.

"I'm *not* your goddamned Acolyte."

His lips pulled back, thinner, straighter, revealing interlocking shark teeth as he loomed over me. "Then you are food."

"Come and choke on it, you evil bastard," I snarled.

He fell on me.

62

The Man in Black descended upon me, swallowing me in his fury. His fist lashed out, and I twisted away, using all the skill learned at the hands of sensei, instructors, and masters.

His knuckles grazed my cheekbone, barely brushing along my skin. The blow knocked me off my feet.

I spun, rolling with the impact, scrambling to stay out of his circle of power. My eye began to swell, pulsing closed with each heartbeat.

He stomped forward, and the ground shook under my feet. The standing stones jittered up and down in their earthwork sockets, and it struck me what I was truly up against.

What have I done?

Daniel, I'm going to fail you.

Movement above caught my eye. I dove to the side.

A capstone the size of a truck crashed where I'd been standing, crushing the grass and weeds, narrowly missing me. A string of black coat tore free from its moorings, snapped by the impact. It whipped through the air, slapping around my calf and latching on.

Music exploded in my head.

The coat was urgent.

Insistent.

I could feel it pushing my magick, its song inside me like a vibrato, dumping raw power into me. The song became clearer in my skull, not sung in English or any human language, but still I understood it.

It wanted me to fight. It wanted free of the Man in Black, and it would help me if only I would fight.

Driven by the song, I lunged, twisting with my hips for power, slashing at the Man in Black with the Knife of Abraham. The point caught him in the arm, gouging a chunk of flesh that flapped open like a big-lipped mouth, *thwap*ping in my direction. Dark yellow fluid ran freely from the cut, thin streamers of what could have been urine from the look and smell.

He stepped back, and I pressed forward.

My hand became a blur as I tried to slash him to pieces.

There was no art to it, no science, no training. Instinct rode my body while my mind screamed for Daniel to be okay.

Hold on. Please just hold on. I'll save you.

In the center of the stone circle, the Man in Black stopped.

Caught in my frenzy, I didn't see him draw up, didn't see his hand, his red right hand, flash out, until it clamped around my wrist, jerking me to a stop.

Viselike fingers bruised my skin, grinding the small bones of my wrist against one another. He yanked me forward, slamming me into his carved teakwood chest. His lip curled, his pinnacled teeth showing wetly.

"ENOUGH!"

Power slammed into me with bone-breaking force, battering

my face like fists coated in acid. He swelled, lifting me like a child into the air. He was all-powerful. Unstoppable. He was death and doom and hot, sweaty destruction all rolled into one terrifying form.

"I have had enough of you, Charlotte Tristan Moore. Your time has drawn to an end." A fat, blister-pink tongue lolled from between his lips. It flicked out, impossibly long, and lapped across my face from chin to cheekbone. It snapped back inside his mouth between rows of shark teeth. "Delicious."

The Man in Black would devour me, and I hung helpless before his hunger.

His arm trapped mine between us, the knife in my hand useless, fingers going numb with no leverage to cut. He squeezed as his head reared, preparing to strike. I couldn't breathe. My head lolled loose on my neck. My free arm flopped in the air, useless.

It was over. Darkness closed in on me. I wouldn't even feel it when his elder-god teeth ended my life.

Something constricted around my calf, tightening into a circle of pain sharp enough to clear my head.

Musical language trilled through my brain.

I.

Am.

A.

Survivor.

I swung my free hand in one last effort.

I slapped the Man in Black across the face with all the magick inside me, all the magick lodged in the Aqedah, and all the magick being given by the coat.

It exploded like a shotgun blast.

He staggered, dropping me. I fell to the ground, knees banging against the hard-packed earth. I was drained, too tired to hurt, empty of everything inside me except my own hot torch of anger at him for trying to destroy me, for trying to destroy Daniel. The

Man in Black looked down at me, his human hand pressed to the side of his face. Around his long, thin fingers was a vaguely hand-shaped burn. One so severe the flesh of his cheek and jaw crackled meat-pink through hard black scorch marks, bubbling and seeping from magickburn.

His hand pulled away, slick and shining with thin, runny fluid. He laughed, his basalt eyes fever-bright. "You surprise me, Charlotte Tristan Moore. I thought you a mewling, broken thing to be easily manipulated." He smiled, and it broke the skin where I'd slapped him. "It appears I have misjudged you."

I spat a bad taste out of my mouth. Even that effort made my head spin. I was almost done.

"You chose to hurt the wrong person." I tried to stop them, but my eyes cut over to Daniel lying on the stone. I could still feel him, faintly, through the residue of magick left inside me.

"It matters not. In the end, my will shall be done on this earth as it is in the heavens. I will seek and find one more of my brethren and take them also, and then shall Azathoth be loosed. Then shall he be free to enjoy all his son has accomplished in his name."

"I'll never help you again."

"There is another. He is almost ripe for plucking."

What?

It hit like one of the standing stones falling on me.

Jacks. He's the same bloodline as me.

"You'll kill me first," I snarled.

He stepped forward. "Oh, that I will. Disobedience must be punished."

Come closer.

He stood before me, looking down on me as I knelt. My head weighed forty pounds as I looked up at him. Exhaustion hooked the corners of my eyes, dragging at them.

He took another step.

Just a little closer.

He bent at the waist, bringing his face low and close to mine. The two god-prison gemstones fell free, rubbing against each other. The larger one swung toward my face, and inside I saw a tiny rendition of Cthulhu. He didn't move much, but his tiny Cthulhu head turned toward me as I stared.

An echo in my head.

three . . . to break the sealthree . . .

The Man in Black smiled, lips parting around his teeth. Ashen chunks of charcoaled skin fell from the right side of his face. His jaw slung down, unhinging and opening. His head swelled like it had in the alternate reality, eyes moving sideways as his throat flapped open, stretching into a ring-tubed trachea large enough to swallow me whole. This close, I watched the teeth slip in flesh-pink gums, sliding against each other like knives of enamel. Black ichor ran from under the gums, dripping down the thin edges of each tooth, bumping along the micro-serrations that would cut flesh like shears through lambswool.

Hot, burning saliva fell on me as his shark teeth grazed the air over my face. He would clamp those jaws shut on me, taking my head off at the shoulders. I reached up, fumbling against his chest until my fingers curled around Cthulhu's gemstone prison, knotted into the coat-scrap necklace. Using it to pull myself up and him down, I thrust the Knife of Abraham *deep* into the side of the chaos god about to eat my face off, pushing with all my strength, twisting from my hips and driving with the large muscles of my legs.

He exploded backward, twisting and writhing around the blade that now jutted from his ribs. Hot-pink etheric energy boiled from the gash, leaking around the magick knife. He screamed, howling in pain and anger. His red right hand scrabbled at the knife handle, trying to pull it free.

That's when the coat fell on him.

It dropped from above us, slapping itself around the Man in

Black. For one horrible second, I thought it would try to rescue him, to save its master, betraying me. Then the scrap around my leg throbbed and the song in my head roared to a crescendo and I felt, I *knew,* the coat was on my side.

It attacked with all the hatred and anger built over centuries of abuse at the hands of Nyarlathotep, fighting with all its strength. The chaos god ripped at it, his body transforming into anything it could, one form flowing to another, flowing to yet another, all deadly with fangs and claws and stingers. Nightmare versions of tiger, wolf, spider, scorpion, and shapes so alien my eyes couldn't translate them.

The coat shrieked in my head as it was torn to pieces.

My head swam as the coat poured information through our connection, gifting me with knowledge as it sacrificed itself.

The Man in Black had been weakened.

He'd used a lot of power fighting the Sushi Priest and then Cthulhu. He depended on the coat to act as a battery, draining its magick to fuel his own, and now the coat in its rebellion had cut that off.

There was a chance.

A tiny, tiny chance.

I shoved myself, staggering, to my feet.

The Man in Black didn't see me, too busy trying to shapeshift into something that could defeat the coat.

He didn't see my hand grab the handle of the knife that still stuck from the side of his body.

But he felt it when I yanked it out and rammed it into his chest, twisting the blade as I did. The point slipped in, the blade sinking to the hilt, stopping as it hit something hard that jarred it to a stop. I felt the knife slice through one of his hearts, the main part of him, felt it as the alien, evil heart continued to convulse around the blade in my hand. Magick burst out over me in a sickly-sweet rush of power.

His scream scoured my brain, flash-burning my nerve endings, before he burst into a million tiny flying stinging shapes and disappeared.

One of the gemstones tumbled to the ground, its tether severed by the impossibly sharp iron blade.

I stumbled until I reached Daniel and fell, landing across his cold, still body. I lay there weeping atop him, the tattered fragments of an alien song in my mind as the world fell into darkness.

SMALL NOISES FILLED the silence of the room. The *whirr* and *hiss* of a breathing machine, the *drip-drop* of an IV bag, the low insect *buzz* of fluorescent lights, and the quiet, turned-down-to-one *beep* of the heart monitor. Little noises adding up to nothing. Adding up to everything.

Two knocks.

The door opened.

A nurse came in.

He wasn't young but had a young face, eyes bright over rounded cheekbones. His name tag read LIONEL. He shuffled in, moving next to the bed, checking the equipment.

"How is he today?"

I didn't move. "The same as yesterday."

He looked over at me.

"How are *you* today?"

Lionel cared, he really did.

"The same as yesterday." The coat rustled around me, whispering between my body and the chair. The nurse pointed at Daniel. "He looks the same. You? Not so much."

Lionel might care, but he's a bit of an asshole.

Daniel lay serenely on the bed, oblivious to the tubes and wires running from him, brow uncreased, muscles relaxed, in the coma he'd been in since I awoke on top of him, both of us covered in the shredded remains of the coat: him with just enough life to live, me with just enough magick to wish all three of us to this hospital.

Lionel moved around the bed, coming toward me. He stopped short when my eyes turned up at him. I didn't know what he saw there, but he didn't want to come too close.

Lionel might've been a bit of an asshole, but he was *not* stupid.

He held his hands up, palms out, class ring twinkling in the low light. Started to speak, stopped.

"It's hard to talk to you when I don't know your name."

"It hasn't stopped you yet." No names was safer. Let Daniel be a John Doe, and I'd be Jane. Names had too much power in the world I now knew existed. So far the case worker for the hospital bought my lack of memory about my identity and his. It had taken a little push of magick to fuzz her mind, but for now, Daniel received treatment and I pretty much got left alone to be by his bed.

It wouldn't last.

But while it did, Lionel could just be all right without a name to call me.

"That's fair." He leaned against the end of Daniel's bed. "You should get out. Go outside and breathe non-recycled air. You don't have to go far, but you *should* go somewhere."

I didn't say anything. We'd done this dance before.

He moved to the bed, checking Daniel's vitals. He kept talking while he lifted Daniel's wrist and took his pulse. I didn't know why he did that; the machine right behind him blipped out Daniel's heartbeat. "You've been here for two weeks. He appreciates it, down where he still knows what's going on, he does, but there's nothing you can do here. Don't you have someone to call? A job to check in with? Wouldn't you like to sleep in your own bed, shower in your own bathroom?"

I didn't care about any of that. I only wanted Daniel to be healed. Even if he hated me for dragging him into the mess with the Man in Black, even if he didn't remember me, I wanted him to be the Daniel he was before.

I stood. The coat flared around me, not healed, but healed enough.

Just like me.

Lionel jumped.

"You're right. I have to go out." My hands soothed the coat, its voice in my head cooing. I ran my finger under the collar around my neck, shifting it to a more comfortable place. Magick thrummed inside me, vibrating my bones as it came to life. It had grown, recharging in the last several days. "I might be gone for a while."

"If he wakes up, I'll tell him you'll be right back."

He wouldn't wake up.

Not without my help.

There was one thing I could do for Daniel. One thing that could restore him.

I stepped to the bedside.

His life force had been locked in a ring, a talisman last seen on the skinless finger of a red right hand.

I leaned down, my lips close to Daniel's face.

I had the magick inside me to find things.

I kissed him gently on the forehead, his skin cool under the warmth of my lips.

I was going to find that ring.

I straightened, turned, and walked out of the room without a backward glance.

And I was going to kill the Man in Black.

ABOUT THE AUTHOR

LEVI BLACK WRITES from the outskirts of Atlanta. Born and raised in the South, he lives there now with his wife, who is also a writer.